# Ink and Intrigue
## at
# Ivy Tree Inn

### Ariadne Winter Mystery

## by Ellen Butler

*Power to the Pen*

# Novels by Ellen Butler

# *Prologue*
# *Ariadne*

## *February 1958*

Had I only taken my mother's oft-given advice and stayed at the Cliff Walk Manor Hotel, it would've been some other poor sod who found the dead man. You see, according to my mother, "the Manor Hotel is the only respectable place for an unchaperoned young girl in your situation to stay."

My situation being—an independent, single young woman, currently residing in midtown Manhattan, at the Webster Apartments for Young Ladies—much to my mother's chagrin, as I did not choose to marry, the very handsome, but rather boring Thackery Youngstown who took me to the senior ring dance.

I digress. My apologies.

You're probably wondering about the dead body. I'd only known the victim for the five days leading up to the murder. Unfortunately, the vision of the cold corpse will remain in the archives of my brain forever. For though it had been staged to look like an accident, it was most definitely a murder. My powers of observation identified the questionable manner in which the body lay and the discrepancy in the timeline.

The cast of suspects, and there were plenty, were also practical strangers to me. On the other hand, the strangers could be quite chatty, and unaware of their surroundings when speaking in confidence. My eavesdropping wasn't *always* on

1

purpose. I accidentally stumbled across a few conversations I'd not been meant to hear. I'd no idea how important those overheard conversations would become when it came to connecting the dots of deceit, lies, anger, envy, and long held grudges.

If I'd realized the danger involved, carrying on my dogged investigation to sniff out a story, I never would have gone down the probing path.

No, that's not true. My curiosity and desperation to obtain my goal would not have been quashed by a little danger.

Some danger.

Okay, a great deal of danger.

To provide a clearer picture, I'd best start at the beginning.

My name is Ariadne Winter.

I know what you're thinking. My mother was on a Greek mythology kick at the time she was pregnant with me. Aunt Ruby once told me, I was lucky Mom didn't saddle me with Persephone or Harmonia—two names under serious consideration.

I work for *Ladies' Lifestyle Magazine,* one of the largest women's magazines in the nation. When I graduated college in 1956, unencumbered by an M.R.S. degree, I naively determined my path would be in investigative journalism. However, after being patronized, lewdly propositioned, and occasionally outright laughed out of at least a dozen newspaper offices, my father suggested I take any journalism job "to get my foot in the door." The reality is, that there are plenty of young girls who would cut off that foot to obtain a job at *Ladies' Lifestyle.*

I'd been at the copywriting desk for the past two years and finally got my shot at writing a feature article. It began a month ago when Aunt Ruby called to tell me about a new movie being filmed near her home in Newport, Rhode Island.

"A musical version of *Arsenic and Old Lace* is being made with top-notch musical talent," Aunt Ruby said. "They're calling it *Marriage, Madness, and Murder*,"

She went on to explain, "A group of superlative actors have been cast. The gorgeous Donna Morgan will be playing the Preacher's daughter, and—"

I interrupted, "Wait a minute, did you say Donna Morgan? Soon to become Her Serene Highness, Princess Donna of Maldinia?"

"The very one," she confirmed.

I let out a low whistle of excitement and scrambled through my desk drawer for a pad. "Wait a minute, let me get a pen." I found a pencil tucked behind my ear. "Okay, shoot. Tell me everything."

"Tommy Tanner will play the hapless Mortimer Brewster. Hollywood standbys Genevieve Pierse and Betsy Thomas are cast as the kindly but murderous aunts, and the director has gotten Frederick Dunbar, fresh out of his stint at the Foxtail Spa and Retreat—a popular spot for famous actors to dry out, you know—for the part of Teddy Brewster. The Tony Baldwin Band will be making an appearance and doing much of the music for the movie."

I scribbled down the information. "And how did you come upon this gossip?"

"Ariadne, I don't gossip," she said in warning tones. "I am stating facts. Apparently, Donna Morgan's regular hair and makeup girl has gone and gotten herself pregnant. The movie studio decided to hire a local makeup and hairdresser for Miss Morgan. I've known Monty, the director, since my modeling days. Once I caught wind the production was coming to Newport, I made a call, and *voilà*. It was done."

The snap of her fingers cracked across the phone lines.

"This is fantastic. I'm sure my editor will want to put it in the 'Hollywood Tidbits' section for the next issue." I dotted the last i and ripped out the piece of paper.

"Tidbits schmidbits. I told Monty my niece is a journalist at *Ladies' Lifestyle*, and I've gotten you a private interview with

Donna Morgan."

The two other girls in the copy pool jumped at my squeal of delight. "Aunt Ruby, you are simply the ginchiest."

"You have forty-eight hours to get back to me before the studio passes the interview on to *Look*."

*Look* was *Ladies' Lifestyle* archrival. I couldn't allow it. Besides, this interview could be my avenue off the copy desk. "When do I need to be there?"

"Filming starts in two weeks."

I burst into the feature editor's office to pitch the article, swearing up and down that *Ladies' Lifestyle* would have one of the last interviews with Donna Morgan, before she became a Princess on June 10, 1958—and quit acting for good.

Howard appeared skeptical about letting a "young gal" take on this meaty article. "I don't know if you're the proper person to send. Those Hollywood starlets must be handled with a certain finesse. You're still wet behind the ears. Chad Reeder, on the other hand, has the experience—" Pondering his options, he shoved his glasses on top of his balding head.

I could feel the story slipping away from me and blurted, "The studio asked for me in particular, and Donna Morgan approved it." I crossed my fingers behind my back—it was just a little white lie. Then I played my trump card. "If you don't send *me*, they'll pass the article over to *Look*."

His pug-like face suffused with anger. "To *LOOK!* Over my dead body!" He threw his glasses across the paper-littered desk and barked "You've got a week, Winter. Get it done! And don't screw it up or it'll be the last thing you write for this magazine!"

I forced myself to walk sedately from his office, while my insides danced with glee.

Before going any further, I should be clear, the dead body was certainly not Miss Morgan, nor anyone associated with the production. However, important information gleaned from my interview with Miss Morgan shed light on the motives of certain suspects.

    We'll get to that later.

    You see, it all started at the delightful Ivy Tree Inn where Aunt Ruby booked me a suite.

# Chapter One
# Ariadne

**Monday**

The 1896 building and had all the charming characteristics a New England Victorian home should have—steepled gabled roofs, a large wrap-around front porch, stained glass windows, and enough decorative woodwork to rival Hansel and Gretel's gingerbread house. And of course, the requisite ivy-covered oak tree took up half the front yard—hence the name of the inn. I arrived in my mother's Ford Thunderbird, which she insisted I borrow—so I wouldn't have to face the horrors of a dirty train and bus—completely ignoring the fact that I rode the rat-infested New York subway on a daily basis.

The first people to say hello were a pair of gentlemen bundled up in coats and hats enjoying a scotch and a smoke on the front porch in the waning light. I surmised the scotch did more to ward off the cold February breeze than the coats.

"You must be the guest we've been waiting for." A white-haired man laid his cigarette in the ashtray, adjusted his wire-rimmed glasses, and rose to his full height a few inches above six feet.

"Hello. Are you the owner, Mr. Wyler?" I removed a leather glove and shook his hand.

"Nope. One of the boarders like you." He winked. "Walter Sullivan."

By this time, the other man had gotten to his feet. He was

the opposite of his friend, maybe five and a half feet tall, bald, with a Hitchcock belly. A pipe still between his teeth, he tipped his fedora and bowed at me. "Cedric Higginbottom at your service."

I believe I heard his stays creaking as he resumed an upright position. "It's nice to meet you both. I'm Ariadne Winter. I just drove up from Manhattan."

"Frank is expecting you. He's either in the library or puttering around the kitchen. If you don't find him, ask one of our wives, you'll find them gossiping in the front parlor." Sullivan's eyes twinkled and he grinned at his little joke as he resumed his seat.

I let myself into the wide foyer and was delighted to find a veritable sea of antique furnishings in keeping with the age of the home. An antique walnut hat rack stood in the corner with a shield back chair next to it and across the way a grandfather clock that must have stood close to seven feet tall. Straight ahead, at the base of a beautifully carved circular staircase, built for a bridal entrance, was an old mahogany counter with a registration book in the center, a phone, and a servant's bell.

On my left was the library. The glass French doors were closed, but I got the impression of dark furniture, and a billiard table surrounded by a lot of dark wood paneling. It was empty.

"Hello?" I stepped further into the foyer.

"Oh, Connie, she's here," said a fluttery voice from the parlor on my right.

The parlor continued the trend of antique furnishings which included seating areas of plump chairs, tufted sofas, and a Louis XV-style card table by a set of French doors. Two ladies sat at the table.

"Oh my, isn't she fashionable?" said a dumpling of a woman with robin's egg blue eyes, whose round face was surrounded by a cloud of blond hair. "What a beautiful coat."

"For heaven's sake, she's not a circus animal, Dottie," the other woman said in gravelly tones rising to her feet. She wore wide-legged trousers, a black turtleneck sweater, and a silver fox stole laid across her shoulders. Her salt-and-pepper hair was cut quite short which did nothing to disguise her horse-faced features.

"Hello. I'm Connie Sullivan, and you must be Miss Winter. Glad you made it. We were beginning to worry." Her handshake went along with her athletic build for it was as strong as a man's.

"Oh? I didn't realize I was expected at a specific time," I replied.

"Frank has been expecting you since early afternoon," Connie said adjusting her stole. "This is my friend, Dottie Higginbottom."

The petite woman minced over to me wearing sky-high heels, and a sunshine yellow dress, with a red belt that sat right below her ample bosom. Even in the heels, she couldn't have been more than five-foot-two.

"Call me, Dot or Dottie. Everyone does. I understand you work for *Ladies' Lifestyle Magazine.* It's my favorite magazine. As a matter of fact, I brought this month's issue with me on the trip. Do you live in the city? I always wanted to live in the city. And I understand you're here to interview Donna Morgan!" she said the last in worshipful tones.

I waited a moment before answering to make sure Dottie had finished prattling questions at me. "Yes, I work for *Ladies' Lifestyle* in New York. Indeed, I'm here to interview Donna Morgan."

"They were filming today, and we saw Tommy Tanner on Ocean Avenue!" Dottie sighed with wonder.

Connie, looking thoroughly unimpressed, crossed her arms. "The movie men blocked up traffic for a solid hour," she said drily. "You must be tired from your drive. I think I saw Mr. Wyler go toward the kitchen a few moments ago." Striding across the floor, she pushed open a pocket door that led to the dining room and bellowed, "Frank, Miss Winter is here!"

Then she returned to her seat at the card table. "He'll be along any moment."

Mr. Wyler hurried into the living room. He was of average height and weight with light brown hair, hooded brown eyes, and a sharp hawklike nose. Wearing a pair of dark corduroys with a plaid flannel shirt, he looked the part of an inn owner, "Miss Winter, we're so glad you made it. I was beginning to worry. Your Aunt told me you'd arrive by three."

I detested the chastising way he greeted me as if I weren't a woman grown. However, I swallowed the impulse to make a smart remark and forced an appeasing smile instead. "I apologize. I left the city late, and there was traffic on the Merritt Parkway. I could use the loo and a freshen up . . . if you don't mind."

"Yes, of course. Let's sign you in, and I'll take you to your room."

I signed the register while Mr. Wyler retrieved my room key.

"Breakfast is served in the dining room from seven to ten. There is a bar in the library, that I unlock for guests to have cocktails from five to six every evening. It's almost six now," he said checking his watch. "Would you like me to fix you a drink while you get settled?"

"A gin and tonic, please," I replied following him up the grandiose staircase.

"I don't smoke, and I've limited the smoking areas to the library and the guest rooms. And the porch of course. No smoking in the parlor or dining room, please. You'll be staying on the second floor. The Conrads and Higginbottoms are in rooms in the new addition, on the main floor," he explained, pointing in various directions as we went. "The Sullivans are on the second level with you, and my apartments are on the top floor. The last room on your level is unoccupied."

I nodded in affirmation when he glanced back at me.

"The front doors are locked at ten every night. Make sure

to take your keys with you if you're planning to stay out later than ten. No overnight guests allowed. You're paying the single rate, if any guests are here past ten, you'll be charged for a double." He gave me a significant look, stopping in front of a door with a rose painted on it.

Tucking an errant curl behind my ear, I glanced at my clothes wondering what would have prompted such a statement. My navy and green plaid swing coat was still buttoned and fell to my calves, my driving heels were a demure one inch high, and the black leather handbag I carried couldn't have been more commonplace. I touched my head to make sure the matching Juliette-style hat hadn't been knocked askew. Perhaps he thought my recently manicured red nails and lipstick were too racy?

He unlocked the door. "This is the Rose Suite, Ruby booked for you. It's been recently redecorated in the modern fashion." With a flick of a switch, the room was bathed in soft light from an Italian glass and brass ceiling chandelier. "This is your sitting room. You'll see it overlooks the front yard. Through that door is the bedroom and bath. My decorator assured me all the fashionable people are doing it this way."

I stepped across the threshold and my heels sank into the wall-to-wall rose-colored carpet. Indeed, the furniture was completely modern with sleek lines, bulbous lamps, and skinny pole-like legs. I disliked the room immensely. The word malapropos came to mind. It held none of the charm of the rest of the house. My fingers ran across the mantel. They'd left the beautifully carved fireplace alone, but it was the only thing in the room that harkened back to the original structure.

"All of the rooms on this floor have been redone. Do you like it?" he asked almost like a puppy dog waiting for a pat on the head.

"It's lovely." I plastered on a smile and turned. "Thank you, Mr. Wyler. Could someone bring my luggage? It's in the trunk of my car."

"Yes, of course." He nodded, accepting the keys.

"And *do* be careful with the portable typewriter. It's on loan from the magazine."

"Of course." He turned to leave, then paused, and twisted his head. "I don't know if your aunt informed you, but we don't serve lunch. However, we can provide a box lunch upon request for additional cost. It includes a sandwich or cold chicken, fruit, and potato or pasta salad. Would you like me to place an order for tomorrow?"

Unsure what my meal situation would be on set, I nodded. "That would be lovely, thank you."

"Dinner begins at seven. Do you have plans to eat elsewhere tonight?"

I shook my head.

"That's fine. I'll let the cook know. While breakfast and cocktails come with the room, dinner does not. It's $4.50 including beverages, wine or beer is extra. It'll be added to your final bill. Will your aunt be joining us?"

*Us?* "Afraid not. It'll be dinner for one, tonight."

"I'll bring up your luggage and a fresh cocktail."

Closing the door behind Mr. Wyler, I leaned against it and rummaged in my handbag for a cigarette. I pulled the packet from beneath my wallet only to find it empty. Crushing it beneath my fingers, I tossed it into a metal wastebasket with a sigh. I'd need that cocktail, before braving the inquisitive Dottie at dinner.

11

# Chapter Two
# Kitty

At half past seven, a stylish young lady strolled through the dining room's open pocket doors.

*She must be the new guest Dottie rambled on about before dinner, the one from the magazine*, thought Kitty.

She wore a dark green velvet, off-the-shoulder, tea length cocktail dress that enhanced her almond-shaped green eyes, which were fringed with long, thick lashes. She had a straight narrow nose and cupid's bow mouth. Her deep brown, chin-length curls were cut into a soft bob that framed her heart-shaped features to perfection. The only imperfection on her face was a tiny beauty mark on her left cheek, but even that feature would be looked upon by some as an enhancement rather than a detractor.

Having grown up just outside Manhattan, Kitty figured she knew exactly the type of person this young journalist would be. Not much different from the gossipy Dot or condescending Connie. Her eyes darted over those women as she listlessly lifted a spoonful of savory stew to her lips.

*Look at them, taking the best table in the room, closest to the warmth of the fireplace.* She glared at the two couples sitting at a cloth-covered, square table in the center of the room beneath a glowing burnished gold chandelier dripping with cut crystals. *While Melvin and I are stuck in front of the drafty bay window. Chatting as if they hadn't a care in the world.*

With her spiteful thoughts, Kitty conveniently forgot her

husband had solicitously asked her which table she preferred when they arrived. It was she who had plopped down in front of the windows.

*It'd been nicer in the morning when they could look out on the holly bushes with their red berries, and the gravel pathways that trailed around the dormant garden flowers,* she reflected squinting past the room's reflection into the shadows of the night. With annoyance, she pulled her cashmere wrap closer around her shoulders and glared at her husband's shiny bald head.

Dot's high-pitched giggle floated above the room. There was a time when Kitty ran in those vaunted circles. Kitty shook her head, wiping the bygone days from her mind.

Her husband, silent and intent on scooping the savory braised meat into his mouth, didn't notice Kitty's sour look, and she returned her attention to the girl standing a little uncertain in the doorway.

Frank came out of the kitchen's swinging door carrying two rimmed China bowls. The steaming scent of cooked onions, garlic, and stewed beef filled the room.

The innkeeper was followed by a boy of sixteen, who'd been introduced to the guests as Edward Massey, the cook's son. The pair lived in the apartment above the detached three-car garage at the back of the inn. His hazel deep-set eyes were magnified by his glasses, he slicked back his short, dark hair with pomade like most of the young boys, and his sharpish nose was made less noticeable by a sprinkle of freckles. The conversation Walter Sullivan had had with him over breakfast revealed a serious, intelligent young man intent on going to a university to obtain an engineering degree in rocketry. He revealed his gratitude to Mr. Wyler for allowing him to work at the inn, so he could save money to attend college.

The teenager's confession had given Kitty pause. However, upon reflection, she'd decided not to allow the teen's aspirations to divert her plans.

"Good evening, Miss Winter," Frank greeted the young woman as he laid a bowl in front of each of the ladies, while the boy set bowls in front of the gentlemen. "Feel free to sit at either table." He indicated the tables set for two flanking the doorway into the parlor and returned to the kitchen.

Dottie twisted, and spotting her newest obsession, let out a little gasp. "Are you alone, dear? Perhaps we can make room at our table. Ceddie, shift over."

"No, really—" The girl started.

"I hardly think there's room, Dot," Connie drawled as Cedric bumped her elbow and mumbled an apology.

"—it's fine. You haven't space, and I have all the company I need." She held up a book with Donna Morgan's face on the front of it. "I've got to do some research before my meeting."

*Right. The woman was here to interview the famous Donna Morgan. Typical, one beautiful girl interviewing another beautiful, famous girl who was marrying her Prince Charming.* Kitty rolled her eyes, but since everyone was focused on Miss Winter, no one noticed the childish expression.

*Of course, it's easy to be beautiful when you're only twenty-five. Wait until she's sixty, and life's thrown its worst at you. Sleepless nights of crying in the dark for the things in life you wanted. Just wait until those pretty features become lined, and gray with fatigue from unexpected burdens,* Kitty thought uncharitably stabbing at a juice-covered carrot.

"Very well." Dottie turned back to the table with a bit of a pout.

Young Edward grinned shyly and pulled out a chair for Miss Winter at the table closest to Kitty and her husband.

Tucking the skirt beneath her, she took a seat. "Thank you."

The boy poured water into her goblet from a pitcher on the buffet, then he ducked his head and murmured, "We have an iceberg salad to start with, and the dinner entrée tonight is either Yankee Pot Roast or Spam Fiesta with a Peach Cup."

14

Kitty wasn't sure what Spam Fiesta was, but she'd eaten enough Spam during the war to last a lifetime and avoided it at all costs.

Perhaps Miss Winter felt the same, because she ordered what the rest of the room was eating, "I'll have the Yankee Pot Roast."

Oh!" His head popped up, and he delivered a full-on smile. "I forgot, we've got a Black Forrest Cake for dessert."

She returned his smile. "My favorite."

He blushed. "Mine too."

"Did you make it?"

His head rotated back and forth. "Nah. Mom made it. But she makes the best cakes."

"Then I look forward to eating it."

The smitten boy continued to stare down at her.

"Was there anything else?" she asked softly.

His mouth twisted. "I'm supposed to ask if you'd like red or white wine with dinner."

"I'll have a glass of red please."

He gave a sharp nod, as if she'd gotten the answer correct, and darted back to the kitchen to deliver the order.

She gave a slight smile to Kitty, who, surprisingly, couldn't seem to resist returning it. Then she laid the napkin across her lap and opened the book.

If she hoped to be ignored by the other couples. It was not meant to be.

"Did you settle in all right, Miss Winter?" Dottie rotated in her seat.

The girl closed the book with the tiniest sigh and turned her attention to the foursome. "Call me Ariadne, and everything is quite lovely. How about you? Did you finish your game of gin rummy?"

"Oh my, yes. I lost five dollars. I'm a terrible card player, but Connie is such a good friend to play with me anyway. She's always trying to teach me strategies, but I can't seem to get them to stick in my head." Dot peeled into giggles.

Edward returned with a glass of red wine for Miss Winter.

"Thank you," she murmured and took a sip.

"I've told you a dozen times, we needn't play for money," Connie interjected.

Dottie's head swiveled back to her friend. "Oh, but where is the fun in that?" Just as quickly, she returned her attention to Ariadne, "Besides, it's so exciting when I *do* win a hand or two!"

Miss Winter gave a polite smile.

"Dottie dear, I think your stew is going cold," Connie said drily.

"Dear me. We'll have to chat after dinner when the ladies retire to the parlor for coffee," Dot insisted.

"Mm, I look forward to it," Ariadne replied in fadeaway tones.

Though there was nothing in her manner to suggest sarcasm, Kitty, nonetheless felt the reply held undertones of it, and her unprovoked distaste of Miss Winter lifted a notch.

Returning her attention to her food didn't shut Dot Higginbottom up. She gave a gasp, which got everyone's attention, and cried, "Did I *tell* you about the most adorable cottage we are looking at buying in Saratoga Springs?"

Her husband drew in a startled breath.

Connie, finally interested in something Dot was saying, looked to her friend. "Why, Dorothy Higginbottom, you know you haven't whispered a thing to me, and we've already been here two days."

Cedric cleared his throat, "Dottie, really. I told you—"

"Oh, pish. I know what you *said*. But it's practically a done deal."

"It is no such thing, my dear," he said with a warning in his tone. "I *said*, I would have to work on the financing." He pulled at his collar.

"Where is it?" Walter asked.

"Right on the water, about twenty minutes away from your place," Dot supplied.

"How lovely," Connie said straight-faced.

Kitty squinted. *That is the thing about Connie, one can never be sure if she's being cutting or if she really means what she says.*

Edward came out with Miss Winter's salad, and asked the room at random, "Can I get anything for anybody?"

Melvin swallowed the last bite in his bowl and his head popped up. "I'll have another glass of the red." He picked up his wine glass waggling it at the kid, like a low-class patron at a divey bar.

Kitty winced with embarrassment. The kid took Melvin's glass with a "yes, sir." The rest of the group declined Edward's offer, and he scuttled back into the kitchen.

"It's on the eastern side of the lake." Dot continued to prattle, "The house was built only three years ago, and it has a dock and everything. Can you imagine? We'll be able to see each other on weekends whenever we want!"

"How are you planning to finance it?" Walter asked Cedric.

"Well . . ." Cedric cleared his throat and sipped his wine. "That's what I'm still working on." He wiped his mouth with his napkin.

Connie turned to her husband. "Perhaps you can help, Walter."

"That's right dear," Dot put a hand on Cedric's arm. "After all Walter *is* in banking. Maybe he can help."

When Cedric said nothing, Walter chimed in, "I can provide a consult on your investment portfolio. It's taken some years to build up, but Connie and I are quite comfortable. And there's always your legacy. Have you thought about, what you plan to leave your children?"

Out of the corner of her eye, Kitty watched Cedric's features flush, and his mouth turn down.

17

"Well, I-I don't know about that. You know the old saying about mixing business with pleasure."

Connie wiped her mouth and stated, "I believe that refers to dating within your office."

"Yes, yes, well . . ." Cedric glanced around in confusion. "Perhaps, I meant the one about business and friendships don't mix. Besides, I'm waiting for an investment to pay dividends to make the down payment."

Dot glanced swiftly at her husband.

Before she could speak, Walter nodded. "Sure, I understand, but let me know if you ever want to discuss it."

Melvin, who'd tuned into the other table's discussion piped up, "I don't mind mixing business and pleasure. I've got some money saved and would like to chew your ear about investments Walter. As you know, Kitty and I weren't blessed with children." Melvin's too-wide-set washed-out blue gaze settled back on her, and he solicitously squeezed his wife's hand, while she closed her features and silently screamed in her head.

After three miscarriages and a stillbirth, that almost killed Kitty, a fearful Melvin had put a stop to their efforts to have a child. He'd never made sexual overtures to his wife again. She assumed he'd had his needs assuaged elsewhere, to her relief, as she'd lost all motivation to continue trying. Those were some dark years for Kitty.

"And a summer house on the lake would be smashing, don't you think Kittikins? Why have I never thought of it?" Upon releasing her hand, he turned back to the Sullivans and Higginbottoms, remaining blissfully unaware of Kitty's slight recoil to his touch. "After all, the Finger Lakes are only a few hours away from Buffalo."

His nostrils flared when he smiled, and those crooked front teeth she once thought were endearing, but now hated, jutted out at her. She'd warned him repeatedly *not* to present a full-on smile out in public. They'd even practiced a close-lipped grin in front of the mirror. Treating it as a big joke, he had laughed at her suggestions.

As usual, she stared past his shoulder to answer, "Why, I think that's a lovely idea Melvin. You know—" she tilted her head and tapped her chin "—Saratoga Springs is only a few hours further east. And since Connie and Walter seem to know it so well, perhaps they could give us some pointers on where to look to buy."

Walter, nodding thoughtfully, agreed with the suggestion. "We'd be happy to help. You could come and stay with us for a weekend to get a feel for the area."

Kitty had to conceal her glee at seeing Dot's initial reaction of gall, while Cedric looked relieved the discussion had moved away from him and the financing. Connie's back was to Kitty, so she couldn't get a read on that woman.

In her usual stolid tones, Connie turned her head slightly revealing a quarter profile, and replied with a noncommittal, "I'll have to check the calendar."

*Oh, but you've no idea, Connie.*

However, Kitty knew.

Kitty knew about her husband's doggedness. After all, he wasn't known as the Vacuum King of Buffalo because he was lazy. She realized if Melvin wanted to buy a place in Saratoga Springs, he wouldn't leave Connie Sullivan alone until a date was set on the calendar.

*Wouldn't it be wonderful if we purchased the cottage right out from under Dot? Better, what if they bought something in a much grander size, leaving Dot's cottage looking pitiful and small in comparison.* Kitty gleefully returned her husband's excited grin which bloomed into the despised full smile, but for once she didn't mind.

"That would be most generous of you!" he stated heartily and leaned over to shake Walter's hand.

At that moment, Frank came out of the kitchen with Miss Winter's entrée. Everyone returned to their table conversations, and the young lady returned to her book. Although Kitty noticed she rarely turned a page and suspected, she spent the meal eavesdropping on the other conversations. Kitty couldn't blame her; Dot's high-pitched voice was tough to tune out.

Walter and Cedric discussed the Brooklyn Dodgers' move out west to L.A. While Dot chattered on at Connie about their private tour of The Elms, along the wealthy Bellevue Avenue—a street known for summer mansions belonging to wealthy New York families dating back to the days of the Gilded age when names, such as Astor and Vanderbilt were upon everyone's lips.

At the end of the meal, Kitty unzipped her purse, leaving it open on the floor for a few minutes before deciding she didn't wish to sit any longer and listen to the two women. Withdrawing a handkerchief, she touched it to her forehead. "Melvin, I have a headache. I believe, I'll skip dessert and go lie down."

Melvin's half rose as she stood up and offered, "I will bypass cigars and pool with the men tonight and return to the room, as soon as I finish dessert."

"No!" Kitty snapped, and, putting a hand to her temple, replied in softer tones, "I mean, there's no need. Enjoy your time with the gentlemen. I'll be fine after I take one of my pills. Don't worry about me. I insist."

She was at the doorway when Dot gave out a screech and leapt up from the table knocking her chair to the ground. "A rat!"

The rest of the table scooted their chairs backwards checking the floor, left and right. Walter swept the tablecloth aside to peer underneath it. Frank, Edward, and the cook in her apron burst through the kitchen door.

"What's wrong?" Frank asked.

"A rat ran across my foot! I felt it!" Dot cried placing a hand on her chest.

"Impossible!" Frank declared.

"It was! It was! I felt it!" Dot insisted.

"I don't see anything," Walter said in muffled tones from beneath the table.

Eyes wide, face tense, Connie's head whipped back and forth searching, while she bent her knees up to keep her feet off the floor. She clutched a small evening bag in her lap. It was the only time Kitty had ever seen the unflappable Connie Sullivan in distress.

"God, I hate rats," she mumbled.

The young journalist put down her book, to help locate the offending vermin. Dot made little moaning noises and fanned her face, while Cedric, much like Sullivan, searched for the supposed rat.

"Ladies, I can assure you the Ivy Tree Inn has never had rats. You must be mistaken," Frank said in firm tones.

With a sly grin, Kitty waited for the backlash. It didn't take long.

Dot, pulling herself up to her full height of five foot two, shot back, "Are you calling me a liar, *sir*?"

"You'd best watch what you're about, *Mr. Wyler*. Nobody calls my wife a liar." Cedric puffed out his chest, although it really was his rather large stomach that stuck out more.

At that point, the innkeeper realized his mistake. "N-no, Mr. Higginbottom, th-that's not what I meant. Perhaps a piece of bread or-or a napkin slipped to the floor, and your wife mistook it for a rat."

"I don't see any food on the floor, but I do see Cedric's napkin down here." Walter retrieved the napkin holding it aloft with two fingers. "Although I'm not sure it didn't fall during the hubbub."

Melvin did a double-take and jumped out of his chair. "There!" He pointed. "I saw movement, near the empty table."

Everyone turned to focus on the empty table.

"Kitty, love, close the pocket doors, so it can't escape."

"Yes, dear," she replied demurely. For a moment she debated stepping from the room and closing them, but she couldn't resist remaining to see how the situation would be resolved.

Frank, Melvin, and Walter bent at the waist and hunted for the rat.

"I saw something move!" Kitty squealed and pointed in the direction of the cook and her son.

The cook gasped and her hands twisted the apron beneath them. "Oh no, not the kitchen." She splayed herself in front of the door ready to block any sort of rodent from entering her domain.

The teen manfully stepped in front of his mother and crouched in a defensive position, as if facing off against an attacker. Melvin, Walter, and Frank rushed toward the kitchen door, while Cedric, Connie, and Dot moved in the opposite direction of where Kitty pointed, joining her near the pocket doors. In the meantime, Miss Winter watched with alertness, but Kitty could detect no panic in her manner.

"I don't see anything," Walter commented scratching his head.

Frank got down on his hands and knees and crawled around on the dark green flowered rug that covered a large portion of the hardwood floors. "Edward, come here. Do you see anything?"

The boy got down beside his employer and scrambled around on the floor with determination.

There was a click, and Miss Winter said with triumph, "Gotcha!"

All eyes directed her way to find an empty water goblet overturned on the floor and a frightened, small, white mouse trapped beneath it.

"I believe if someone can locate a piece of paper or cardboard, he can be safely returned to the outside," she suggested.

"Good catch, Miss Winter." Edward rushed over to the young woman and paused staring down at the critter. "But . . . that's not an outdoor mouse. That is the kind we have in science class. They run the mazes we make. You can buy them at the pet store."

"I wonder how he got here," Connie commented.

Edward's mother glared at him and said with warning in her voice, "Edward . . ."

He frowned. "It wasn't me, Mom, honest."

"You've been known to bring critters home," the cook pushed back a whisp of hair that escaped from her bun.

"Edward?" Frank stared at the boy.

"Best to come clean, boy," Walter suggested.

"No, sir." Edward's head shook back and forth. "I only brought an injured bird home that one time, *Mom*. Besides, that was a long time ago. When I was ten . . ." he said in a manner only youth can claim. As if six years was a lifetime ago.

"Well . . ." Frank hesitated.

"I believe the young man," Miss Winter calmly folded herself into her seat.

Connie, behaving as if Edward's guilt had been dealt with, waved her hand in the air and moved across the room to the table. "The question now, is what's to be done with the creature? If he's not an outdoor mouse, he'll never survive the cold."

Melvin took a paper dinner menu off the buffet and slipped it beneath the glass. Holding the critter up high he grinned. "It's a cute little fella. You are right son, I'm not sure he'd survive if we plopped him outside."

"I saw an old aquarium in the attic. I could put him in there until tomorrow and take him to school. I'm sure Mr. Jenkins wouldn't mind another one." He looked to his mother for permission.

The put-upon cook placed a hand on her hip and sighed, "I suppose . . ."

Edward grinned. Melvin passed the glass and paper to the boy who quickly retreated through the kitchen door.

"Only for a night, *niño!*" she called firmly to his retreating back.

"Now that's been settled, why don't I refill your wine glasses? On the house! Maria, go ahead and begin plating the dessert." Frank pulled out Dot's chair for her while Walter helped his wife into hers. "You ladies are in for a treat. Maria makes the best Black Forrest Cake.

To Kitty's disappointment, the cook disappeared into the kitchen, the Sullivans and Higginbottoms started discussing their plans to play bridge after dinner, and Melvin flopped down on his seat with a guffaw as if he'd just enjoyed a great lark. Her gaze swept past her husband and met the piercing green stare of Miss Winter. Her brow furrowed as if trying to solve a difficult math problem.

Kitty slipped between the pocket doors and retreated to her room.

# Chapter Three
## Ariadne

**Tuesday**

I woke to a cozy warm room. The radiator beneath the window clicked and ticked as the hot water ran through the pipes. It was still dark outside, and I snuggled deeper beneath the blankets to get a little more beauty sleep. Alas, my little travel alarm clock announced the time with its rattling ring. Sighing, I flung back the counterpane and swung my legs to the floor.

After dressing, I stuck a fresh handkerchief in my handbag, gathered my pad and pen—compulsory equipment for a journalist—and headed downstairs.

The rising sun pushed away the last gray tendrils of early dawn, as I sauntered down the circular staircase at quarter past seven. A shaft of light speared through the transom window above the front door transforming the dark heavy furniture in the front hall from menacing to welcoming.

Breakfast items were already laid out in chafing dishes across the walnut breakfront. Mixed scents of fried onions, coffee, and sausage pervaded the room. The space was empty except for the woman everyone called Kitty. She'd chosen to sit at the four-top table by herself.

"Good morning." I nodded at her before heading to the buffet.

I nipped a piece of toast, and a hardboiled egg, bypassing

something that looked like fried onions, spam, and potatoes. Probably leftovers from last night's unpopular Spam dish.

The canned peaches had been cut up with maraschino cherries, canned pears, and coconut to make an ambrosia salad. After adding a spoonful to my plate, I headed toward the table where I'd dined the night before.

"Oh, do join me, please. I hate eating alone." Kitty indicated the seat next to her. "I don't believe we've been formally introduced. I'm Katherine Conrad, but everyone calls me Kitty."

I laid my plate down, choosing the place across from her. "Ariadne Winter. Is that coffee?" I searched the buffet for a carafe or urn.

She grinned, "Yes. Edward can bring you a cup."

As if summoned by Kitty saying his name, Edward pushed through the door. "Hello, Miss Winter. What would you like to drink? Orange juice? Grapefruit juice? Tea? Coffee?"

"Coffee with cream and sugar please."

Edward retreated, and I returned my attention to Kitty. "Isn't that kid in school?"

"Oh yes. He leaves around eight. He's on the basketball team, but he returns home in time to work the dinner service."

I examined Kitty as she spoke. Like yesterday, she wore no makeup, and I desperately wished to show her how. Not that Kitty was ugly, but her face could use a little color. Her lips held so little pigment, they were almost gray, and her pale cheeks left her looking older than I suspected her true age to be. Pretty sapphire blue eyes behind her thick black spectacles were surrounded by surprisingly long straw lashes, which would have been accentuated with simple mascara. The lines around her eyes would have been less noticeable as well with proper makeup. Grey streaked through her beige-brown hair which she wore brushed away from her face and twisted into a chignon. A few wispy pieces on top floated above her head defying gravity. I longed to tamp them down with some spray.

The brown wool dress she wore was of fine quality, but too large. It would have looked better tailored to her reedy figure, instead, it gave her a frumpy appearance. However, the yellow and olive silk scarf tied around her neck—a Hermès would be my guess—was quite lovely. Unfortunately, the colors increased her sallowness.

"I understand from Connie and Dot that you're a reporter." She cut a miniature piece of spam and stuck it in her mouth.

"Yes, I work for *Ladies' Lifestyle Magazine.*"

Edward brought out my coffee along with the small pitcher of milk and sugar bowl on a tray. Carefully, he laid them in front of me. "Can I get you anything else? Mom can cook you an egg. Would you like one scrambled or fried?"

"Maybe tomorrow. Hard-boiled is fine for today, thank you." I scooped a teaspoon of sugar into the dark brew and lightened it with a bit of cream.

He nodded and left the room.

"Tell me about yourself, Mrs. Conrad," I suggested taking a sip of coffee.

"Call me Kitty. Melvin and I live in Buffalo. He owns half a dozen vacuum shops in upstate New York."

"How nice." I buttered my toast wondering why they weren't staying at a fancier hotel like the Cliff Walk Manor. "And how did you end up here, in Newport? Vacation?"

"Yes, but it's more than that." Kitty explained, "Frank, erm Mr. Wyler's mother and I were great friends. From girlhood. You see, we went to school together—"

"We all did," Connie interrupted.

Her entrance startled Kitty into dropping her fork. The wide-legged trousers were back, very Katherine Hepburn-esque. Today they were pea-green and topped with a black cashmere sweater set and pearls, but the fur was missing this morning.

Kitty's mouth flattened as if frustrated by the interruption, but she said in balanced tones, "Hello, Connie."

"Kitty. Miss Winter."

"Mrs. Sullivan." I nodded at her.

"Good old Saint Mary's Academy for Girls. Not a place I'd wish on my worst enemy." Connie voyaged through the buffet offerings filling up her plate.

"Oh, it wasn't so bad," Kitty off-handedly replied.

"Perhaps you've blocked out the scratchy uniforms. Or Sister Mary Claudette. The woman was a sadist with a ruler," Connie drawled and pulled out the seat next to me. "You girls don't mind if, I join you."

Kitty immediately hid her irritation, but I saw it flash across her face. "Yes, well . . . perhaps the nuns weren't great, but we did gain a top-notch education. After all, you got into Radcliffe."

"Mm," Connie rose, to push the kitchen door open. "Edward, be a dear and bring me a cup of coffee and a glass of grapefruit juice."

"Besides, we made friends for life," Kitty defended. "Look at you and Dot. And Irene and me."

Resuming her seat, Connie delivered Kitty an odd look.

Kitty gave a sad sigh. "It's simply wretched how her mental health has declined in the past few years."

I cracked my hardboiled egg on the side of the plate and began to peel it. "You're all friends with Mr. Wyler's mother?"

"We grew up together in Brooklyn," Connie cut a sausage into bite-sized pieces.

Edward came out with Connie's drinks and laid them in front of her. "Would you like eggs this morning, Mrs. Sullivan?"

"Two. Scrambled, please."

"Do any of you still live in Brooklyn?" I asked, picking at a stubborn piece of shell with my nail.

Kitty shook her head. "Irene was the only one who settled anywhere near where we grew up. After high school, Connie went off to Radcliffe, while Irene went to Rutgers. Dot had been dating Cederic during her senior year. They married, as we all knew they would. After Cedric graduated from NYU, his job took them to Connecticut."

"How did you meet Mr. Conrad?" I prodded wondering how she met and married a man she'd so obviously grown to disdain.

"After high school, I began working for the Red Cross," she explained sipping the last dregs in her coffee cup. "He was in town for a vacuum exposition. We met on the train."

I cut my egg into quarters and turned to our tablemate. "What about you Mrs. Sullivan? Where did you meet your husband?"

She put down her grapefruit juice and adjusted the napkin in her lap before answering, "Walter was at Harvard. We met at a mixer during my sophomore year. He was a senior. After he graduated, he got a banking job in Boston, and we married at Christmastime."

"Did you finish college?" I asked.

"Oh, yes. Walter was quite proud of me the day I graduated with my degree in mathematics. I taught high school math for two years before our first child arrived. We have three—" Connie wiped her mouth cutting off what she was about to say.

Kitty gave her a glance of pity.

Connie cleared her throat and started again, "Two grown boys. Both smart as whips. *I* saw to that," she explained with pride. Thanking Edward for the plate of eggs he placed in front of her, she proceeded to douse them with salt.

"Connie was always the smartest among the four of us," Kitty put in.

Connie eyed the pale woman. "If I recall, you also received good marks, Kitty. Especially in English class. Why didn't you go to college?"

Kitty's cheeks bloomed crimson, giving her some color,

and she glanced away from Connie's scrutiny to pick at an invisible piece of lint. "My- my father didn't think it necessary."

Connie waited with a forkful of egg lifted halfway off her plate. When Kitty was unforthcoming with further explanation, she merely let out an unsatisfied, "humph."

I wasn't certain about the real reason behind Kitty's inability to attend college, but I would bet my last penny that it wasn't related to her father.

The room went quiet. Kitty fidgeted with her napkin, and Connie tucked into the meal.

I finished my egg and decided to break the awkward silence. "Then, you've all come here to enjoy a vacation at your friend's son's new inn."

"Of course, Walter and I wanted to support Frank," Connie responded. "After all, it can't be inexpensive to put up Irene in that Whispering Pines place, or whatever they call it. It's ridiculous how much they charge to care for an aging parent."

"Whisper Willow Ridge Nursing Home," Kitty supplied.

"Yes, yes." Connie gave her hand a flick as if waving off a gnat. "It's bloody unfair if you ask me. Losing your marbles like that. I still recall when Walter's father went senile. Couldn't remember to put on pants. Forgot his own children. Terrible. Simply terrible. I sympathize with poor Frank."

Kitty cleared her throat and rose from the table. "If you'll excuse me."

# Chapter Four
## Dottie

"Don't leave on my account." Dottie stood in the doorway wearing her favorite dusty rose dress with the matching pink pearls Cedric had gifted her for their twentieth anniversary. The two petticoats she put beneath the skirt made the dress flare out, making her waist appear smaller. At least that's what the lady at the dress boutique claimed . . . four years ago when she purchased the dress. Lord knew Dottie could use the illusion of a smaller waist. It was just too darn hard to keep thin, unlike Connie and Kitty. They never seemed to gain an ounce.

"I'm not. I'm . . . I'm going to check on Melvin. He came to bed quite late last night." Kitty fumbled and bent to pick up the napkin she dropped on the floor.

*She's wearing another one of her ugly frocks that does nothing for her complexion. Poor dear, she hasn't aged well,* thought Dottie.

"They all did, dear." Connie slathered butter across her toast without looking up. "I understand there was a poker game in the library. Walter didn't come in until midnight. I rather doubt he'll be up before nine."

"Well then. Goodbye," Kitty quickly slipped out of the dining room.

Dottie glanced at the two remaining guests. The pretty Miss Winter wore a smart black and red plaid suit which accentuated her tiny waist, and her dark hair curled around her creamy face. Connie's athletic build was clad in her usual pants and cashmere cardigan set that looked brand new.

Dottie sucked in her gut, pushed her shoulders back, and minced her pale blue suede stilettos—which she'd purchased, on sale, at Bergdorf's last month—over to the buffet. She hadn't told Cedric, and so far, the bill had yet to arrive. *Really, I've no idea why he's been such a skinflint these days. He keeps talking about economizing. After all the shoes were on sale.*

Edward popped out of the kitchen. "What would you like to drink this morning Mrs. Higginbottom?" he asked in deferential tones.

"A cup of English Breakfast Tea, and no eggs for me today, dear," she chirped opening the first chafing dish. "What do I want this morning? Oh! Fried ham and potatoes. Lovely."

Dottie filled her plate with a bit of this and that—potatoes, toast, ambrosia—she began to take a sausage, but thought better of it. She placed her plate across from Connie, and, after much rearranging of her skirt, she settled in a manner so the petticoats wouldn't itch the backs of her legs. Inwardly she sighed, *what women do for fashion. Speaking of fashion . . .*

Her blue gaze speared the young Miss Winter. "What fascinating things were you two discussing with Kitty? Did you talk about the magazine? The latest fashion trends?"

"Hardly." Connie snorted. "Kitty was telling us about her *close friendship* with Irene."

The comment sent Dottie into a peal of twittery laughter which only halted when Edward brought out a mini teapot along with a cup and saucer. "Is there anything else I can get for you ladies?" he asked, staring at the young woman. "More coffee Miss Winter?"

"*Niño*, it's time to leave," his mother called from the kitchen.

Answering for the table, Connie said, "I think we're fine. You'd best hurry. You don't want to miss the bus."

Edward didn't budge but continued to stare at Miss

Winter. Dottie couldn't hold back the giggle that escaped.

The boy blushed.

Taking pity on him, Miss Winter calmly replied, "No thank you. Have a good day at school." She bestowed her lovely smile on him.

The boy reddened and couldn't help returning the smile.

"Edward! You're going to miss the bus," his mother warned.

"Coming, Mom!" He skipped back through the kitchen door.

"I believe you've made a conquest there," Connie commented.

Miss Winter pursed her lips and turned to Dottie. "What do you find so funny about Kitty and Irene's friendship?"

Dottie fumbled the teacup in the saucer. "Well . . . I mean . . . nothing was funny, per say. It's because, well, you know . . ."

Uncomprehending, Miss Winter waited for further explanation, her eyes bright with interest.

Dottie squirmed and glanced over her shoulder to check and make sure they were alone.

Connie apparently had no qualms, "What she's trying to tell you—Kitty and Irene *weren't* friends."

Miss Winter's head tilted with interest.

"I'd go so far as to say they were mortal enemies," Dottie couldn't help adding.

The journalist must have sensed a story, for she prompted, "Oh, really?"

With one more glance around the room, Dottie leaned into her audience and whispered, "You see, our junior year Irene stole Kitty's boyfriend, George Poppleton. The Homecoming Dance at Bishop Xavier High School, was coming up and everyone assumed George would ask Kitty to go with him."

"How long had they been going steady?" she asked.

"Almost two years," Connie supplied slathering jam on a piece of toast. "Everyone assumed Kitty and George would be walking the aisle one day."

"Yes." Dottie's curls bounced lightly against her shoulders as she nodded. "Kitty was smitten with George, and we all assumed he with her—"

"He *was* smitten," Connie interjected again.

"What happened to cause a change of heart?"

Dottie picked up her teacup and began unwinding the tale. "The summer before our junior year, Kitty spent a month visiting family in California. Meanwhile, Mr. Poppleton, who worked for Irene's father, invited Irene's family out to their house in Montauk for a week. Unbeknownst to everyone, Irene and George embarked on a secret tryst."

A V formed between Miss Winter's thin brows.

"Once the new school year started, Kitty and George were back together. Meeting at the drug store for sodas, going on dates to the movies, and studying together." Dottie's shell pink nails fluttered. "Nobody had any idea George and Irene were secretly dating. Until the Homecoming Dance, when, to everyone's surprise, George asked Irene to go with him, effectively breaking up with poor Kitty—"

"It was a surprise to everyone, *but* Irene." Connie tsked and said with disdain, "George was too cowardly to break it off with Kitty, while she was in California."

"Why didn't he do so once she returned? Before school began?" Miss Winter asked.

Connie pinched her lips together. "I believe he was hedging his bets. Trying to determine which girl he preferred."

The young woman's lips made an O. "In the end, he chose Irene?"

"Who could blame him." Dottie tittered scooping up a potato cube. "I mean, Irene was very popular, and *quite* beautiful back then. Kitty was pretty and all, but nothing compared to Irene's dramatic dark beauty." She popped the potato in her mouth.

"I disagree." Connie gave a sidelong glance. "I believe his parents played a part. Once Kitty returned home, George realized what he'd been missing. However, with Irene's father being the President of the company—" she shrugged "—perhaps George's father made it clear, that breaking the heart of the boss's daughter would *not* be in the family's best interest."

Dottie swallowed. "I've never thought of it that way." Her forehead furrowed, and her pouty lips turned down. "I assumed he and Irene were in love. I mean, he asked her to marry him."

"Eventually," Connie confirmed.

Miss Winter picked up her mug. "But . . . she didn't marry Poppleton?"

"No." Dottie chased a slippery peach around her plate with a fork. " *That* was a bit of a kerfuffle."

Connie snorted. "A bit."

"Irene refused George's proposal. A month later, George went groveling back to Kitty." Dottie triumphantly stabbed the runaway peach.

Miss Winter waited for Dottie to swallow the fruit before asking, "What did Kitty do?"

"She refused him," Dottie replied.

"She did," Connie confirmed dabbing her lips with a napkin. "Though, I believe she was still in love with him. She'd never take second place to Irene. Too much pride."

"I don't blame her." Dottie took another sip of tea. "He'd made her look like a fool. After all, George asked Irene to the dance in the middle of Ken Mattson's birthday party. With Kitty sitting at the same table!"

A gasp escaped the young woman.

"Poor Kitty ran out of the party in tears," Connie said with pity.

"What happened to Irene? Was she snubbed by the other girls for her despicable behavior?"

"No one dared," Dottie breathed spearing a potato.

"No. *You* didn't dare," Connie practically snapped at her friend.

Dottie's mouth dropped open, revealing a half-eaten potato.

"When *I* heard what happened, Irene and I had words, behind the bleachers. We didn't speak for two months!"

Dottie's mouth shut and she swallowed hard.

The room went silent.

The young woman patiently folded her hands on the table and spoke, "You must have reconciled. No?"

"Of course, we did." Connie dismissively flapped her hand. "In the long run, I decided Kitty was better off without that spineless sack George Poppleton. Eventually, they both got their comeuppance." She patted her mouth one last time and rose from the table. "I'm going to see if Walter is awake."

Miss Winter watched Connie leave before returning her attention to Dottie who'd tucked into her breakfast plate with gusto. "What did she mean by their comeuppance?"

"Mwall . . ." she mumbled with her mouth full. Quickly she chewed and swallowed. "George married that harpy Linda Diebold, who buried them in debt. And everyone knows, Irene's marriage wasn't happy."

Miss Winter sat back in contemplation nursing the last of her coffee clearly mulling over the information she and Connie had just shared.

Dottie sipped her tea in thought. "I suppose Kitty didn't end up much better. I mean, less than a year after she graduated, she met and married the Vacuum King of Buffalo," Dottie commented in a derisive tone.

"It sounds to me Melvin is quite successful, and he seems to adore Kitty," she commented.

Before Dottie could respond, Maria the cook came out of the kitchen carrying a yellow metal tin with a black handle on top. "Here's your lunch, Miss Winter. There's a thermos of coffee inside, along with cold chicken, potato salad, and snickerdoodle cookies. You can leave the empty tin on the buffet when you return tonight," she spoke with a slight Spanish accent—Mexican or Argentinian, or something like that. As far as Dottie was concerned they all sounded the same.

"Thank you, Mrs.—"

"Massey. Maria Massey."

"Ariadne Winter." She took the tin from her and laid it on an empty chair. "Your son sounds like an industrious young man. Mrs. Conrad was telling me he's on the basketball team, along with working at the inn."

"Yes, he's a fair player, but he has stars in his eyes." At Miss Winter's puzzled look, Maria went on to explain, "He wants to attend MIT to become an engineer in rocketry."

Comprehension cleared her features, and she suggested, "I suppose most of the kids have stars in their eyes ever since the launch of Sputnik."

"A noble profession," Dottie chimed in. "We need all the smart brainy ones we can get to outmaneuver those Commies."

"I suppose so." Maria sighed, twisting a bit of apron between her fingers, "I've no idea how we'd afford it."

"Edward seems to be a determined young man. Perhaps a scholarship?" Miss Winter helpfully suggested.

"Where there's a will, there's a way!" Dottie chirped proudly voicing her husband's oft-repeated mantra. When no one said anything, Dottie blundered on, "Did he remember to take the mouse with him to school this morning?"

"He did." Maria blanched. "I best get back to the kitchen." She gave a quick head nod and retreated to her domain.

Dottie, thoroughly sick of talking about Irene, Edward, and the boring people at Ivy Tree Inn, struck out on a new avenue of conversation. "Tell me more about your work at *Ladies' Lifestyle*. Are you meeting Donna Morgan today?"

"Oh!" Miss Winter checked her watch. "Yes, and I must run if I'm to pick up Aunt Ruby on time." Scrambling, she retrieved her handbag, pad of paper, and lunch tin. "Have a nice day."

The young lady swept out of the dining room leaving a disappointed Dottie alone with her thoughts.

# *Chapter Five*
# *Ariadne*

Exiting through the front door, I found Mr. Wyler on a step stool hammering a piece of woodwork in place. I felt a smidge of guilt over encouraging Dottie and Connie to gossip about his mother, but I doubted he'd heard all the way out here.

"Hello, Mr. Wyler. I'm glad I ran into you. The lightbulb on my bedside table has burnt out." The man came down the ladder as I spoke, and, when he turned, I realized my mistake. "Oh! I apologize. I thought you were Mr. Wyler."

He had a similar body type and the same slicked-back, light brown hair as Wyler, but his eyes were bottle green, and his features were softened, rounded, and more attractive. I estimated he couldn't be much more than thirty-two or thirty-three. At least ten years younger than the innkeeper.

The man casually removed the cigarette dangling from his mouth and grinned at me. His eyes crinkled in the corners. "I'd be happy to fix that bulb for you. You're the young lady staying in the Rose Suite, right?"

"Er, yes, Miss Winter. And you are?"

"Johnny Wexler. Gardener, handyman, and all-around dogsbody." He took a drag on the cigarette and blew smoke toward the ceiling.

I noticed a pack of Chesterfield cigarettes, sitting on a nearby chair. "Do you mind if I bum a ciggie? I ran out yesterday and didn't have a chance to pick up a new pack. I'm simply dying for one."

"Help yourself." He pulled a silver Zippo from his pocket and lit it for me. "Where are you from?"

"New York City. I'm on assignment for *Ladies' Lifestyle Magazine.*" Drawing a deep breath, I allowed the smoke to fill my lungs before releasing it. "I'm here to interview Donna Morgan." I don't know why I was trying to impress the handyman. Perhaps it was his beguiling smile.

"Are you now? I hear she's about to marry a Prince."

I nodded. "Prince Rinaldo of Maldinia—"

"Johnny, have you finished fixing the eaves yet?" snapped Mr. Wyler, as he stepped out the door. "I'm not paying you to take a smoke break every—Miss Winter! I didn't see you there."

"I'm afraid, I was the one distracting Mr. Wexler. I begged a cigarette." I glanced between the two men, and again noted the similarities in height and build, they also had similar ears and hands.

"It's no problem, I didn't realize Johnny was speaking with one of the guests," he replied in an apologetic tone.

"She mistook me for you." The handyman seemed to take pleasure in saying those words.

The inn owner reddened.

"Yes, the bulb by my bedside is out and needs replacing," I explained.

"I'll see to it," Wyler said. "Johnny after you finish up here, I need you to look at the stove. Maria said it's acting up, again. Have a nice day, Miss Winter."

"Goodbye," I said to his retreating back. When my gaze returned to Johnny, I saw a look of naked animosity as he watched the owner go. In a blink, his features shifted into pleasantness, and I wondered if my own eyes had deceived me.

"What time is your interview?" he asked.

My diamond-encrusted Elgin watch read ten past eight. "I'd better dash. My Aunt will be waiting."

Pulling out of the parking space, I maneuvered around an older model Chevy truck with a wooden ladder sticking out of the back. Rust spots showed along the running board, and scratches and dents marred the paint and chrome bumper. I remembered hearing a car backfire, along with the grinding of old gears at breakfast. I figured this old jalopy was the culprit, and that it belonged to the handyman.

Aunt Ruby waited for me in front of her shop wearing a mink coat, matching fur hat, and a pair of alligator heels that I coveted. Even in middle age, her beauty was still evident with creamy skin and a mane of silky autumn red hair she'd pulled back into a chic French twist. We loaded the salon's travel case in the trunk, and she navigated me to Castle Hill Inn, where Donna Morgan was staying.

"Turn right at the next stop sign," Aunt Ruby directed. "I've arranged for you to visit the set today. I see you're wearing gloves and a warm coat. Good, you'll need it. They're filming exterior shots today, although most of the movie will be filmed on set in California. You'll be at Kingscote Manor. The winds can be vicious this time of year. Miss Morgan is allowing you to ride in her car. You may conduct the interview questions at that time. You may not ask questions during filming."

"Like the old saying—I'm allowed to be seen but not heard?" I drawled.

"Precisely." She dug into her purse and pulled out a cigarette. "Now, how do you like Ivy Tree Inn? Any problems?"

"It's charming. Although, I find the owner a tad stiff."

"Frank? Really? Hm. Well, he's under quite a bit of pressure to make a go of the inn." Her lighter flared and she lit the cigarette. "He's sunk an obscene amount of money into renovating it."

"Well, there's something between him and his handyman Johnny Wexler. They're a bit waspish with each other."

"Oh, those two."

41

I gave a sideways glance. "That's a loaded response."

She rolled the window down a crack. "An old rivalry. Before your time."

"Have you ever noticed a resemblance between them?" I asked.

Aunt Ruby blew a stream of smoke that ribboned out the window. "Your father is right. You are rather observant. Not much gets past you. Turn left ahead." She indicated with a wave of her hand. "Frank and Johnny are brothers."

"Brothers?" I braked and wheeled around the corner.

"Actually, half-brothers." She exhaled. "Poor Johnny was born on the wrong side of the blanket, if you know what I mean. Robert Wyler was their father. He was a famous choreographer during the twenties and thirties. He started in New York, but eventually Hollywood came calling, and he moved to California. Irene, his wife, refused to move out west with him. She was East Coast born and bred and insisted on remaining in New York with Frank, to be near her parents. He must have been about seven or eight when Robert left. I think she always believed Robert would return to her."

When Aunt Ruby didn't elaborate, I prompted, "But he didn't."

She paused a moment to study her cigarette. "Mitsy Wexler was a dancer in his first film. I can't recall the title. He won an Oscar for it, you know. Anyway, Robert took up with her right out of the gate. I believe he asked Irene for a divorce, but she absolutely refused, though she knew he was seeing another woman. Even after Johnny was born, she still refused. Robert was a brilliant choreographer, and he must have been bringing in pots of money. Enough to keep up homes on each coast. It all went to Irene when he died unexpectedly in a car accident."

I brought the T-bird to a stop at a red light. "What happened to Johnny and Mitsy?"

"She danced for a while, but, you know, there's always a

new starlet waiting in the wings to replace you." She shrugged away the old sordid story. "It's just up ahead on your left."

Castle Hill Inn is a gorgeous waterfront estate overlooking Narragansett Bay. It put Ivy Tree Inn to shame, and I could see why the studio chose it for their female star, who happened to be standing on the front porch when we arrived.

"Good, she's waiting for us," Aunt Ruby commented.

In her black ballet flats, Donna stood an ordinary five foot six. However, when she broke onto the Hollywood scene six years ago, *Movie Life* magazine labeled Miss Morgan a "tall, cool blonde" and compared her to the likes of Joan Fontaine. Her ocean blue eyes were covered by dark glasses that sat on a slightly upturned narrow, straight nose. Her hands were tucked into the fitted, cerulean-blue, velvet coat trimmed in white ermine fur, and she looked every inch the princess she would soon become.

‡‡‡

My initial interview with Donna Morgan went swimmingly. She could not have been more charming or kinder to me. I got a close-up gander at the 9.68-carat, pink Cartier diamond engagement ring given to her by Prince Rinaldo. She told me it was the same ring she would be wearing during the movie. We talked about how they met—on a skiing holiday in Gstaad, Switzerland. Two months later, they met again at the International Film Festival in Cannes, where the Prince invited her to dinner on his private yacht. A quiet year-long courtship blossomed through written correspondence and clandestine meetings.

We discussed her wedding plans. They were to marry at eleven o'clock on June 10, at Saint Benedict Cathedral in front of 700 family members and guests. The guest list would include plenty of VIPs—princes and princesses from England, Denmark, and Sweden, along with America's First Lady. Donna's hometown priest, Father Joseph Ferguson would escort her to Maldinia and guide her through the ceremony presided over by the Bishop of Cordaine.

The extravaganza would be filmed and broadcast by RKO. A reception would follow at the Hotel de Maldinia. Donna remained mum about the wedding gown itself. Award-winning costume designer, Violet Helena, who'd dressed Miss Morgan in four other films, was working in secret along with half a dozen seamstresses to create the gown.

"I'll tell you, it's got lace and a thousand seed pearls," she said with a sideways glance. "And that's the most I've told anyone."

When I commented, "Miss Morgan, the press is hailing this event as the 'wedding of the century,' what do you think about that?"

She replied with nonchalance, "I believe the papers make too much of it."

"But it *is* every girl's fairy tale. Isn't it? I mean to say, a young woman from New Haven, Connecticut becomes an Academy Award-winning actress, and *then* she falls in love with a prince and marries him. It's a dream come true."

"Really? Is it your dream?" she asked in soft tones.

Taken aback I sputtered, "W-why, *my dream?* Um, sure, I-I guess. I mean, er . . ."

"I'll be giving up that award-winning career and my citizenship. And I will permanently move to another country to become their princess." Her blue eyes stared at me with a steely intensity.

I gave a shaky laugh. "Well, to be honest, no, it is not my dream."

"Then perhaps the media *is* making a bit too much of it."

The woman was only three years older than I, but in the face of her quiet reserve and determination, I felt like a child. "Perhaps it is."

The limousine rolled over the graveled drive which led to the back of Kingscote and our morning discussion came to an end.

The first thing I learned about movie making—it was boring. There seemed to be a lot of standing around waiting for lighting people, sound people, and camera people to assemble everything, and then Donna and her castmates would run through the scene a few times before moving on to the next scene or camera angle, which included more set up time.

By three cloud cover caused the production to move inside for interior shots. However, they didn't include Donna, only Tommy Tanner and Frederick Dunbar.

Miss Morgan kindly offered me a ride back to Castle Hill Inn. After two questions, I realized Miss Morgan's responses were succinct and faded away. Her tight eyes and pulled features led me to believe she was exhausted. Knowing we'd have time tomorrow for more interview questions, I tucked my notebook into my handbag and sagged against the seat back.

"Shall we speak off the record?" I suggested.

The leather creaked as her head pivoted in my direction. She glanced at my empty hands before agreeing. "Off the record."

"I thought about what you said, and I'm wondering, *why* are you giving it all up? Is the draw to become royalty that strong?"

"It's not about becoming a princess at all." Her head rolled back and forth against the backrest. "I'd prefer it if he wasn't the Prince of Maldinia. It would certainly have made things easier."

"How so?"

She held up the diamond ring and stared at it, deeply contemplating her next words. "In order to marry the Prince, I've got to pay a three-million-dollar dowry to the House of Aaldenberg."

I sucked in a breath. The House of Aaldenberg was the Maldinian royal family's name. The little tidbit about a dowry had *not* gotten into the papers. I'd done my research and knew her net worth was about a million and a half. I desperately wanted to place the scoop in my own article but realized Donna had only spoken because we were off the record. *Darn it!*

"A dowry!" I exclaimed. "That sounds like something from the Middle Ages. I wasn't aware any of the royal families still expected a dowry."

Her ocean-blue gaze shuttered, and a sigh escaped between her lips. "I'm a commoner. I bring no connections from other European royalty. It's the agreement the Aaldenberg family reached, for the Prince and I to marry."

Without thinking, I blurted, "*How on earth will you pay that?*" Immediately realizing my gaffe, I felt my face burn and tried to backpedal, "I apologize that was crass. It's none of my business."

Her head rotated and I felt her eyes upon me. "We are still *off* the record. Correct?"

"Yes, of course." I picked at a hangnail.

As if she'd been holding on tight to this secret, and needed to tell someone, the story tumbled forth, "I've my own money, and my salary for this movie will go directly to the family which covers one point four million. My father paid another six hundred thousand."

Weldon Morgan, her father, was a prominent attorney and came from old money. He could afford the $600,000. He could probably afford more than that, but I dared not ask. I couldn't imagine he'd been pleased when an upstart prince of a minuscule European country requested money to marry his smart, stunning, and renowned daughter.

Would my father pay a dowry for me? My mother might empty the bank account to marry me off. However, I reckoned my father might have something to say about it.

My training kicked in, and I prodded, "What about the rest?"

She hesitated a minute. "The prince took money out of his

private accounts to fund this movie. RKO guaranteed to double his return on investment, which will more than cover the balance of the dowry. Any additional profits will be returned to the prince's private coffers."

"What's the movie budget?" I ventured.

"Two million. RKO also has sole rights to televise the wedding."

I'd no doubt the box office would pull in more than four million. It was set to be released a week before the wedding. Audiences would clamor to see the movie-starlet-turned-princess in her last film.

Still, Donna was giving up her career, her citizenship, *and* all the money in her bank account.

That seemed an awful lot to me. I wasn't sure I could do such a thing—even to become a Princess. Not that I was deluded enough to believe that I could become royalty. However, I understood such a position could become a gilded cage for a woman. Granted, a pampered, privileged, gilded cage, but a cage, nonetheless.

I couldn't help digging deeper. "It seems there are an awful lot of obstacles to overcome. Why do it?"

Her cheekbones rose and a peaceful smile spread across her perfect features, "I love him, of course. Wouldn't you give up everything for love?"

The vehicle remained silent for the rest of the ride, as I mulled over her question. Having never truly been "in love," I couldn't render an appropriate answer.

# Chapter Six
# Edward

The growl of a 372 horsepower V8 engine rumbled into the Ivy Tree parking lot. Edward dashed over to peek out the parlor window and observed Miss Winter step out of her 1957 Starmist Blue Thunderbird. The door closed with a solid thunk. She slipped the white cat-eye sunglasses from her face and popped them into her pocketbook.

*That dame is wicked cool,* Edward thought.

He tucked his shirttail into the back of his pants and brushed an errant lock off his forehead. Fast walking to the foyer he found the mannish Mrs. Sullivan coming down the stairs in her usual pants outfit, her hand glided along the polished oak railing.

"Hello, Mrs. Sullivan," Edward greeted her with a wave.

"Good evening, Edward," she said in her scratchy voice before turning to Mr. Wyler who was standing at the check-in desk beneath the stairs, "Frank, Walter, and I have decided on the White Horse Tavern for dinner tonight. Go ahead and make reservations for four, I imagine the Higginbottoms will join us."

Edward strode out of the front door in search of his quarry. The creak of a metal hook and eye had him turning left to locate her at the end of the deck. She'd settled on the white porch swing—her legs tucked up beneath her coat with a lit cigarette in hand. Her shoes lay in a tumble on the porch deck boards along with her pocketbook and a notepad. The waning sun settled into the horizon, its orangey pink rays shot through the branches of the distant baren trees, and backlit Miss Winter creating an ethereal effect around her dark hair.

A stream of smoke slithered out between her rosy lips as she exhaled. "Hello there. What's the rush?"

He shortened his stride stuffing his hands in his pockets. "No rush. I came out to tell you that the kitchen stove is broken. There will be no dinner service tonight, and we're making reservations for all the guests."

"I see. How unfortunate," she replied and languidly took another puff.

He stood in front of her with his spine straight and shoulders back. "Would you like me to make a reservation? I can suggest a few restaurants."

Her head rotated back and forth. "Not for me. My aunt has already arranged our dinner reservations. She'll pick me up at seven."

He wilted a bit realizing she wouldn't need him to perform this task for her. "Then . . . uh . . . Mr. Wyler opened the bar early, due to the inconvenience. Shall I fetch you a drink?"

"In a moment." She flicked her ash into a tray sitting on the porch railing. A bit got on the blue and green striped cushion, and she dusted it off.

Edward rolled back and forth on his heels waiting for her drink order.

"How was school today?" she conversationally asked. "Did your science teacher appreciate the mouse?"

"Oh, yes, he did." Edward bounced up and down on the balls of his feet. "He looks like a good maze mouse." Edward frowned, wondering again how a laboratory mouse got into the house. "My teacher told me the mouse can be mine for the next experiment . . . along with the other thing."

She gave a close-lipped half smile.

Edward continued to bounce on his toes in front of Miss Winter, his hands tucked behind his back.

"Edward, be a dear and have a seat. All this bobbing about is making me seasick."

He couldn't believe his luck! Ariadne, he rolled the exotic name around in his brainbox, had asked him to sit with her.

After he plopped down on one of the rocking chairs, she said, "Now tell me about the 'other thing' your science teacher revealed."

Edward couldn't help the wide grin that split his features, any more than he could help leaning toward Ariadne as he hastened to explain the exciting news, "Today, me and eleven other students, were taken to the auditorium to meet engineers from MIT and NASA. They are running a summer space program for students with top marks in science and math. We'll have a team project to complete over the six-week course. The top three teams will win a two-thousand-dollar scholarship for each person and increase their likelihood of acceptance into MIT." He spoke so quickly his words practically tumbled over each other. The rocker rolled backward as he gulped in air.

"Congratulations. That is quite an opportunity," she praised. "Is there an application process?"

His head dipped. "Those of us in Mr. Jenkins' advanced physics class completed it at the beginning of the school year. I filled out the acceptance paperwork during study hall. I just need a parent signature."

"Wonderful. Good luck to you." She sucked on the cigarette.

"Thanks." He bit his lip and stared down at his feet. "There's only one problem," he confessed.

Her mouth twisted and smoke snaked out of her nose. "Don't tell me . . . money."

"Yeah," he breathed. "It's a hundred and fifty bucks."

Her eyes widened. "When is the money due?"

"A fifty-dollar deposit is due now. The rest at the end of May," he sighed.

She took another drag in thoughtful silence. "For an opportunity like this, I'm sure you will figure out how to make it work. Perhaps you can add to your hours here at the inn. Do odd jobs in the area. Or find a different job that pays more."

"Maybe." He lifted a shoulder. "My mom kind of needs the help here."

"Mm. Something to think about." She tamped out the cigarette, swung her legs down, and slid her feet into the shoes. "I believe, I'm ready for that drink now."

Edward leaped out of the chair so fast the rocker slammed back against the siding. He bent and scooped up the pocketbook and notepad for Miss Winter, then offered to help her rise. She placed her soft supple palm in his, and her elegant fingers tipped with red polish curled around his hand as she rose. His entire body warmed from her touch, and he felt his cheeks burn.

"Thank you, Edward." Gently, she pulled her hand free and shifted her pocketbook into it. "I'm going to run these things up to my room and powder my nose. Can you ask Mr. Wyler to make me a gimlet with a lime, please? I'll take it in the parlor."

"I can make your drink," he volunteered holding the front door open. "I've been reading the *Bartenders Guide.*"

"Aren't you clever? Hello." Ariadne waved at Mr. Wyler who was still at the reception desk, his ledger opened in front of him.

"Good evening, Miss Winter." His boss replaced the telephone handset into its cradle. "Did you have a good day?"

"Yes, Donna Morgan is most charming. Young Edward here has told me about your difficulties with the stove. No need to worry, Aunt Ruby is taking me out tonight."

A flash of relief crossed Mr. Wyler's features, and his shoulders visibly relaxed. "Then I believe all the guests are taken care of. I'm about to open the bar, would you like me to fix you something."

Edward had hung back as his favorite guest spoke to Mr. Wyler, but when cocktails were mentioned, he stepped forward.

Before he could speak, Ariadne half-turned and indicated him, "I've given my order to Edward. He offered to take care of it for me. I'll be back down in fifteen." She swept up the circular staircase, her heels tapping lightly against the treads.

The boy watched in admiration until she disappeared. When his gaze swept down, it collided with the inn owner's.

Mr. Wyler gave Edward an assessing look.

Edward felt the back of his neck prickle with unease. "I'll go fetch her drink," he mumbled pivoting to the library.

"Edward."

The boy stopped and glanced over his shoulder.

Mr. Wyler held up a chain with a key dangling off the end of it. "You'll need this, to unlock the bar. Mr. and Mrs. Sullivan would like a Manhattan and an Old Fashioned. Do you think you can handle that?"

"Yessir. Right away." Edward retrieved the key.

"And Edward . . ."

Once again, he paused. "Yes?"

"Please take care of the Higginbottoms when they return. I need to go check on some rotting molding out back."

Edward nodded and skipped into the library to locate the *Bartender's Guide* where he'd left it on one of the lower bookshelves.

# Chapter Seven
## Ariadne

I retreated to the second floor diverted by the boy's infatuation, writ so clearly across his features anytime he set eyes on me. The crush itself was harmless, and I'd be gone soon enough. His tender little heart wouldn't be too devastated when I left. This summer program seemed to be a great opportunity for his future success. I sincerely hoped he and his mother could get the money sorted. I made a mental note to leave him a good tip during mealtimes.

Reaching the top of the stairs, I came to an abrupt halt, when my heel caught on the fringe of the red Aubusson hallway runner. As I knelt to untangle it, Mr. Sullivan came out of his door studying a piece of paper in his hand. A cloud of smoke followed him into the hall.

Rising to my full height, his shoulders jerked in surprise.

Quickly, he crammed the paper into his pants pocket. "Miss Winter, I didn't notice you there. Drop something?"

"My heel caught on the rug."

"Ah. I see." He shoved a hand into the same pocket as the paper. "How was your day on set? I think that's what they call it. Right? On set?" he said in an overly jovial manner.

"That's correct. My day was—" *How was my day?* I screwed up my face thinking about Donna's disclosures during the car ride home. "Illuminating."

His brows rose at my description. "Is the movie going to be a hit?"

"Undoubtedly. After all, *it is* Donna Morgan."

"Quite a looker, that one," he chortled.

"Yes. She's as beautiful in person as she is in the movies."

When I didn't elaborate, Mr. Sullivan cleared his throat and set about patting his coat. "I know, I've got a cigarette somewhere," he murmured.

"I've one if you like." I retrieved the newly opened pack from my purse. Giving it a quick shake, one of the white tubes popped up.

"Thank you." He stuck it between his lips and retrieved a silver lighter from his pocket. The paper he'd shoved in there earlier, fell out and fluttered to the ground. "Best head downstairs. Connie will be waiting. Will I see you down there?"

"After I freshen up."

He stepped away without noticing he'd lost the note. For a note it was. I read the typed, opening line.

Dear Mr. Sullivan,
Be at the Ivy Tree Inn, in Newport, R.I., on the date of February—

I bent to pick it up. "Mr. Sullivan, you dropped—"

Before I could finish my sentence, he'd snatched the piece of paper from beneath my hand, so swiftly, it brushed the tips of my fingers.

"I've got it!" He registered my shocked expression and sought to cover up his impoliteness. "It's financial business. Highly confidential."

I tilted my head and waited, but there was no forthcoming apology.

"See you downstairs for cocktails." He strode away and clomped down the steps faster than a Kentucky Derby racehorse.

Dropping the handbag on the divan in my room, I slipped out of my shoes and flicked on a light. The chamber was stuffy, and the radiator's metallic odor hung heavy in the air. I cracked open a window beside the fireplace to allow the winter breeze to freshen the room.

# Chapter Eight
## Cedric

"Slow down, I can't walk that fast," Dot's silly heels tip-tapped along the sidewalk, and the hand wrapped around his elbow tugged at him.

Begrudgingly, Cedric slowed his pace.

The sun was almost completely set as the pair trotted up the flagstone walkway to the inn. Dot had insisted he come with her to the ladies' boutique and watch her try on the hat she'd seen yesterday, in the window. That was almost two hours ago.

Not only did she drag him to the boutique, but also the shoe store two doors down, and a little souvenir shop where she'd insisted on purchasing birthday gifts for the grandchildren. In the meantime, the sun had set, dropping the day's unusually mild fifty-three-degree high at least twenty degrees colder.

Cedric's wallet was significantly lighter—much to his dismay—but his ears and nose were red with chill. Since he'd also forgotten his gloves, now his hands were stiff with cold from carrying all the shopping bags. Moreover, his feet and knees ached from the walk. He was ready to warm up and settle down with a drink and his pipe in front of the library fireplace. Perhaps he'd enjoy a game of snooker with Walter or Melvin.

Dot gasped, pulling him to a halt. "Cedric, I just saw Frank go around the side of the house. He was alone. Do go, talk with him about the money," Dot urged.

Cedric grunted, "I'm sure he's busy, perhaps it should wait

until later."

"You said that three days ago. It is later *now*. Go! Speak to him. We *need* that money for the house in Saratoga Springs," his wife hissed. "You *saw* Melvin Conrad poke his nose into our discussion with Connie and Walter. I won't allow them to snatch that perfect cottage out from under us."

Realizing his wife wouldn't give up, Cedric sighed. "Very well. Go on in." He unloaded all the shopping bags into her greedy hands. "Have someone pour me a Scotch. The Glenfiddich. Not that cheap stuff Frank tried to pawn off on me the day we arrived."

Cedric waited until the door closed behind Dot before waddling around the corner of the building.

The innkeeper wore a brown corduroy coat, and knit hat, and was winding a garden hose around a large pair of hooks sticking off the side of the house.

"Frank!" Cedric hailed him.

Frank's head jerked up in surprise and he squinted into the gray gloom. "Why, Mr. Higginbottom. I didn't see you there." Dead leaves crunched beneath his feet as he strode over to Cedric. "How was your walk?"

The library lights flickered to life, and the glow from the windows illuminated the two men.

"Oh, fine, fine. Dot found a hat in one of the shops, and gifts for the grandkids. She'd fill up the entire station wagon with presents if I let her," Cedric said the latter out of the side of his mouth.

Frank nodded as if understanding, though he wasn't married, and didn't have progeny of his own. "I don't know if you've heard, the stove is broken."

"No, I hadn't," Cedric replied with a touch of irritation. Visions of a relaxing evening playing pool after dinner dissipated like his breaths in the frigid air. "I suppose we'll have to eat out."

"Mrs. Sullivan requested I make dinner reservations for the

four of you at the White Horse Tavern at seven."

With an agreeable grunt, Cedric removed a pipe from his pocket, tapped the bowl against his palm to loosen the ashes, and dumped them on the ground.

"Edward is making drinks for everyone tonight. I'm trying to give the young man more responsibility." Frank checked his watch. "He should be in the library. Would you like your usual? Scotch on the rocks?"

"Yes, the usual. Dot will take care of it." Cedric packed tobacco into the pipe. "That's not what I came to speak to you about."

"No?" Frank's gaze darted around as if searching for a distraction.

"No." Cedric made a show of finding a match and running it around the bowl to light all the tobacco while puffing multiple times.

Frank shifted his weight back and forth, while his guest went through the ritual.

"You've done quite a nice job here." Cedric indicated the building. "And you opened your doors when—at Christmas time?"

The other man visibly relaxed. "Yes, it's come a long way since you originally saw it."

"Precisely." Cedric's head bobbed up and down, as he puffed the pipe. "Therefore, I believe it's time to discuss your repayment of my investment. When I gave you the money, a year ago, you assured me I'd see a quick return."

"Erm, uh, yes, well you see, your investment . . . it . . . uh . . . wasn't used for Ivy Tree."

Cedric's eyes widened. "I don't understand. When we met here last year, you led me to believe the money would be used for improvements for the inn."

"Yes . . . that *is* what we discussed. However, something better came along. You see, a lucrative investment came across my desk. Which, since you'd been so kind to me, I decided *your* money should be the cash to get in on the ground floor of this investment opportunity."

Cedric's bushy eyebrows practically met in the center above his nose. "What in the blue blazes are you talking about? When I gave you the $5000, I expected it to be invested here." He pointed to the building for emphasis. "This property."

"I understand Cedric—"

"That's *Mr. Higginbottom*, to you, young man," Cedric commanded.

Frank's face turned a bright shade of magenta. "Right. Apologies. I'm trying to explain."

"Go ahead, then." Cedric's lips pursed around the pipe stem.

"You may recall my father was in Hollywood, an Oscar winner."

"I've heard tell. What's it got to do with my money?" He placed a hand on his rotund belly willing to hear the younger man out.

Frank nodded with affirmation. "An opportunity came along that was *not* to be missed."

"Such as . . ."

The innkeeper drew in a breath leaned forward and in hushed tones declared, "Movies."

"Movies!" Cedric's bushy brows rose in surprise.

"Sh . . ." Frank's eyes darted wildly around and drew Cedric further down the side of the house away from the front porch.

Cedric lowered his voice, "What on earth are you talking about?"

"I've invested that money into a movie," Frank declared "And you're sure to reap twice the amount you invested."

"I am, eh? How do you figure?" he asked in a disbelieving tone.

"We gather a percentage of the profits."

"Hm. Interesting." Cedric puffed on his pipe and

contemplated the nervous man before him. "Tell me more."

"There isn't more to tell. You know that journalist who is here to interview Donna Morgan?"

"The pretty young thing speeding around here in that blue roadster? What's she got to do with it?" Cedric barked.

"That's my point." Frank winked conspiratorially. "I invested your money in the movie Miss Winter is writing about. You'll receive a percentage of the profits."

"What if the movie is a flop?"

"A Donna Morgan movie? A flop?" The innkeeper hooted. "No such thing. The movie people have *guaranteed* it'll be a blockbuster. You know, she's marrying a prince in a few months."

"So, I hear," Cedric harrumphed. "My wife won't stop talking about it. Says, 'It's the wedding of the century.' Bunch of nonsense if you ask me," he muttered.

"I expect to see returns by the summer."

Cedric chewed on his pipe in thought.

Frank cleared his throat and rocked back on his heels. "I can see you're uncertain. If you'd prefer, I can take the five thousand out of the inn's profits and return your loan by the end of the month."

Cedric remained silent thoughtfully puffing on his pipe. This opportunity could bring in more money than expected.

Frank slung an arm across Cedric's shoulders and pointed into the darkened distance. "Mr. Higginbottom, you seem like a man with long-term vision. Wait a few months, and you'll see double that amount."

"Double you say?"

"Double," Frank stated.

"Why didn't you tell me about this earlier?" Cedric puffed up his chest and slapped the younger man on the back. "Brilliant strategy, my boy."

Frank coughed. "I-I didn't want to spoil the surprise."

"Dot will be thrilled. We'll be able to purchase an even

grander house on the lake."

"Yes, erm, well . . . about that. I suggest we keep this on the QT. While Mrs. Higginbottom is a lovely woman, I'm not sure she'd be comfortable keeping the secret from her best friend. And, as I didn't invite the Sullivans, to invest with us . . ." Frank trailed off.

Cedric thought of the demeaning discussion they'd had over dinner the previous night. When Walter had the gall to suggest he "help Cedric with some financial planning." The mortification still stung. As if he couldn't figure out how to provide for his family. Granted, there had been that stock investment that unexpectedly took a nosedive. Cedric had been assured it would bounce back . . . eventually. Boy-o if this movie investment paid out in spades, he'd be back in the black. Then he could rub it in Walter's face.

However, what Frank said had merit. He wouldn't want Walter horning in on their investment. "You're right. They might feel slighted. Wouldn't want to hurt anyone's feelings now, would we?"

"No, sir." The innkeeper shook his head.

Cedric drummed his fingers against his belly. "I agree, it is best if we keep this to ourselves."

"That was my thinking."

"Good. Well, then, I suppose I'll go inside and see about that Scotch. I could use a celebratory drink." Cedric meandered his way back to the front of the house. A noise caused him to glance upward.

Miss Winter stood in the window looking down upon him. She waved, and Cedric gave a little salute. He didn't notice her window was open as he strolled beneath it.

# Chapter Nine
## Ariadne

To my right came the crack of billiard balls slamming against each other as they rolled across the green felt.

"Nice shot," Walter Sullivan's voice filtered out through the library's open doorway.

On my left, Connie's gravelly amusement became overshadowed by Dottie's high-pitched giggle as the friends laughed at some anecdote. My foot hit the final tread of the staircase and Edward glided out from the library, as if he'd been lying in wait. Admittedly, it'd taken quite a bit longer than the fifteen minutes I'd promised, when I ascended the stairs.

"Miss Winter, I've got your gimlet." The drink was filled to the brim, and he carefully balanced the triangular martini glass on a silver tray taking care not to spill a drop. A white tea towel hung from his forearm. He'd garnished the drink with a circle of lime.

With two hands, I carefully removed the glass. "Why, thank you, Edward." Immediately, I sipped the liquid to keep from spilling it. "Mm, nice job."

He beamed at my compliment. "The ladies are in the parlor with Mr. Conrad, while Mr. Sullivan and Mr. Higginbottom are playing snooker in the library."

"I'll join the ladies."

Turning the corner, I found Dottie and Connie sitting together on one of the tufted, blue-velvet sofas across from Kitty and her husband who sat on the matching counterpart.

The sofas flanked a beautiful green tiled fireplace with a scrolled walnut mantel.

Dottie spotted me the moment I darkened the doorway. "Here she is! We were wondering if you would come down for cocktails."

"Good evening." I strolled between the couches to take up residence by the fireplace, so I could watch for Aunt Ruby.

The clatter of a dropped tool and a muffled curse came from the kitchen region, and I glanced toward the closed dining room doors. Someone must have been working on the stove.

"I do hope they're able to fix the problem in time for breakfast," Melvin commented to no one in particular. Kitty elbowed him in the ribs. "What? You know, I like my eggs and bacon in the morning."

"Oh! I adore that dress you're wearing, Miss Winter." Dottie clapped her hands together. "Who is the designer?"

"It's Dior." I sipped my tangy-sweet drink.

"Dior," Dottie nodded in reverent tones.

"My, my. La-di-da," Connie condescended.

My face burned. The tea-length, peacock-blue silk gown with bow accents, and quarter-length sleeves had been provided to me by Edna, the wardrobe mistress at *Ladies' Lifestyle*. It was a couture dress by Dior from two years ago. Even so, I'm certain the price tag was more than I made in a year.

The magazine was given dozens upon dozens of designer clothing items. They ended up in "The Wardrobe," and were used by the models for photo shoots. Plenty of the models walked away from the shoot with the latest fashion trends under their arms. Working girls at the magazine, like me, were allowed to borrow the unwanted or past seasons' clothing; a perk I rarely made use of.

However, upon learning of my interview with Donna Morgan, Edna had hunted me down in the bowels of the copy desk pool, and demanded I accompany her to The Wardrobe.

She then proceeded to pile a tower of dresses, shoes, belts, gloves, and hats into my arms for me to take on my journey.

"We can't allow a *Lifestyle* reporter to show up to a Hollywood interview wearing something off-the-rack." She'd said in clipped tones, eying my simple but elegant forest green suit. "Even if it did come from Bergdorf's."

I could have easily told my audience this information, however I decided it was really none of their business where my dress came from.

"I think it's lovely," Kitty contended. "I wouldn't have the courage to wear that color, but it's quite becoming on you, Miss Winter."

"Thank you," I murmured.

Kitty turned and admonished her husband, "Melvin why don't you go join the men in the library and allow Miss Winter to sit in your seat."

Melvin immediately jumped up from the couch and with great flourish bowed in my direction. "My apologies, Miss Winter. Please, *do*, have a seat.

"No, really, I'm fine," I demurred.

"I insist," he replied.

"Very well."

Kitty patted the empty spot next to her. In doing so, a bracelet flew off her wrist, landed on Dottie's foot, and slithered to the floor.

"MOUSE!" Dottie screeched bolting off the sofa, her arms flailing.

It was just my bad luck that I was passing in front of her to take Melvin's seat. Dottie swatted the gimlet out of my hand where it crash-landed on the tile hearth.

"Blast it!" I muttered beneath the cacophony of Dottie's hollering and shook the drips off my hand.

The commotion brought the men in from the library post haste.

"What's going on?" Cedric demanded.

Dottie danced around on her tiptoes. "It ran across my foot! I felt it!"

"Not another one!" exclaimed Walter taking in my dripping hand and shattered drink. He pulled a handkerchief from his pocket and handed it to me. "This is too much."

Melvin cleared his throat loud enough to capture the audience's attention. "It was no such thing—" he knelt "—I'm afraid it was my wife's charm bracelet. If you would, Mrs. Higginbottom?" He tapped her foot with his knuckle.

Dottie stepped off a broken golden bracelet which now held a handful of mangled charms—a key, a heart, an apple, and an unidentifiable scrap of gold.

Melvin straightened studying the charms, his face downturned and regretful. "The clasp broke." He slid the damaged jewelry into his pocket. "We'll look for a jeweler to fix it tomorrow, Kittikins. After all, it carries my heart on it. Can't break my heart," Melvin guffawed.

"Of course." Kitty stared down at her lap.

"Oh, my. *That* is a relief." Dottie fanned herself flopping back down on the sofa.

"Are you alright Miss Winter?" Walter asked.

I ran a dry hand down the front of my dress. Thankfully, none of the drink had spilled onto the silk. I couldn't imagine what Edna would say if I brought the Dior back to her with a stain on it. "Yes, I believe the rug and fireplace got the most of it." I returned the damp handkerchief to him.

"Well, you can't blame me," Dottie cried defensively. "After last night, I thought . . ." She glanced around seeking approval for her actions.

"Yes, Dot. We all remember last night," Connie shifted to sit straighter.

Edward, who had followed me into the room, squatted and began picking up the larger pieces of glass placing them in his palm.

"Careful." I seized a waste can, with a hunting scene

painted on it, and placed it next to the boy. "Put those in here. Don't cut yourself."

"Use your towel to gather up the smaller pieces," Walter suggested.

"Oh, my nerves are shot," Dottie dramatically draped her arm across her forehead.

"Perhaps you should retire to your room and lie down," Kitty suggested.

*Is that a hint of malice in her tone?* I couldn't determine, as she continued to keep her head down.

Dottie didn't respond to Kitty's suggestion, and I witnessed the glint of a narrowed eye peek out from beneath her elbow to glare at the other woman.

Edward dropped a large piece of stem into the can with a clang. "I'll make you another gimlet, Miss Winter. As soon as I finish—"

"Don't worry about it, my boy!" Cedric boomed. "I'll make her one. Does anyone else need a refresh? Dottie? Connie?"

Dottie, not receiving the sympathetic response she sought, gave a harumph and straightened up. "Yes, dear, that would be lovely. A Manhattan, please."

As Cedric lumbered out of the room, Edward made a sucking noise between his teeth. I glanced down to find a slash of blood dripping from his middle finger.

"Oh, dear. Does anyone have a clean hankie?" I asked.

"Here." Melvin proffered his.

I folded it over a few times to create a narrow dressing and wrapped the white cotton around the appendage.

"Put some pressure on that, son," Walter suggested.

Edward pinched his fingers around the makeshift bandage, and blood immediately seeped through the multiple layers. He stood frozen, his face a mask of confusion.

Gently taking Edward by the elbow, I guided him toward the dining room, "Come on, let's get you cleaned up."

We entered the large kitchen to an interesting scene.

Edward's mother knelt on the floor with a toolbox in front of her, a screwdriver in hand, while the buttocks and legs of Mr. Wexler or Mr. Wyler—I couldn't discern—stuck out of the butter-yellow stove. His head and torso were buried inside the oven opening. A scarred wooden table had been shoved up against the far cabinetry to allow better access to the stove.

Finding the pair in the kitchen surprised me. I suspected Dottie's screeches, or the crash of my glass, would have reached the confines of the kitchen. If they did, clearly neither one of the inn's workers felt the need to investigate the noise.

Maria's face dropped upon our arrival. "Miss Winter? *Mí niño?* What is going on?"

"I'm afraid Edward has received a cut."

The screwdriver landed amongst the other tools with a clank, and the cook leaped to her feet grabbing her son's hand. "What happened?"

Edward snapped out of his stupor. His face bloomed rosy, and he snatched his hand back. "It's nothing, Mom. Just a small cut."

"It should probably be cleaned and bandaged," I recommended.

The man in the oven wriggled his way out. As I initially assumed, it was the inn's handyman.

Maria pulled her son over to the big farmhouse sink. Gingerly unwrapping the bloody handkerchief, she ran the injured finger under a stream of water.

"Have you a first aid kit?" I asked Johnny.

Without taking her eyes off her son's injury, Maria responded, "It's on the right, top shelf in the pantry."

"I'll get it." Johnny wiped his hands on a dirty rag and disappeared through a door to the left of the sink. A moment later he returned holding a square, white metal box, with a red cross emblazoned across the top. He laid it on the counter and flipped it open.

Now that the pair had things under control, I could have

slipped away. Honestly, I preferred the company in the kitchen to the group in the parlor, and once his cut was taken care of, I wanted to explain how it had happened so no blame fell on the young man for the broken glass.

"There should be a bottle of Betadine," Maria said.

Johnny passed her a small reddish bottle and a piece of gauze. She turned off the water and patted Edward's finger with the gauze.

"It's fine, Mom. I don't need the Betadine."

"Of course, you do."

"Listen to your mother," Johnny softly admonished. "After all, you wouldn't want an infection keeping you off the basketball court."

Edward hissed as his mother squirted a dropperful of yellow liquid on the cut and put on a stoic face. Johnny passed her some clean gauze and then pulled out the white medical tape, ripping it off with his teeth. The pair made short work of it, and soon Edward had a cleanly bandaged finger. The pink tip that poked out of the bandage reminded me of the pigs in blankets that my mother would make for parties.

I gave him a soft smile. "Better?"

He shuffled his feet and nodded.

"Now tell me what happened," Maria suggested wiping her hands on a lemon-colored towel.

Before I could begin the story, the back door opened. A cool gust of wind swept in with Mr. Wyler, along with brown leaves. He removed a wool cap and wiped his feet on the rag rug.

His gaze took in the mother and son at the sink, the first-aid kit, and flickered over to Johnny. "What happened? Are you hurt?"

"Not me." Johnny shook his head and indicated Edward. "The kid got a cut."

Frank turned his attention to Edward. "Are you all right?"

Edward gave an "aw shucks" half-shrug and said with as

much nonchalance as he could muster, "It's no big deal."

Frank opened his mouth to interrogate further, when I interrupted, "Unfortunately, there was a broken glass . . . mine to be exact."

It became clear that Frank had not noticed me upon entering, and my voice startled him.

"Edward was cleaning it up," I finished.

"I'm sorry to hear that, Miss Winter. Were you injured?" he asked solicitously.

"No. The glass was accidentally knocked out of my hand by Mrs. Higginbottom. It landed on the hearth."

While I'd noticed the family resemblance between Frank and Johnny, something else occurred to me, as the two men and the boy stood side-by-side. Edward also had familial similarities to the brothers—ears, sharp nose, squared hands with short nailbeds, and blunt fingers. Edward's skin tones were slightly darker than the two men, but not by much. If I didn't know Maria was his mother, I never would've guessed he had Latin ancestry.

My gaze went to Maria. I observed her brown skin, coal-black hair, wide nose, and high cheekbones. The only resemblance between mother and son that I could detect was their dimpled chins and rounded lips.

"Would you like me to fix you another drink?" Frank offered.

I blinked back to the present. "No thank you, Mr. Higginbottom has seen to it."

The innkeeper grimaced.

I pivoted the conversation, "Mrs. Massey, I wanted to give you my congratulations."

She laid the towel down with a confused expression. "I do not understand."

"Edward told me about the opportunity he's been given for the summer program at MIT. Sounds like the opportunity of a lifetime," I said. "You must be very proud. Surely, he will show those MIT folks what he's made of." I glanced at Edward and was rewarded with a sheepish smile.

Frank's brows rose with interest. "What's this about MIT, Edward?"

Edward went on to explain the opportunity he'd been afforded at the prestigious technical university.

"Fantastic, young man! I'm positive you'll be up to the task." He clapped Edward on the shoulder.

Maria swallowed. "Yes, well, we're still discussing it."

"What's there to discuss?" Frank demanded.

"It's a hundred and fifty bucks," Edward stated baldly.

Frank's mouth snapped shut, until he finally replied, "Ah."

"I-I was thinking—" Edward picked at his fresh bandage "—maybe I could do some more work around here to earn some extra money."

"Erm, I'm stretched pretty thin at the moment, with three staff members to pay, and now the stove." Wyler scratched his elbow, and his eyes darted around the room.

"Perhaps his father . . ." I tossed out, wondering if there was a father in the wings who could come to the kid's rescue. I'd gotten the feeling Maria was a single mother, and assumed she'd been divorced.

Maria went pale, Johnny's sardonic expression never changed, while Frank's facial features slackened.

Edward, the one person's features whom I failed to notice, until he murmured with a saddened but resolute look, "My father's dead."

My cheeks flamed with embarrassment. It wasn't the answer I'd been expecting. "I'm terribly sorry. I didn't realize . . ."

If I didn't feel like enough of a heel, to my utter shock, Edward went on to explain the tragedy of it. "He was hit by a car in front of the hotel where he worked when I was ten."

"Oh, dear. Yes, I see," I cleared my throat and suggested, "Perhaps, Edward could find another job that would give him more hours." Silently, I added, *and better pay.* Somehow, I had a feeling Frank was a bit of a skinflint when it came to his staff.

Johnny, wiping his hands with the rag, gave his half-brother a steely-eyed glare. "I'll loan him the money."

"NO!" All eyes went to the cook's fierce features, which she quickly tempered, "What I mean is, I'll figure it out. If this will help Edward obtain a scholarship to the college he wants to attend, we'll make it work." She put an arm around her son.

"But how, Mom?"

"Don't you worry about it? I have a few ideas." She ruffled his hair. "Since you're not on dinner service duty tonight, why don't you head up to the apartment and finish your homework?"

"Okay."

"Keep that injury elevated." Frank opened the door, allowing another brief gust of cool air to fill the room.

Edward shuffled out into the dark night.

An awkward silence ensued, and I suddenly wished I'd never mentioned the father, much less brought up Edward's MIT opportunity. I regretted sticking my nose into a place where it didn't belong. "Well—" I checked my watch "—Aunt Ruby should be along shortly. Goodnight."

I slipped out of the room, breathing a sigh of relief as the door closed behind me.

# Chapter Ten
## Ruby

"I hadn't heard about the dowry, but it doesn't surprise me." Ruby tapped the linen napkin against her lips. "The Principality is desperate for money. Although I don't doubt Donna Morgan's name alone will bring plenty of tourists to the tiny country."

Her niece leaned forward and glanced from side to side as if checking for unseen listening ears. "You mustn't say anything, please, Aunt Ruby. We were speaking off the record when she told me."

"Were you speaking in confidence?"

"Well, the exact words weren't spoken, but it felt like it was a confidence." She sat back allowing her head to rest against the red leather of the tall banquette booth.

The Lobster Seafarer restaurant was filled with circular booths. The sides went high up to provide privacy, and the decorator had gone as far as draping chiffon fabric between the booths, to dampen the sound. The tables were quite isolated, which is why men were known to bring their mistresses—though Ruby would never reveal that information to her niece.

However, it wasn't the privacy that made Ruby choose the restaurant. The stuffed lobster tail happened to be a most tantalizing experience for the tastebuds. The combination of garlic, herbs, butter, and lobster meat baked into the crimson shells until they were crisped to a golden brown, was the main reason Ruby patronized the establishment.

"Either way, I shan't say a word," she assured Ariadne. "But, you realize, the press is bound to get ahold of the information sooner or later."

The girl sighed and her shoulders drooped. "I know. It's positively killing me, and I can't do a *thing* about it."

"Are you sure?"

Her nostrils flared and she shot Ruby a look of irritation. "Off the record, *means off the record.*" She tapped the table emphasizing each syllable. "I cannot . . . no . . . I will not sacrifice my journalistic integrity for a juicy piece of gossip. If I do it now, I can kiss my investigative reporting dream goodbye. I'd never get a source to trust me again."

"Well, the Prince will make his money back and plenty more." Ruby ran a finger around the rim of her empty wine glass. "I suspect this movie will be Donna's highest-grossing film of her career."

"So, *all* the investors will make a pretty penny?"

"Sounds to me like the Prince is the only investor. I can't imagine he'd want to share the profits with anyone else."

Ariadne's brows furrowed, she opened her mouth and then closed it. "Hm."

The tuxedoed waiter, a middle-aged fellow who possessed a nose like Jimmy Durante, and ears like Clark Gable sidled up to Ariadne's side. "Ladies." He bent slightly at the waist and poured the remainder of the bottle of Bordeaux into the glasses filling them to the brim. "Shall I bring another bottle?"

"Goodness no!" Ruby tempered the abrupt words with a smile. "We've jobs to get to in the morning."

He gave that slight bow again and asked, "Is there anything else I can bring you ladies? Perhaps a parfait for dessert? Slice of Black Forest Cake? Lemon pie?"

Ruby looked at her tablemate.

Ariadne shook her head. "None for me."

"Just the check."

The waiter took the bottle and disappeared from view.

Ruby flipped open her silver cigarette case and offered one to Ariadne. When she shook her head, Ruby took one at random and lit up. "You'll be able to find the hotel on your own tomorrow?"

"Oh yes. Do you need me to pick you up? Same time?"

Ruby blew a cloud of smoke upward. "I'll drive myself. Plan to be over there by nine. You'll ride to the set with Donna again." She took another puff feeling that comfortable calm envelope her as only a cigarette could do. "Oh, and you needn't bring your sad little tin lunch box. The studio pays for catering. Might as well take advantage of it."

"Mm-hm." Ariadne took to staring off in the middle distance, clearly her mind had wandered to other pastures.

It wasn't the first time she'd been distracted during dinner. Her lipstick had rubbed off, but she'd nary a hair out of place. While she had the beautiful unlined face of a twenty-four-year-old, her features were pinched with uncertainty.

"Penny for your thoughts?"

Ariadne's attention came back to earth. "I'm not sure they're worth a wooden nickel." She picked up the wine glass and took a sip.

"No?" One of Ruby's faultlessly hand-drawn eyebrows rose.

"How do you know Mr. Wyler?" Ariadne asked.

"Frank?" Ruby tapped the ash off her cigarette. "I met Irene at a fashion fundraiser for war orphans. Irene was on the coordinating committee. I modeled some of the clothing. Irene held a party after the event. All the models were invited."

Ariadne ran her thumb and forefinger up and down the stem of her wineglass. "Did you know Johnny by then?"

"Yes, of course. Of the two brothers, I'd say, I know Johnny better than Frank. Unfortunately, I had a front row seat to poor Mitzy's downward spiral. There were plenty of us girls who tried to give her a hand. Unfortunately, the booze and pills got ahold of her." Ruby shrugged and took another drag recalling the sad headline of Mitzy's death.

*Variety* saw fit to place the article on page four. By that time Mitzy had been out of the limelight for years. All but forgotten in Hollywood. It wasn't the headline or the glamorous photo of Mitzy from her heyday that struck a melancholy chord for Ruby. It'd been the mention, at the very end of the article, of her young son, Johnny, who, at the impressionable age of fifteen, was now an orphan.

"I was the one who suggested Frank hire his brother to help at the inn. I knew Johnny had been working in New York, building sets for Broadway shows," Ruby confessed. "With Irene packed away at that nursing home, I hoped the brothers could bury the ax, so to speak."

"I think you mean hatchet, and I'm not sure that has happened," Ariadne commented.

"Oh? What makes you think so?" Ruby stubbed out the cigarette and brought the wine to her lips.

Ariadne's mouth twisted as if weighing her next words. "Whenever I've been in the same room with Johnny and Frank, the animosity they hold toward each other is almost . . . palpable."

"Shame, really. Irene was unspeakably harsh to Mitzy, and by extension, Johnny, when Robert died, leaving them out in the cold. Johnny was the foreman for the recent renovation work Frank did at Ivy Tree. He's quite handy, from what I understand. Not sure if Frank could've gotten it off the ground *without* the help of his brother."

"Indeed. I witnessed it today. Johnny was fixing the oven." Ariadne drank her wine deeply, down to the halfway mark, then proceeded to fidget with the napkin in her lap. "Do you know the cook, Maria Massey?"

"I met her once. When Frank opened the inn."

Ariadne cleared her throat and then her eyes pinned her aunt. "Is she related to Johnny and Frank?"

"Maria?" Ruby laughed at the thought. "I don't believe so.

Why do you ask?"

"There's something about her son." Ariadne shook her head as if trying to shake loose the answer to a knotty math problem. "I don't know. A family resemblance? They have similarities."

"I've not met her son," Ruby replied tapping a cherry-red nail on the table. "Now that you mention it, I recall hearing Maria's got a bit of a tragic story as well. Her husband was the manager at the Grand Park Hotel in New York City."

"How on earth do you come by your knowledge?" Ariadne grinned, shaking her head in disbelief.

"Dearest, I run a hair salon," Ruby drily replied. "Do you want to hear the rest of the story?"

"Please, continue." Her niece indicated with a sweep of her hand.

"If I recall, the story went something like this, it was the blizzard of fifty-two. Mr. Massey, I don't know his first name, was going home for the night, heading toward the subway. A taxicab lost control, slid across the lanes, jumped the curb, and plowed the poor man down."

Ariadne gasped. "That's horrible."

"Yes tragic. From what I understand, there wasn't much money saved. Maria found work doing odd jobs—sewing, cooking, cleaning, and such, to support her young son."

"That must have been difficult. I can't imagine . . ." Ariadne turned a palm to the ceiling.

Ruby gave a half shrug. "Neither can I." She dug into her purse and pulled out a gold compact. "She and Frank were friends, from childhood. An odd pairing if you ask me." She tunneled in search of her favorite Elizabeth Arden lipstick. "They must have stayed in touch. Or she reached out after her husband's death. Ah, there it is." The golden tube appeared. Ruby took off the top and wound it up to reveal a well-used, red-pigmented tip. "When he opened Ivy Tree, he hired Maria on to be the cook and clean the rooms."

"So, they aren't related? Cousins perhaps?"

Opening the compact mirror, she swept the stain across the top and bottom, smacking her lips together to even it out. "I doubt it." Ruby snapped the compact shut.

The waiter appeared, bowing obsequiously, and depositing a brown leather check holder next to Ruby's elbow.

"Thank you for dinner, Aunt Ruby."

"It's a pleasure, dear. I enjoy your company." Ruby placed a handful of bills into the check holder. "I even enjoy your far-fetched ideas about Frank and Johnny being related to the cook."

Her niece blushed. "It's silly speculation."

"Nonetheless, you have piqued my curiosity." She tapped off a length of ash. "I've determined to join you for dinner. Tomorrow night."

# Chapter Eleven
## Ariadne

My watch read quarter past nine when Aunt Ruby dropped me off at Ivy Tree. The gravel pathway crunched beneath my heels. Movement from above had me glancing upward, where I found a silhouette in the third-floor window above mine, backlit by a soft lamp inside the room. Initially, my heart skipped a beat, until I remembered that Frank had said he lived up there. I gave a wave. After a moment, he returned it, then the heavy curtains closed shutting out the light except for a tiny sliver.

Things appeared rather quiet as I let myself in the front door. The library on my left was dark, and only one lamp burned in the empty parlor. The fire had been banked for the night, and a cool draft nipped at my ankles.

I shivered and hurried up the steps to my room. To my relief, the radiator emitted heat making it cozy and warm. I slid out of my stilettos and took a moment to enjoy the plush carpet beneath my tired toes. While I didn't care for the aesthetic, I had to admit, it made for comfort beneath the feet.

I ran myself a hot bath in the clawfoot tub pouring in a packet of sweet-scented, powder bubbles—an amenity left in the bathroom by the proprietor. A nice touch in my opinion. I wondered if it was Maria's idea, or Frank's to provide bubble bath for guests.

While it filled, I rolled my hair into curlers and mulled over the day's events. For some reason, I couldn't get thoughts of Donna Morgan's revelations about the dowry out of my head. To me, it sounded archaic.

My mother would happily pay a man to "take me off her hands," though I no longer lived at home and am quite independent. Mom's desperate need for a grandchild came with a pressure like none other. Over the years, there were many times I'd wished my older brother, Nathan, had survived.

My parent's firstborn succumbed to scarlet fever before the age of two. Thirteen months after his death, I came along, and my parents never had another child. If Nathan had survived, at least there would have been another sibling to take on some of Mom's pressures and high ideals of marriage and family.

Twisting off the taps, I gently lowered myself into the steaming heat. The soft crispy crackle of popping bubbles surrounded me, and I sighed with pleasure as my body adjusted to the water temperature.

I reviewed the notes from the day and jotted down new topics of conversation relating to Donna's childhood, parents, and her younger sister, who would be her maid of honor. Eventually, the questions came to an end, and I allowed the pad and pen to drop to the floor. Laying my neck against the rim, I closed my eyes, and my mind drifted away from work.

Voices coming from the room next to mine woke me out of my stupor. The Sullivans must have returned from dinner. The toilet flushed, and the pipes groaned as the taps were turned on.

My water had turned lukewarm. I tugged the plug loose, before I got chilled, and rubbed myself with a fluffy pink towel. The cold air against my skin made goosebumps rise. I slipped on my blue-and-white-striped pajamas, then climbed into bed. One last question popped into my head before unconsciousness consumed me.

*Ask Donna about the other movie investors.*

# *Chapter Twelve*
## *Johnny*

### *Wednesday*

Johnny's pick-up truck rumbled and screeched to a stop in front of the two-story garage behind the inn. It backfired as he cut the engine. The old truck needed new belts and brake pads. He'd be able to replace the brakes himself, but the belts would have to be done by a professional. A cost he could ill afford considering the paltry salary Frank provided.

Johnny shook his head wondering why he didn't move back to New York. But he knew the answers were the same as the last time--the city was expensive, and work was sporadic. He could be on a job for six months, and then out of work for four. Moreover, he didn't have the capital to start his own company, yet. Work at the inn was steady, and with the odd jobs he'd been picking up around town, Johnny was slowly saving his pennies to purchase the necessary tools, and a better truck to go into business for himself.

Edward came loping down the stairs alongside the garage wearing a heavy wool coat, his schoolbooks fastened together with a worn leather strap.

"Good morning!" He greeted Johnny and climbed onto the running board.

Johnny rolled down the window. "Morning kiddo. Everything go okay with the breakfast service? Is the stove working?"

"Seems to be. Mom baked an egg casserole for the guests." He scrunched up his nose. "She also made some swell pancakes."

"Which did you eat?"

Edward rolled his eyes. "The pancakes, of course. She put pumpkin in them, and something she calls an apple compote on top. Which are just stewed apples in cinnamon and sugar. I poured some hot syrup on top, and it was crazy good, man."

Johnny grinned at Edward's slang. When he was working at the inn, his mother insisted he speak properly and respectfully to the guests. He also made sure to keep up the act whenever he was around his uptight half-brother. Only Johnny got to hear this side of him. Edward was a good kid who'd had some tough breaks in life. Johnny could relate. He wanted to do anything he could to help Edward and decided to speak to Maria about this MIT program.

"Well then, I guess I'll go in and see if I can sweet talk your mom into fixing me a plate of those pancakes. Are you headed off to the bus?"

"Yeah."

Johnny pulled the key out of the ignition. "Did you finish the paperwork for the MIT program?"

His head bobbed once.

"Did your mom look it over?"

"Yeah." He scratched his nose. "But I'm going ask my English teacher to look it over one more time before I send it off to MIT."

"That's a sound idea."

"I mean, mom's a good cook, the best, but she's not a Pulitzer Prize writer, you know. I just want to make sure we've done it right." Edward glanced over his shoulder back at the house. "Don't tell her I said that. Okay?"

Johnny swallowed a grin, and answered levelly, "No, I won't."

Edward hopped down from the running board. "Bus

should be coming any minute. I'd best run." He set off at a jog down the driveway.

Johnny let himself in the back door to be met with the tantalizing flavors of baked pumpkin, cinnamon, apples, and hot coffee. Three of the six burners on the stove had blue flame heating pots. Maria wore a frilly yellow apron over a plain black dress, the ties accentuating her hips. She stirred one of the pots.

"Good morning. How is the oven holding up?"

Maria spun around holding a wooden spoon in one hand while pushing a whisp of dark hair away from her face. "Everything is working fine, thanks to you." Her mahogany brown eyes softened, and she shot him a grin, before returning to the pot on the stove. "I was worried, I'd have to resort to making a purchase from the bakery to serve breakfast this morning."

"Glad I got it working." Johnny helped himself to the percolator warming on one of the stove's back burners. "I hear tell there are pumpkin pancakes with apple compote."

"You must have talked to Edward." She stirred a sweet maple syrup mixture.

"Saw him on his way to the bus stop."

She nodded.

"What are the chances, I could get a pancake?"

"One hundred percent! My hero." Maria laughed and placed a lid on the pot. "I'm heating more syrup."

"Busy morning?"

"Not too bad. It seems everyone is having a bit of a lie-in. So far, the Conrads are the only ones who have had their breakfast."

He cracked open the swinging door, to check the dining room. "Still empty. Has Frank been about this morning?"

"I haven't seen him."

Johnny sipped the hot, slightly bitter brew. "I wanted to talk to you about Edward's opportunity at MIT and reiterate my offer to help."

She started shaking her head.

Johnny plowed on before Maria spoke her mind. "The kid deserves to go. He's incredibly intelligent, not to mention kind, resourceful, and a hard worker. You've got a swell kid there, Maria."

"I know he is a great kid." Maria stated with pride. She grabbed a towel and opened the left side of the oven to pull out a pea-green Dutch Oven. "But he is not your responsibility."

"You're right. He's Frank's responsibility," Johnny declared.

The oven door snapped shut. "Johnny, don't," she warned.

"What? Tell me I'm wrong." He lifted his palms to the ceiling.

The cook only shook her head. "Please, pass me a plate from that cupboard."

He handed her a dish rimmed with pink flowers. "I feel some responsibility for the kid."

"That is kind of you, but I couldn't." She piled three steaming, orange-tinged pancakes onto the plate.

"Why not? I'm his uncle."

Maria stiffened and the plate clattered onto the counter. "Sh." Her gaze darted around. "Someone could hear you," she hissed.

"There's no one out there." He pointed over his shoulder with his thumb. "Remember?"

Maria picked up the plate and scooped the cinnamon apples out of one of the saucepans and plopped them on top of the pancake mound. "Would you like hot maple syrup?"

"Of course."

While she drizzled syrup from the smallest pot over the delectable breakfast pile, Johnny took his coffee over to the table and lowered himself onto a chair. "Did you ask him for the money?"

"Absolutely not!" She thumped the plate on the table so

hard Johnny wouldn't have been surprised if she cracked it. "Listen up, when Frank and I made our deal, we agreed never to talk about it again."

"Why?"

Her gaze narrowed. "What exactly do you know?"

"I know Frank is that boy's father. Were you pregnant when you met your husband? Did he know?"

Squeezing her eyes shut, she ducked her head away from him mumbling, "You do not understand. It was not like that."

Johnny cut off a triangle of pancake stack and jammed it into his mouth. When Maria didn't continue, he prodded, "Help me to understand. Because right now, all I can see is Frank shirking his responsibility, like a waster."

"It is a long story."

Johnny indicated the feast in front of him. "I've got time."

Maria checked the dining room once more, then paced around the kitchen table mumbling to herself in Spanish and throwing her hands about. Though she wore no makeup, and was almost ten years his senior, Johnny thought the cook had an exotic prettiness, and believed, in her younger years, Maria would've been a knock-out. It came as no surprise his brother would have found her attractive and engaged in a tryst. However, because of Frank's almost pathologic desire to please his mother, he *never* would have married a girl of no consequence or background, much less the daughter of Puerto Rican immigrants.

Johnny swallowed a bite of a pancake and washed it down with a gulp of coffee. He watched the cook pace a minute longer before offering, "Shall I ask my *brother*–" he said the word with a snide intonation "–instead?"

The Spanish diatribe halted as she spun around to face him.

With a frustrated grimace, she began her story, "As I said, it is *not* what you are thinking. Jack and I had been married for six years. Five of those years, we tried to have a baby. I never got pregnant." Her mouth puckered with sadness.

"I'm sorry, Maria. I didn't realize—" He looked down at his pancakes and scratched his prickling neck.

She drew in a deep breath, "I thought it was my fault. But the doctors couldn't find anything wrong with me."

Turning her back, she retrieved the flowered coffee mug that matched Johnny's dish, poured herself some coffee, and leaned against the counter rather than taking a seat. "Jack got the manager job at Grand Park, and he barely had time for me. I started working part-time at the hotel to give myself something to do. Occasionally, we'd catch a few moments together."

"Jack didn't mind you working?" Johnny asked.

She grunted drumming her short nails against the mug. "He never noticed I was gone, and he appreciated the extra income. It was not a lot, but after he'd been working at the hotel for a year, he received a raise. I talked him into moving closer to work. Our rent increased, but I figured we could afford it. Besides, he was working so many hours. Sometimes he'd leave at six in the morning and wouldn't come home until midnight."

Johnny thought about the hours his mother and father worked during his childhood. Rehearsals could last well past midnight. When they weren't at work, they'd be out on the town, going to glamorous parties, and movie premieres. His nanny, a grandmotherly type named Irma. took care of him while his parents were gone. In between movies, he'd see them more often.

Those were the times Johnny loved the best because his father lavished attention upon him. They'd have grand adventures—spending the day at the beach or maybe take a trip to a cabin in the mountains owned by a studio exec. Sometimes, they'd go to Las Vegas. Johnny loved to see the showgirls or sit on his father's lap watching the candy-colored wheels in the slot machine spin and spin.

With a mental headshake, Johnny returned to the present. "What did you do about it?"

"As time passed, our marriage became detached. I considered the unthinkable . . . divorce," she whispered the last and crossed herself.

"Sounds rather dramatic," Johnny teased.

"You laugh. My mother was distraught. Divorce was unimaginable to her. Over a tearful dinner—without Jack, again—I confessed everything. She refused to believe the marriage was over. Being a strict Catholic, she refused to consider the possibility of our divorcing. Our anniversary was approaching, and she suggested we take a trip. 'Get away from New York. Go to Niagara Falls,' *Amá* told me."

Maria stared into her mug with a bittersweet grin lifting the corners of her mouth as she reminisced. "I remember she gave me thirty dollars from her stash of money in the raisin tin. She recommended a hotel where the lady across the hall once stayed."

"She thought Niagara would rekindle the love?" Johnny forked another mound of pancakes into his mouth.

"Something like that. I had to beg Jack to take off work and come with me."

He couldn't imagine a wife who looked like Maria having to beg her husband to come away on a romantic vacation.

"Just for three days, I promised. It was not asking much. Initially, he hedged, saying he couldn't get away from the hotel. I asked him point blank if he was seeing another woman."

Johnny's brows winged upward. "What was his reaction?"

The whisper of a smile crossed her features, lifting her soft butternut cheeks. "He was so surprised he choked on the olive in the martini I'd made him. He denied seeing anyone else. I asked if he wanted a divorce, and he agreed it wouldn't be a bad idea to go on vacation for a few days."

"Did the trip rekindle the marriage?" Johnny asked, finishing the dregs of his coffee.

"We arrived in time for dinner. Everything was wonderful." Maria took the empty mug and refilled it. "The following morning, the hotel called. There'd been a water main break. He hopped the first train heading south," she said in a flat voice.

Johnny paused with a forkful of food halfway to his mouth. "You stayed behind?"

She gave a curt nod and sat across from him. "That afternoon, I ran into Frank. I hadn't seen him since our school days."

Sipping her coffee, her eyes got a faraway look as memories rose to the surface. "My family owned a bodega not far from Frank's private school. Lots of the boys would stop in after class to buy candy, sodas, and comic books. *Apá* would specifically stock ones the white boys liked to read."

"Did your mother work alongside your father in the bodega?"

"Of course. We all did. *Apá* expected my brother Mateo to take over the business. But then the war came." She shook her head. "It was not meant to be."

Johnny gave her hand a sympathetic and understanding squeeze. Too many lost loved ones.

After a moment, Maria asked, "Where was I?"

"You met Frank at the bodega."

"Right." She snapped her fingers. "Frank and I became friends—although we never told our parents about our friendship. None of them would understand how a white boy from a good family, and a poor Puerto Rican girl could be friends. We used to sneak cigarettes behind the alley of the store. Frank was always telling me about his dreams to go out to California, to be with his brother and father."

Johnny's face registered surprise, but Maria didn't notice as she got up from the table to renew her pacing.

"When Frank found out I was in Niagara alone, he invited me to lunch." Maria checked each pot on the stove, turned the flame down on one of them, then checked the dining room again, to confirm it was empty.

Johnny, sensing a revelation was coming, laid his fork and knife down, and leaned back against his chair.

"After a glass of wine, our sob stories poured out. Frank's fiancé, Carol, was supposed to be there, but she'd jilted him three days before their trip and ran off with some stuffy British university professor. Lunch ran into cocktails at the bar. And then martinis with dinner."

Maria's head bowed and she picked at a hangnail.

"Go on."

"One thing led to another, and we ended up in bed." She whispered and continued to stare down at her hands. "The following morning, we both realized the mistake we'd made. I knew Frank was not in love with me. I was not in love with him."

She shook her head, and her anguished gaze rose to meet Johnny's. "I packed up, but before I left, I phoned Jack to tell him I was returning home. He met me at the train station and apologized profusely. He was angry at himself for leaving. The water main break was fixed before he got there, and his assistant manager had taken care of the clean-up. That night, he gave me sapphire earrings from Tiffany's and promised to take more time off. We made love that night, and I knew he still held my heart in his hands. I couldn't leave him."

Johnny laid his fork and knife together on his empty plate. "Did he stay true to his promise?"

"He did. He hired two more assistant managers and created a new work rotation. He took Sunday afternoons and Mondays off. Nine months later, Edward was born. A healthy baby boy. It was a miracle." Maria took Johnny's empty plate and placed it in the kitchen sink.

The room remained silent except for the wall clock that went tick-tick-tick.

Johnny broke the silence. "When did you realize the baby

wasn't Jack's?"

Her back stiffened straight as a rake handle, and she gazed out the window. Fingers curling around the edge of the sink, she spoke in stilted tones, "By the time he turned six, I realized the resemblance to Frank." She spun around to face him. "Luckily, he also looked like Jack's maternal grandfather."

Drumming his fingers on the table, Johnny considered all she'd revealed "When did you tell Frank?"

"After Jack died. Edward was about twelve. *Amá* took us to a Broadway show. We saw Gwen Verdon in *Can-Can*. The upper tier." Maria got a faraway look in her eyes. "It was the last time we went to see a show together. *Amá* loved going to see musicals. I couldn't afford the apartment in the city after Jack died. Edward and I moved into her apartment over the bodega. I took my old room and moved Edward into the one that had been my brother's. I helped her work the shop . . . until she got sick with the cancer. Then, I hired a neighbor's son to do it. The surgery and medicine were so expensive. Within a year of seeing *Can-Can*, she was down to ninety pounds, and by the following year—" her expression twisted in pain "—we'd buried her."

The silence lay over the room like an itchy blanket. Johnny strained his mental capabilities to find the proper words to say. "Maria. I—"

Maria sniffed and gave herself a little shake. "Where was I?"

He cleared his throat. "You went to the theater."

"Right. We ran into Frank during intermission, and he invited us to join him for a late-night dinner. It was a Friday. Edward didn't have school the next day, I thought, *what can it hurt?* I never believed Frank would perceive the similarities, or else, I never would have agreed to join him."

"But he did."

She sighed. "Yes. He did. He said he saw his own father . . . your father, in my boy."

"Certain traits run deep."

"The nose, expressions." Her chin jerked his way. "You possess the same hands."

"He has my father's eyes." Johnny stared at his strong square hands, calloused from hard work, scarred by nicks and cuts. The tips of two fingers yellowed from cigarettes.

She startled him out of his contemplation. "Frank came to the funeral. We stayed in touch. I'd gone through what little savings Jack had left me. The two funerals ate up Jack's life insurance policy. I was cooking at a diner and taking in washing on the side. The rent above the bodega kept increasing, and I had to move twice, putting us further and further away from Edward's school."

Rubbing her hands up and down her apron, she licked her lips. "When Frank decided to open this place, he threw me a lifeline. We agreed never to tell Edward, because we do not want to sully the memory of his father. And Jack was a true father to Edward, up until the day he died."

Johnny's brows rose in disbelief. "Jack never suspected?"

Vehemently, Maria shook her head.

"What about your mother?"

More head shaking. "No."

Maria paused mid-shake. "Except . . . there was a moment. Once. That dinner, after the show. I remember her scrutinizing Frank, and I thought, *she knows.*" Her shoulders bobbed. "If she had any suspicions, she never let on. She adored Edward more than life itself."

Shoving back his chair, Johnny cleared his throat and rose to his full height. "Still, Frank *is* Edward's father," he stated emphatically. "And now the inn is making money. Also—"

"But Irene's bills," Maria protested.

Johnny squinted and snorted in disgust.

She took the towel off her shoulder and vigorously wiped down one of the pots in the dish drainer "Besides, I already know, I'm getting some mon—" she coughed. "I-I mean, I'll figure out a way to get the money."

He scrutinized her for a moment, but she wouldn't turn to face him. "My offer remains open."

Maria paused her drying. "You're a good man, Johnny Wexler."

He frowned. "Don't tell anyone. You'll ruin my reputation."

"One day you'll make some lucky girl a wonderful husband," she declared.

He placed his empty coffee cup in the sink and gave Maria a pat on her shoulder before exiting into the dining room.

Miss Winter stood at the buffet in a forest green suit with a pencil skirt that accentuated her tiny waist. A plate in hand, she seemed to be debating between the egg casserole and the pancakes.

"Eat the pancakes."

She must not have heard his entrance. The chafing lid slammed down with a clang, and she spun around with a gasp, "I-I didn't hear you come in."

"The pancakes—" he pointed to the buffet "—You won't regret it." Johnny jammed his hands into his pockets and with a whistle shuffled through the pocket doors in search of his dear brother.

# Chapter Thirteen
## Ariadne

My banging clumsiness brought the cook into the dining room. The one person I didn't want to see. As usual, whisps of Maria's hair escaped from the low chignon she had twisted at the base of her neck, the yellow apron had splotches of brown on it.

"Good morning, Miss Winter. Would you like coffee or tea?" She seemed a bit wooden with me this morning.

*Irritation from my nosiness last night? Or is it more? Does she know I heard?*

I cleared my throat and tugged at the pearl choker around my neck which suddenly seemed too tight. "Coffee, please. Cream and sugar."

"Juice?"

"Just the coffee." I turned back to the chafing dish before remembering I needed to tell Maria something. "Oh! I forgot to mention, my Aunt Ruby will be dining with me tonight."

She ducked her head, and I couldn't read her features. "Very well. Do you need a lunch today?"

"Not today." I shook my head. "Smells like the oven is back in working order. I was trying to decide between the egg dish and the pancakes. Mr. Wexler suggested I take the pancakes."

Her gaze swept up to meet mine. I didn't see anger, but rather . . . trepidation? Fear, maybe? The glance was so fleeting, I could have imagined it. Did she realize I'd overheard

Johnny's declaration?

"Try the apple compote on top of the pancakes. I'll bring out a pitcher of warm syrup with your coffee." She pivoted and returned to the kitchen.

I took a seat at the table by the bay window which overlooked the back garden. Pathways with crushed gravel wound through islands of dormant grass and plants. Evergreens like arborvitae and boxwoods sprinkled in among the brown plants that would revive in warmer weather. A pair of blue spruces flanked an iron arbor arch. Tendrils of a dead vine wound around the side legs and across the top. I imagined the garden turned into a beautiful summertime oasis. Even now, it invited me to wander through the winding passages in search of woodland nymphs. Perhaps there would be time to take up the invitation later in the week.

Maria returned with my coffee, sugar bowl, and creamer. She also placed a small pitcher of syrup in front of me. I murmured, "thanks," as she returned to her kitchen domain.

Popping the first bite of pancake, syrup, and compote into my mouth, I instantly understood why Johnny had recommended them. The sweet apple combined with the savory of the pumpkin melted on my tongue. I gave a small moan of delight and wished my figure could handle a plate piled a foot high of the fluffy flapjacks.

Savoring the last morsel, a movement outside had me pausing mid-chew. A blue jay landed on one of the boxwood topiaries, and I watched as his little head bobbed and rotated in short, quick movements. He plucked at a dead stem—

"Top of the mornin' to you, Miss Winter!" Cedric bellowed in a funny Irish accent.

"Eep!" I practically jumped out of my skin.

"Caught you daydreaming, did I?" He chuckled and began perusing the buffet's offerings.

"Good, morning," I croaked and cleared my throat. "Yes, I suppose I was in my own world."

Cedric loaded his plate with culinary delights from each chafing dish and bowl on the sideboard. Maria bustled out of the kitchen to take his drink order. While she did so, I checked the yard once again, but the bird had flown away with his prize.

To my relief, Cedric toddled over to one of the tables by the door and lowered himself into the chair with a wheeze and a crackling of knee joints. "Oof," he groaned. "The old body isn't what it used to be."

"Um-hm," I murmured still watching out the window.

"How is your interview going with the princess?"

With an inward sigh, I put on a tolerant smile. "Very well. She's a fascinating subject."

"Subject, eh? Sounds like a science experiment."

"No, nothing like that. I meant to say, she's traveled a fascinating road to arrive where she is now—on the brink of becoming a Princess of Maldinia."

"Never heard of the country, until all this hullabaloo about the marriage."

"It's a small province in Europe. It's becoming quite a draw for those who enjoy the casinos and gambling."

Maria came out to deliver Cedric's coffee.

He hmphed and leaned around her to speak to me. "Never could abide throwing my money away like that. Now give me a good investment that can grow. That's where I put my . . ." he trailed off. Now it was Cedric who stared out the window. "What the devil do you think that's all about?"

Raised voices in the garden drew our attention. Frank gestured towards the house with a wild swing of his arm, his face flushed with temper. The pair were too far away for us to understand their words through the thick windows, but their body language alone spoke volumes. Johnny shoved his half-brother who shoved back.

Maria slammed Cedric's coffee cup on the table and bolted from the dining room.

The men continued their argument. I believe, I heard the words, "cheap bastard," but couldn't be sure.

A moment later we witnessed Maria, coatless with her frilly apron flying into the air, race over to the pair. In her mad dash, she ignored the laid-out pathways crossing directly through the dead grass and fallen leaves. She attempted to quiet the two men when Frank rounded on her.

His face pinched with anger when he spoke. Maria's back was now to us, and we couldn't hear her response, but she did point in our direction.

Both men looked our way.

I presume they saw me at the table in the window, and Cedric, who'd labored to propel himself out of the chair. His nose smashed against the window and his breath made round patches of steam, as he watched the contretemps with unguarded fascination.

Frank's mouth slammed closed. Johnny threw back his head and laughed, which only sought to anger his brother more, turning his face into a puckered thundercloud. Maria's hands fluttered around like a pair of angry robins establishing their territory.

How I wished I could have heard the exchange.

A moment later, Maria tapped Johnny on the shoulder and indicated one direction. With the other hand, she gripped Frank's biceps and coaxed him to follow her. Everyone exited our line of sight.

"I suppose that's the end of that. I thought for a moment it might come to blows, and I'd have to intervene." Cedric sighed, returned to his table.

I doubted Cedric would have made it outside in time to be helpful should the pair have started a fist fight.

Cedric checked his watch. "I imagine Dot will be along shortly."

I rose to gather my things. "Give her my best. I must leave soon if I'm to arrive on time. Have a lovely day, Mr.

Higginbottom."

A door closed in the hallway behind the stairs, and I surmised it would be Dottie going to join her husband. My feet darted up the stairs to avoid interacting with her. Once in my room, I collected my purse, verified I had at least two pens to accompany my notepad. I put on lipstick and a coat, checked my watch, and realized I needed to get a move on.

Hurrying into the hallway, I plowed directly into Kitty Conrad. She fell back against the wall with a metallic clank, while I bounced painfully off the door frame.

"Ouch." I gripped my left shoulder which would be bruised by the end of the day. "Are you all right Mrs. Conrad?"

She straightened upright. "So sorry, my fault."

"No, it was most definitely mine. I'm late and was rushing."

"I wasn't looking where I was going." She wore a navy-blue dress with a sunflower pin at her throat. Plain, but good fabric, except it hung lopsidedly on her, and it could have used a bit of tailoring. Otherwise, I found it a vast improvement over yesterday's awful brown frock.

I frowned in thought. "Isn't your room on the main floor?"

"Yes . . . I-I, uh . . ." She rubbed her head. "Came up to, uh, see Connie."

"The Sullivans are in the Blue Suite, there." I pointed in the opposite direction. The Green Suite is empty."

"Of course, I-I forgot," she said with confusion.

I squinted at her and was about to ask again if she was okay, when she declared, "You'd better go."

I blinked. "What?"

"You said you were running late. I'm perfectly fine. You should go." She made a scurrying motion with her fingers. "Don't want to keep the Princess waiting."

"If you're sure." Checking my watch again, I felt my stomach drop. At this rate, I'd barely make it on time.

"Yes, go."

Needing no further encouragement, I flew down the stairs,

96

wishing I could hop on the banister and slide down it. Like I did when I was a child.

On my way to the car, I found Frank speaking in low tones to Maria.

Faltering, my steps came to a halt, and I vacillated. I was loathe to interrupt them, but I needed to get cracking and didn't know how much longer their discussion would last.

More strands of hair had escaped Maria's bun, as her head rotated back and forth in the negative. She still wore no coat, and she rubbed her arms up and down to keep warm.

Frank grabbed her by the shoulders. From where I stood, I could see his thumbs dig into the muscles.

Maria winced.

"It's done. The estate will be his one day," he proclaimed. Abruptly, he released her, and, without a backward glance, Frank stomped toward the garage.

Maria, her face pinched white, glanced up to find me frozen in place, keys in hand.

I swallowed and croaked, "Everything fine?"

That gaze narrowed, but she didn't speak. Instead, she reached for the kitchen door and slipped out of sight.

# Chapter Fourteen
## Maria

Maria shoved the door closed with a decided thud. *That nosey reporter is everywhere I turn!*

Leaning her head against the solid wood, she closed her eyes and willed her racing heart to slow. Initially, she thought the young woman to be nice enough. She'd been kind to Edward in the face of his obvious crush.

That is, up until last night when she'd invaded the kitchen—most inappropriate for a guest—and started asking questions about the MIT summer program, which was certainly *none* of her business. Her comment about Edward's father helping with the money was a slap in the face. Edward may have taken discussions about Jack in stride, but to Maria, every time Edward spoke of his father, it took her breath away.

*What does that wisp of a girl know about raising a child? Much less on her own?*

Jack's death had deprived Edward of so much. Edward's clothes mainly came second-hand, or they were sewn by Maria. The bike he rode, he'd found at the dump, and, thinking it was a lark, rebuilt it with the help of his friend Bobby. His Converse basketball sneakers had been purchased as a Christmas gift last year. Realizing the cost was one they could ill afford; Edward never wore them off the court. Nonetheless, Maria realized only last week, Edward had been covering up a hole, next to his pinky toe, with tape.

Though Frank cut the rent for the apartment over the

garage, and they were able to eat from the breakfast and dinner menu she cooked for the inn, money was still tight. Her one saving grace—Maria had never taken the money Edward had offered from his measly paychecks. She'd insisted he use it for his own spending money, which allowed for occasional splurges on things like ice cream with the team after winning a game.

Last night, when she'd come into Edward's closet-sized room—barely big enough for his twin bed and dresser—to say goodnight, Edward told her about the fifty-dollar deposit due with the paperwork. Maria's heart wept when, with embarrassment, her beautiful son had asked if he could borrow money, as he'd only saved up seventeen dollars and eighteen cents.

"Keep your seventeen dollars. I've got the deposit covered," she'd told him.

"I'll get another job to pay for the rest. I promise," he'd declared.

"Don't fret, *mi Corazón,* I'll find a way to make it work." He'd allowed her to kiss him on the forehead before she left the room.

Maria had fifty-two dollars—saved up in the tea tin she kept beneath her bed. She'd been planning to use it toward a down payment for a used car. But she had a line on more money. Lots more. Something she'd put into action, before Edward's acceptance to the program. If she had the guts to go through with it, their money worries would soon ease.

The sound of male voices drew Maria back to the present. Breakfast guests gathered in the dining room. She pushed stray wisps of hair off her cheeks, smoothed down the apron, and put a smile on her face.

"Good morning, Mr. Sullivan, Mrs. Sullivan, Mrs. Higginbottom, what will you have to drink?"

# Chapter Fifteen
## Ariadne

The morning began ordinarily enough. After driving my mother's car like Formula One racer, Juan Manuel Fangio, I arrived at the hotel only five minutes late. I endured a silent but clearly disapproving look from Aunt Ruby at my tardiness.

However, Donna didn't seem to detect the delay, and we climbed into her waiting car. Silently, I noticed we had a new driver.

Flipping open the pad, I began asking about the palace and her living quarters. "Will you redecorate?" I paused and rethought the question. "*Can* you redecorate?"

"That's the question, isn't it? Can I?" One side of her mouth lifted. "Only the private bedchamber, and the Princess's receiving room. Certain items in the receiving room will have to remain, due to their cultural and historical importance to the family. It's going to take a bit of getting used to."

"Getting used to?"

"Asking permission to change things in my own home," she replied ruefully.

"Hm," I tapped the pen against the pad and stared past her profile at the passing scenery of midnight blue water. "I suppose that's because it's not really yours . . . or his, for that matter. It is the country's home. The family members technically own it, but they will come and go. The palace will always remain standing as a symbol of the country itself."

Her head rotated to face me. She didn't speak. An indecipherable mask had come down, and I felt my ears begin to burn.

*Were my musings insensitive?*

I knew if I wanted to become an investigative reporter, I had to become comfortable asking difficult questions. On the other hand, this was a human-interest story. A bit of fluff for the ladies, not an interrogatory. While I had enough material to fill my inches, I wasn't satisfied and wanted more. Maybe it was the curse of a reporter, we always want more.

Clearing my throat, I glanced at my notes. "What are your plans for the décor? Color scheme?"

"How old are you?" The façade was still there, but I didn't see any censorship in her crystal blue gaze.

I cleared my throat. "Twenty-four. Why?"

"What you said is accurate. While I believed, *I* was the visitor, the guest at the palace, who would have to find a place to fit in. It's the entire Aaldenberg family." Her gloved fingers gripped the red clutch in her lap. "Even my children, who will grow up in the palace, are passing through."

"I believe it's that way with any historic home. Especially those belonging to royal families. The Aaldenberg family is the curator of the palace. One day your children will be the guardians of that history." I brushed a lock of hair behind my ear. "Besides, the prince has plenty of other properties, which belong to him—not the family. Those will become yours."

"Greens and blush."

I blinked. "I beg your pardon."

"Color schemes. Blush for the bed chamber, and greens for the receiving room."

I nodded and scribbled down the information. "Have you heard from the Prince recently?"

Donna pulled a cigarette from her bag and intoned, "Yes, we spoke early this morning."

Nothing further was revealed regarding their topic of conversation.

The rest of the trip, I dug deeper into her knowledge of the palace and the Aaldenberg family. My questions were rather innocuous. She answered stiffly, providing nothing I couldn't discover with minimal research on my own. Obviously, she'd been coached how to answer questions about the family. I pivoted to questions about the flowers for the ceremony and she relaxed. Neither of us touched on the dowry discussion from the previous evening.

We arrived at Kingscote. The moment the vehicle came to a halt, Donna's manager, Bronson Hughes, hurried over to open the door and help Donna out of the car. To my surprise, he didn't acknowledge my presence. Whispering in her ear, he pulled Donna behind one of the movie production trucks. I was left to find my own way about the place.

It didn't take much to locate the crew. Today, filming was set up in the foyer. The room felt heavy with parquet wood floors, and dark walnut wood paneling along the walls and ceiling. Plenty of lights had been set up to brighten the space, and the camera was on some sort of crane. Four men adjusted giant white pieces of board to bounce the lights and brighten the room. A couple of sound engineers stood nearby holding poles with microphones attached at the end and chatted quietly with each other. The room felt tight and humid with all the bodies and equipment. Eventually, I tucked myself into a recessed doorway to watch the action.

Donna appeared at the top of the stairs. She'd changed into her costume, a fabulous full-skirted blue dress, with a striped fabric underneath blue chiffon. She floated ethereally down the stairs rehearsing her lines. The dress swished—a cloud of chiffon and crinoline as she touched a hand to her pearls, her eyes wide and ignorant of the murders done within the walls of the home. Mesmerized, I watched her play the innocent ingenue.

At quarter to eleven, the director yelled cut, and a balding man in a pinstriped suit along with Donna's manager bustled over to speak in his ear. The director told everyone to break for ten minutes. The pinstriped man hailed Donna, and the four of them disappeared into the library. The crew randomly milled around or tinkered with their equipment.

Ten minutes later, Donna, her head bowed, exited the building with her manager and drove away in a black sedan. The director came out of the library scratching his head and reassembled the crew. I slinked into the back of the pack to hear what he had to say.

"Donna has taken ill. Since Genevieve and Betsy are here today, we're going to reset in the parlor to film scene fourteen," he declared.

Aunt Ruby had not come to set today, and Donna's ride from the Castle Hill Inn was long gone. Everyone seemed to have forgotten about me.

I wandered aimlessly around the main level searching for a telephone to call a cab. A few of the doors were locked, and I suspected a telephone may have been in one of the rooms. I didn't want to bother any of the crew members resetting the front room for the new shots and decided to see if there was a phone upstairs.

My intentions were cut short when someone called out, "Excuse me, Miss!"

I paused on the landing halfway up the staircase.

The fellow in the pinstriped suit stood at the bottom step. "Yes. You. The reporter." He made the "come hither" signal with his index finger.

Languidly, I retreated down the steps explaining, "I'm looking for a telephone. I didn't realize Donna was unwell. She seemed fine in the car, on our way over?" Upon closer inspection, I determined the man's bespoke suit was made of silk, and his shoes Italian leather.

He gazed at me like one would a nasty piece of gum stuck to the bottom of a shoe. "Miss Morgan has left set for the day. You will go," he said with a French accent.

I blinked, stung by the abrupt dismissal. I cleared my throat and replied evenly, "Sure thing, Bob. Like I said, I need a telephone to call a cab?"

"My name is not Bob, it is Gaultier. I am the Cultural Attaché at the Maldinian Consulate."

"Very well." With an ingratiating smile, I went on to explain in French, "Gaultier, I rode in Miss Morgan's limousine this morning. My car is still parked at Castle Hill Inn."

"We are aware," he stated in English. "Transportation has been arranged." Taking me by the arm, he guided me firmly to the front door, and said in clipped tones, "You may wait, outside for the car."

"My father once told me, 'Never allow a man to touch you who does not have your permission,'" I admonished lifting my arm to remove it from his grasp. "He is a lawyer."

Uncertainty crossed Gaultier's arrogant features.

Taking advantage of his doubt, I decided the only way to deal with arrogance was to meet it head-on, and imperiously pronounced, "I need to fetch my coat and hat."

"I will fetch them for you. Where—"

"*You* will *not* touch my things. *I* will get them." Before he could utter another word, I stepped around him. My stilettos clicked across the parquet floor, as I fast walked into a den, decorated in flowers and yellow chintz.

Dozens of coats, hats, and gloves had been tossed into the room along with other random cases and boxes of production equipment. My hat was still on a hook above the mantel where I'd left it, and I found my swing coat, beneath a leather jacket on a dainty chair. Gaultier followed me into the room. Turning, with my outerwear in hand, I lifted my chin and slipped past him swishing my coat in a theatrical circle to drape it regally across my shoulders.

I threw open the front door, and imperially exited, striding down the stairs like a queen . . . or a princess. To my utter relief, a powder blue car rolled to a stop right in front of me as if scripted.

A beanpole of a fellow wearing a plaid cap with ear flaps got out. "Someone need to go to Castle Hill Inn?"

"That is me." The door behind me remained open, but I refused to allow the Maldinian the satisfaction of a backward glance. Instead, I slipped on my sunglasses and slid into the backseat of the car.

Twenty minutes later, I nosed the T-bird down the incline, away from Castle Hill Inn, my thoughts churning, a hard lump in my gut.

*How dare that smarmy man, put his hands on me. Why am I suddenly being treated like a leper? Donna seemed physically fine this morning. What changed? Is the end of my interview with the Princess?*

The morning clouds burned away leaving behind pure azure skies. I arrived back at Ivy Tree to find the sun's rays bouncing off the chrome bumper of Johnny's green truck and pulled in next to it. Shading my eyes, I glanced up to find him climbing down a ladder perched against the roof of the porch. He fiddled with the tool in his hand and headed toward the truck.

"Good afternoon, Miss Winter," he said cordially.

"Hello, Mr. Wexler. What are you working on today?"

"Gutter came loose." He indicated with a jerk of his head. A piece of gingerbread molding had been removed, and the water-diverting channel hung lopsidedly on the wooden facia.

"Seems like there's always something that needs fixing around here," I commented.

"Tends to happen with old houses," he explained with the lift of a shoulder. "Especially ones built before the turn of the century."

I continued staring up at the Victorian gables and fussy molding. "Keeps you in business."

"It does that. Are you well?" He squinted at me. "Your face seems particularly flushed."

Embarrassment from my summary dismissal from Kingscote still stung. I waved away his concerns with the flick of my wrist, and smoothly lied, "It's nothing, we were outside for the morning."

The screwdriver clattered among the other tools, as he tossed it into the case sitting on the liftgate of the pick-up truck.

"Have a good day." I skirted around him and hustled up the front steps.

Frank glanced up from the ledger he'd been studying and closed the book. "Good afternoon, Miss Winter."

"Hello." I trotted over to him. "Have I any messages?"

"You do." He reached into the cubby titled "Rose Suite" and pulled out a slip of paper. "A gentleman by the name of Howard Bradley was most insistent you phone him."

"My editor. Is there a phone I can use?"

He pointed to a door with a frosted glass window across from the reception desk. "Light switch is to the right."

I let myself into what must have originally been a coat closet. The booth smelled faintly of mothballs, and there was just enough room for the hard wooden chair and shiny black pay phone. My handbag balanced precariously on the minute shelf, as I dug out my coin purse. I gave the operator Howard's number and waited impatiently for the call to connect.

A few minutes later the operator said, "I have Mr. Bradley on the line."

"Hello!" he bellowed.

"Good afternoon, sir."

"What?"

The lines crackled and I spoke louder, "It's Ariadne Winter, returning your call."

"Winter! Where have you been?"

I blinked in confusion. Had he forgotten my assignment? "I'm in Newport as we discussed."

"I damn well know that! Why haven't you phoned sooner?"

Ah. He'd asked for regular reports. I hadn't realized he'd been expecting them daily. "Well, sir, it's only my second day—"

"Don't tell me you haven't got a story by the second day."

"Of course not," my voice pitched. "I've got a good start."

This seemed to placate his irritation, for he simply huffed, "Tell me."

"Well . . . I, ah . . . haven't begun typing the story, yet. I've been formulating my notes."

"That's fine. Give me what you've got so far."

I fumbled to pull the notebook from my handbag. Wrenching it free, my purse flipped off the shelf and rolled down my lap to slide between my feet. I bent to retrieve it and knocked my cheek against the corner of the payphone in the process.

"Ouch," I whimpered pressing cold fingers against it.

"Winter? Are you still there?"

"Yes, sir. Here's what I've got so far." I gave him the rundown of our discussions about the wedding. The flowers. The palace redecoration.

"Not bad. Not bad at all, Winter."

*Is that a tinge of approval in his voice?*

"Anything juicy?"

"Juicy, sir?"

"About the Prince? Scandals? Proclivities? What about his family?"

I paused thinking about the dowry. "I don't take your meaning."

He got down to brass tacks. "You don't get my meaning, eh? I received an officious phone call from some Frenchie. Claimed to be a minister of communication or some such thing. From the palace. He inquired about you. Wanted to know what your intentions were for the article. If you were trustworthy."

"I believe we made our intentions clear. As for my

107

trustworthiness—"

"Of course! That's what I told the fellow!" his voice boomed at me. "He was a bit cagey when I questioned what he meant by that. Told him all my journalists were above reproach. Have you any idea what he was talking about?"

"Nothing comes to mind."

"Well, those royal types can be a bit tetchy about their business. Believe me, I know," Howard intoned with the full gravity of his twenty-five years in the business.

"Yes sir." I replied.

He fell into one of his smoke-laden coughs.

"Sir?"

Howard cleared his throat. "Winter! I can't have you kicked off this story. We'd never get another journalist in there. So don't go putting your nose where it doesn't belong."

My editor, piling on top of my run-in with Gaultier elevated my blood-pressure, and I couldn't seem to help the sarcastic words that popped out of my mouth. "Of course, we wouldn't want to dig up anything untoward, like a real journalist. Keep things simple and uncomplicated. A nice bit of fluff for the ladies."

There was a pause, and I wondered if he'd fire me on the spot. On the other hand, Howard had given himself away with his earlier statement. He needed me to finish this for the magazine or *Look* would take over.

"Miss Winter, I've heard the stories," he said in deceptively dulcet tones, and I readied myself for a complete dressing down. "You don't think I realize your young little heart goes pitty-pat at the thought of getting a reporter job with the *Times* or the *Herald-Tribune*. You dream of working in a man's position as an investigative reporter. No?"

I realized the question was rhetorical and remained mute.

"May I remind you, *this* is *Ladies' Lifestyle Magazine.* Our readers want pretty pictures and princess dreams. If you're lucky, it'll be a steppingstone to bigger stories. So, if you want to keep your job at this magazine, you'll keep your nose clean. Am I clear?" he barked the last line.

"Crystal, sir."

"Good. I expect a report tomorrow."

"Yes, sir."

The line went dead, and I slammed the phone back on its hook. Closing my eyes, I rested my forehead on my palm. It wasn't shaping up to be a banner day, and it was only—I checked my watch—one-fifteen.

Something dripped onto my hand. I sniffed. It didn't have a smell. My eyes swept upward. Another drip fell onto my cheek and the lights went out.

109

# Chapter Sixteen
## Connie

Wiping her hands on a white towel, Connie stepped out of the bathroom and studied her husband as he sat in the blue flowered armchair staring sightlessly out the window. They'd returned home after lunch instead of going on the Block Island ferry because Walter pleaded a headache. While Dottie's prattle could get on one's nerves, it was unusual for it to affect Walter's even-keeled personality. He'd turned over the car keys to Cedric and heavily encouraged his wife to go with them. While she'd considered his suggestion, there was something that had her returning to the inn instead.

Connie had watched the furrow in Walter's brow deepen the longer they stayed in Newport. His half-burned cigarette lay untouched in the ashtray. The fingers on his right hand worried something in his pocket. Unconsciously, he pressed his left hand against his temple.

"Darling, are you *sure* you don't want one of my headache powders," she asked for the third time.

Walter pulled the hand away and picked up the cigarette tapping off a snake of ash. "No, I'm fine."

"At least the handyman has stopped all that racket. I swear, I could feel that metal against metal hammering in my teeth." She sat in the matching overstuffed chair and pulled a cigarette out of the packet he'd left next to the ashtray.

Walter struck a match for her and lit it, but offered no further conversation, instead choosing to return his attention to the baren oak tree outside their bedroom window. The pair had been married long enough, not to feel uncomfortable with long bouts of silence. Connie was a great reader of biographies and memoirs. She often enjoyed sitting next to her husband in silence, while he reviewed the *Financial Times* or work reports. However, they were not at home, and this silence came with a heaviness Connie couldn't quite put her finger on.

Not one to prevaricate or mince words, she decided it was time to put an end to this melancholy. "So, why don't you tell me what's going on? Problems at work?"

"Going on?" Confusion drew down his mouth to match his brow line. "To what are you referring?"

"Come now, Walter. Don't treat me like a fool. We've been married forty years. I know your moods like the back of my hand."

The ghost of a smile drifted across his features. "Oh? And what mood am I in now?"

Her eyes narrowed. "Pensive. Worried."

"Try worn out." The hand that picked up the cigarette shook the tiniest bit. "Remember, the headache." He tapped his forehead with the cigarette dangling between his first and middle fingers.

She took a deep drag on her cigarette, allowed the nicotine to fill her system, and then blew the smoke toward the ceiling. "Honestly, I cannot remember the last time *you* suffered from a headache. You have the constitution of an ox."

"Occasionally, Dottie Higginbottom can wear even *my* nerves to the bone. I didn't get much sleep last night. There was an owl in that tree that kept me awake. Did you hear it?"

"No, I didn't."

"It's probably why I'm out of sorts." He yawned.

That was the answer? A bad night's sleep?

For a moment, Connie's eyes narrowed analyzing her husband. *Why doesn't he just tell me what's eating at him?*

She crossed an arm over her meager bosom and cupped

her elbow. A waft of smoke slithered from the glowing tobacco to disappear into the air. "If that's all it is?"

"That's all it is," he spoke in a manner that did not reassure her. Pushing to his feet, he said, "You have a book sitting on the bedside table. Shall I get it for you? I'm going to lie down and rest my eyes." He settled on the side of the bed waiting for her answer.

She decided to leave it alone. Stubbing out her cigarette, she rose. "Why don't I close the curtains, and take my book to the parlor? Allow you to take a refreshing nap." Not waiting for a response, she pulled the curtains shut with a whoosh.

"Thank you, dearest." Walter slipped off his shoes and sank into the fluffy down comforter.

Connie scooped up her book and slid her feet into loafers.

She passed the Rose Suite on her way to the stairs. *That's where the young journalist is staying. At least she's not a noisy neighbor.*

It's the thing Connie hated about staying at a small inn. One guest could ruin the experience, and with so few rooms it's not as though they could request to move to a different room, like a large hotel. Still, she felt it was important to support Irene's son.

The carpet squelched beneath her feet. Stopping, she rocked back and forth. Sure enough, the red hallway runner had a distinct squish. Upon closer inspection, she saw water seeping from beneath the door to the Green Suite.

"Hullo, is anyone in there?" Connie knocked and tried the doorknob, but it was locked.

"Was there a spill up here?" Miss Winter's heels tapped their way around the curve of the stairs. "Water is dripping in the phone booth."

"It's coming out of the Green Suite. Best find Frank and Johnny."

She pivoted, and hurried back down calling, "Mr. Wyler, are you still at the reception desk? No."

Connie heard the library door open and close, then Miss Winter's pumps traipsed across the foyer as the young lady headed into the parlor.

"Yoohoo! Mr. Wyler! Mr. Wexler!" Her voice and footsteps dissipated as she searched the far side of the house.

Water continued to drift along the wood floors and carpet. The liquid stain spread further almost reaching the Rose Suite. Connie twisted the knob again and shoved her shoulder against the door. A foolish action that only sought to give her a sore shoulder. She rubbed it silently chastising herself. The doors in this old building were inches thick and made of solid hickory. Since there was nothing more she could do, Connie stepped away from the pooling water to await reinforcements. It wasn't long before they clattered up the stairs.

Frank led the way looking wild-eyed. Johnny directly behind, while Miss Winter brought up the rear. Connie indicated the Green Room.

Frank fumbled with the lock and dropped the keys.

Johnny scooped them up and with a sharp, "Let me do it," keyed into the room.

His work boots left imprints on the sage green carpeting and there was a distinct squelch as he walked. "It's coming from the bathroom."

The women followed the men into an explosion of verdant and coral hues. Floral curtains hung in the windows, peach and green wedding ring coverlets spread across the twin beds, a modern green loveseat with blush striped pillows sat between the two windows, and grass cloth paper covered the upper half of the walls, while the lower wood paneling had been painted peach. Miss Winter let out a sad sigh.

"Damn it! How did *this* happen?" Frank lamented.

Tiptoeing through the soaked bed chamber, Miss Winter and Connie made their way to the bathroom door to find Johnny bent under the sink twisting off the water valve. A frustrated and bewildered Frank stood to the side with his arms akimbo.

The cold-water handle had come off and water glugged out of the top of the fluted escutcheon. Johnny gave the valve one last twist, and the fountain stopped. The leak wouldn't have been a problem, except the heavy porcelain lever landed on the stopper and pushed it closed. Once the water filled the sink, it had nowhere to go except over the edge to leisurely work its way past the bathroom threshold into the bedroom.

Johnny retrieved the lever sending more water cascading over the rim of the sink and released the stopper plug. "Fetch my toolbox. It's in the back of my truck," he directed.

Frank's face suffused into an angry red. "Tell me how this happened!"

"How should I know? Ask the plumber who installed it," he shot back. Johnny picked up a small screw from the back of the sink. "Looks to me like it wasn't screwed on correctly."

"It was *your* job to oversee the workmen."

Johnny got into Frank's face. "I warned you about cutting corners. Bring in a cut-rate crew, and *this* is what you get."

"If you'd watched them complete the work—" Frank chastised.

"I was *watching* half-a-dozen subcontractors the week the plumbers were here. I remember telling you not to overlap like that," Johnny spat back. "Contractors were in here tripping over each other."

"We were on a deadline!" Frank barked.

"I told you to move it. And now look what's happened!" Johnny argued.

"Gentlemen!" Both males turned their angry faces toward Connie, and she spoke in the stern tone she often used on her boys when they would bicker. "While you're arguing, water is seeping deeper into the carpets, and the wood flooring beneath them, and into the ceiling on the first floor. Now is not the time to place blame. I suggest you work together to solve this problem before it gets worse."

When neither man argued with her valid points, she continued, "Johnny, why don't you go and fetch your tools? Frank, you'd best see about calling a service to mediate the flooding and fetch as many towels as possible."

"There was water dripping from the light fixture in the phone booth. You'll want to clean it out and make sure the water hasn't damaged the electrical circuit," Miss Winter put in. "My room is next door. I'm going to see if the damage spread that far."

Once the room emptied, Connie put down her book on a bed and rolled up her sleeves. Pulling the sage towels from the rack, she laid them on the linoleum floor. They were sopping wet within moments, and she flopped them into the tub. A quick search discovered more towels in the wardrobe, and she laid them in the hallway to stem the outflow.

Johnny, toolbox in hand, came up the stairs two at a time. Glancing down at the already-drenched towels in the doorway he grimaced. "Not sure that'll do much good."

"We do what we can," Connie replied tartly to his receding back.

Miss Winter came out of her room carrying two fluffy pink towels. "I thought these might help."

She'd changed into slim black ankle pants, a soft pink Angora sweater, and exchanged her pumps for white Keds.

At least the girl had changed into something practical. She could feel the water seeping through the leather of her loafers and considered changing into the snow boots she'd brought. "Are you sure you want to sacrifice all your towels to the cause?" Connie asked.

"I kept one for my bath tonight." The girl spread them across the wet hallway carpet stepping on them to soak up the liquid. "Funny how Mr. Wyler has had a string of bad luck," she mused.

"What do you mean?" Connie stared at her bowed dark head.

Those cunning green eyes swept up. "The mouse, the oven, and now this flood," she reeled off. "Don't you find it odd?"

Though the comment seemed innocent, her sharp gaze let Connie know the cogs were turning. From the outset, Connie had found something disconcerting about the young woman. She was not what she seemed. Her couture fashions and fluffy women's magazine job belied a cleverness most people wouldn't bother to notice.

She spoke little but observed everything.

Connie, too, was an intelligent woman used to being overlooked—though never by her husband. Perhaps that's why she felt a twinge of annoyance over the fact that Miss Winter had identified and grouped all of Frank's recent maladies. Indeed, when one viewed them as a cluster, it appeared the poor man was having a bad time of it.

"I believe there's an old saying—bad things happen in threes," Connie replied. "Let's hope this is the end of Frank's rotten luck."

She moved a towel over the threshold. "I wonder where everyone's gone. We're making a racket."

"Kitty and Melvin left around ten. I believe they were driving to a museum in Providence today. Dottie and Cedric took the one o'clock ferry over to Block Island."

"Cold day for the ferry." There was a pause before she probed, "You didn't go with them?"

"Walter wasn't feeling well. He's lying down."

"I'm sorry to hear it." She tamped down the towel, leaving a dirty shoe print behind.

Turn about being fair play, Connie asked her a question, "What are you doing back so early? I thought you had a front-row seat to the filming."

Miss Winter's ears visibly reddened. "Donna Morgan wasn't feeling well either and she returned to her hotel."

Connie grunted. "Must be going around."

Frank came up the stairs at a fast clip, his arms loaded with towels. "Thank you, ladies," he puffed. "I appreciate the help, but I'll take it from here. Go enjoy your day."

"Nonsense, young man," Connie said. "I've nothing better to do. I'll remain to help."

Miss Winter cleared her throat. "If you've got things under control, I have an article to draft." She stepped back.

"Has there been any damage to your room, Miss Winter," Frank asked.

"None that I could see. Would you like to take a look before I start?" she pointed to her door.

"It's not necessary." He dropped the pile of towels on a dry spot in the hallway "Be sure to let me know if something crops up."

She nodded and retreated to her room. Johnny cursed, and the clank of a tool reverberated out of the bathroom. Frank stared into the Green Suite with a defeated look on his face. "The carpet is only three months old. Do you think it can be salvaged?"

Connie doubted it, but she didn't want to be the one to break the news. "Let's see what the professionals have to say about it." She laid a motherly hand on his shoulder.

"What happened here?"

Startled Connie jerked her hand away. "Walter! I didn't hear you. I thought you were going to take a nap."

Frank began laying down a path of towels from the hallway to the bathroom.

Walter removed his glasses and rubbed them with a handkerchief. "Couldn't sleep with all the noise."

"What about your headache, dear?" Connie scrutinized her husband. The worry lines were still etched on his forehead, but the tension around his eyes had eased.

He gave a sheepish look as he replaced his glasses. "Took one of your headache powders."

She patted his arm. "Good."

He cleared his throat. "Looks like we've got a leak."

"Bathroom sink," she confirmed.

"What can I do to help?" Walter asked.

Connie let out a swooshing breath. Her husband was truly a good man. "Frank, pass us some of those towels."

The faint clack of a typewriter came from the Rose Suite.

# Chapter Seventeen
## Ariadne

The conversation dipped and swayed through the parlor, and, for the most part, covered the low hum of the industrial fans brought in by the company Frank hired to dry things out. They'd spent the afternoon ripping up the green wall-to-wall carpet. Two fans were set up in the room, another in the hallway. The phone booth was out of order until a professional electrician came in the next day.

Tonight, all the guests gathered in the parlor. By unspoken consent, we'd chosen to mute our evening finery, as if in deference to Frank's latest calamity. Everyone, that is, except Dottie, who'd swathed herself in sea foam green chiffon and no less than five strands of pearls of varied lengths. Kitty and I had chosen simple black dresses, and Connie wore a navy-blue skirt with a polka-dot blouse. In her dry manner, she retold her discovery of the flood. Kitty had an almost macabre fascination with the overflow, asking about each detail and hanging on to Connie's every word.

Meanwhile, Melvin pulled a rather frazzled Frank into the parlor and lectured him on the vacuum the company should have used to suck the water out of the carpets. "I'm telling you! If the company had used the new bagless Hoover vacuum, you would've been able to keep those carpets. The machine's a dream. I sold three to a feller in Buffalo who runs one of these flood recovery companies. Sucks that water right up. You just dump it out in the street when the canister is full. Wish I'd been here when it happened. I could've given him a call for you."

Melvin, holding a bottle of beer in one hand, slapped Frank on the back with the other. "I can set you up with your own bagless vacuum if you like. In case it happens again."

Frank gave a weak smile. "Thanks for the offer, but I'm hoping never to need such a contraption again."

Melvin gazed around the room, up the wall, and across the ceiling. "I wouldn't be so sure about that." He made a sucking sound between his teeth. "These old houses . . . you never know."

Kitty's head swiveled away from Connie. "I'm sure Frank knows what he's doing, dear. Besides you *promised*, no business while on vacation," she chastised in a harsh nasal tone.

Melvin guffawed at Kitty's reprimand as if it was a joke.

Dottie, bored with the entire discussion—or perhaps jealous she'd missed all the action— injected, "Oh, Connie, I wish you and Walter could have come with us over to Block Island. The wind was something fierce on the ferry ride over, but the water simply glistened in the sun!"

She pivoted on the couch to speak directly to me. "Miss Winter, you *must* go over there before you leave. It had the most adorable shops. You, in particular, would love the boutiques."

I wasn't sure why I, of all the women at the inn, was to be singled out for such a treat. "I'll see if I can fit it into my schedule."

"If Donna Morgan is still sick tomorrow, surely you'll have time to do some sightseeing," Connie commented.

Dottie gasped, "She's ill? How awful. What is her malady?"

"I wasn't told," I said in clipped tones.

"Probably the vodka flu," Cedric snickered making a drinking motion with his empty hand. "Those Hollywood types, they're all the same." Ironic considering Cedric was on his third drink of the evening while the rest of us nursed our first.

"Ceddie! Surely not!" Dottie admonished.

"I've not seen evidence of it," I commented irritated by such an aspersion being cast upon the future princess of Maldinia.

Cedric must have recognized my displeasure, for he shrugged, and turned to Walter. They fell into a discussion about the upcoming baseball season.

Because Frank had been dealing with the flood remediation company, he'd given Edward the key to the liquor cabinet and told him to make the cocktails.

I'd chosen a martini, and the kid had done a damn fine job of it.

"Shall I pour anyone another drink?" he asked solicitously.

A general negative murmured through the company, although, out of the corner of my eye, Cedric took a large slug of his Scotch, as if preparing for another, a move witnessed by Frank.

"Edward, I believe your mother needs help in the kitchen. Run along," he suggested. "I'll take care of the drinks."

I fell quiet, sipping my drink while listening to the conversations around me. The front door banged open silencing the room as it caught everyone's attention.

In walked Aunt Ruby.

She was magnificent in leopard fur over a bark brown pencil dress with her tresses pulled up into her signature French twist. As usual, not a hair was out of place and her expertly applied makeup highlighted her cheekbones and eyes.

"Well, my pet, it's happened. You've been scooped."

A folded newspaper dropped on the coffee table.

The headline jumped out at me as I picked it up, *Prince Funds Morgan's Latest Flick.* "What paper is this?" I asked flipping it over.

"*Providence Chronicle,* front page of the—"

"Lifestyle section. Above the fold," I murmured reading

the article.

Overall, it didn't have much to say beyond the headline. The article stated that the Prince of Maldinia, in an act of love and affection for his fiancée, was the sole financier of his soon-to-be wife's last film. It outlined information about the production being filmed in Newport. It didn't mention the dowry payment.

"Hello, Frank." He nodded at Ruby as she stripped off her black gloves. "I assume you are not the anonymous source who the reporter quotes."

My eyes flew upward, and I slapped the newspaper on the coffee table. "No!"

Dottie subtly leaned over slipping the paper off the table.

Aunt Ruby gave me a hard stare.

"Absolutely NOT!" I gave my head a vehement shake.

"I didn't think so," she sighed. "I received a phone call from Monty about an hour ago."

My mouth dropped.

"Don't worry." She flicked her wrist. "I assured him you'd never give away a scoop such as that to a rag like *The Providence Chronicle*."

"You're damn right I wouldn't." I surged to my feet, and realized the entire assemblage hung on our conversation. "Pardon me," I softened my tone. "Perhaps we should finish this discussion in my suite."

Aunt Ruby trailed me out of the parlor and up the stairs. Meanwhile, the events of the day replayed in my mind. The suspicion and rudeness from the Maldinian. The call to my editor. Donna's reserve in the car.

My aunt's eyes alighted on the equipment. "What happened here?"

"Bathroom sink overflowed. Watch the cords." We stepped around the snaking cables, and I keyed into my room. Once the door was closed, I rounded on her. "I know *I* didn't reveal any information. Did *you*?"

Unperturbed, Aunt Ruby walked through the sitting area, running her hand across the back of the sofa, the mantel. She glanced at each piece of furniture and decided on the loveseat. Draping herself onto it, she crossed her legs and lit a cigarette.

I paced from the front windows to the fireplace and back again watching her movements. After she'd taken a puff, I cracked out, "Well?"

"Frankly Ariadne, you're lucky I don't put you over my knee for such an impertinent question," she voiced in arctic tones.

Rooted to the spot, my shoulders fell. "I beg your pardon. I've had a rather unnerving afternoon. Starting with an unceremonious dismissal from the set, and a pointed dressing down by my editor. After reading the article—" I fell onto the sofa next to her and stared gloomily at the mint green portable Smith-Corona typewriter the magazine had provided for this assignment. The roller held my partially typed article.

*Can I write a full spread article with what I have?*
*Probably.*

And it would be good. But to get off the copy desk permanently, I needed great.

I sighed. "What should I do? Will Donna speak to me?"

"Well, pet, after I got off the phone with the director, I made a few phone calls myself. It appears the leak came from the driver." She passed her cigarette to me.

It wasn't my favorite brand, but right now, I could have smoked an entire pack of unfiltered Lucky Strikes. "Who hired him?"

"The studio."

I cast my mind back to the drive home yesterday. "He must have heard us talking about the dowry. Why wasn't it in the article?"

"It seems as though the Maldinian Consulate stepped in, and requested the entire article pulled. Since the *Chronicle* was able to obtain confirmation about the funding from a secretary at the studio—who will likely be fired tomorrow, poor girl—" Aunt Ruby shook her head, pity writ across her features "—they ran with the little they had."

"Do you think I'll be able to continue the interview?"

"Tomorrow morning, I will pick you up and take you over to Castle Hill Inn. Be ready to go at seven. I'll assure her of your integrity, and if she banishes you, she'll have to do her hair and makeup on her own," Ruby said.

"Oh, Aunt Ruby! You can't."

"I can, and I will," she firmly stated. "Nobody blames my niece for another's naughtiness. Besides, you work for *Ladies' Lifestyle Magazine.* Not some tittle-tattle rag."

I gave a lop-sided grin. "Thanks."

She pulled me into a side hug. "You can count on me."

I stubbed out the cigarette, rose to my feet, and offered my hand to Aunt Ruby. "Shall we go down to dinner?"

"I thought you'd never ask."

# Chapter Eighteen
## Dottie

"It's clear he takes us for a couple of fools," Dottie hissed at her husband, her hands gripping the filched newspaper. They stood in the short passage that led to the back rooms, where she'd dragged Cedric after reading the article about the Prince of Maldinia. "He's been lying from the beginning." So angry, Dottie felt as though her head might explode like one of NASA's rocket ships. Fire might spurt out of her ears.

"Now, now." Cedric patted Dottie's shoulder. "We don't know that for sure. The *Chronicle* is known for printing false reports."

She swatted him away. "Cedric! How foolish can you be? I'm going to speak to him right this moment." Her chiffon skirt rustled as she spun on her heel.

"Now hold up there Dorothy Higginbottom." He grabbed her tightly by the wrist before she could take two steps. "This is a man's discussion. I will talk with him. *After* dinner," he stated firmly.

"Why?" Dottie's voice rose high and pitchy. Though it was childish, she stamped her little foot. "Why not now?"

"I don't wish to cause indigestion." Cedric stroked his rotund belly.

The sound of women's pumps tapping across the hardwood floors halted any further arguments from Dottie. Rearranging her features, she uncurled her fingers and pressed the paper against Cedric's chest. Huffing out, "Fine. Let's go eat. But I expect you to have it out with Frank *after* dinner."

As they entered the dining room, Dottie ran into a new problem. Miss Winter and her aunt were taking their seats at the table in front of the window. However, it wasn't the young woman and her guest that put Dottie's nose out of joint. One of the two-person tables had been stuck at the end of the four top normally occupied by the Conrads and Sullivans. Walter sat at the head of the table with Connie to his right, both studying the menu. Kitty had taken the seat to the left of Walter, and her husband on the other side of Connie, leaving two spaces free. Neither of which Dottie cared to occupy.

Kitty turned to Dottie and Cedric as they entered. "Isn't this charming? We've made it a six-person table, so we can all sit together, and continue our conversation. Cedric, come sit next to me, so we can be boy-girl. Dottie, you're there, at the foot of the table next to Melvin."

Her already sour mood worsened, and Dottie couldn't help the slight wince that crossed her features as Kitty pointed to her husband. Luckily, Melvin's attention was turned to the menu, and he missed the face she made.

Dottie couldn't decide if she was more infuriated by Kitty's heavy-handedness at arranging her seating chart, or Frank Wyler for lying about the money he owed them.

Frank walked out of the kitchen carrying a tray with four wine glasses.

The cottage on the lake flashed through Dottie's mind, and her eyes threw daggers at Frank's back.

Without bothering to help his wife into her chair, Cedric took his seat with equanimity, if not downright pleasure. "Well, isn't this a nice change?"

Connie looked up from the menu to accept the glass of wine Frank handed her. "Dot, do sit down and look at the menu so we can order. I find I'm ravenous tonight."

*Et tu, Connie?*

Melvin noticing Dottie had not been seated jumped to his

feet, the only male at the table to do so, and pulled out Dottie's chair for her. "Madame," he said with a grandiose flourish.

Dottie batted her lashes at him. "Thank you."

In an effort to punish Kitty for her perfidy, she began flirting mercilessly with Melvin. Kitty seemed not to notice, or care, and the tactic backfired on Dottie. Melvin, taking her interest seriously, proceeded to list the top five vacuum cleaners on the market, and the reasons why Dottie should buy one for her home.

*How on earth does Kitty put up with it?*

# Chapter Nineteen
## Walter

The paper, crumpled from being folded, refolded, and jammed in his pocket, sat innocently enough on the laminate tabletop. There was nothing innocent in the threatening words typed upon it.

Walter draped his arm across the back of the vinyl chair. His robe splayed open revealing an undershirt and the gray slacks he'd worn to dinner. He reached for the bottle and poured another finger of Canadian whiskey into the tumbler. A stripe of moonlight filtered through the amber liquid. Walter spun the tumbler watching the liquid move through the light and darkness, then he clinked the rim of his glass against the bottle and downed the shot in one go.

The swinging door gave the slightest creak as it opened, and a figure in white glided into the room. Walter blinked wondering if it was the lack of sleep or the drink which brought on the hallucination. The apparition drifted over to the refrigerator and opened it. Light emanated from the appliance and the apparition morphed into a solid and recognizable human form wearing a white dressing gown with little pink slippers peeping out from beneath the hem. The back of her hair was wrapped in a net thing, he believed it was called a snood, or something equally strange.

"Good evening, Miss Winter."

She jumped and spun around putting a hand to her chest. Now backlit, Walter couldn't see her face in the dark, but by her gasp, he presumed, his presence startled her.

"My goodness! Mr. Sullivan! I didn't see you sitting there."

"Pilfering Wyler's food?" He pulled out a cigarette from the pack on the table.

"I-I couldn't sleep, and thought I'd make some hot milk," she stammered. "I plan to tell him in the morning so he can put it on my bill." Her gaze landed on the bottle and her spine stiffened. She returned fire, "And you? Pilfering Mr. Wyler's liquor?"

He softened. "I'm ribbing you, Miss Winter. I can't imagine he'd notice if a glass of milk went missing. You can count on my discretion."

"Nonetheless. I'll notify him." With determination, she took a quart of milk off the refrigerator door, retrieved a small saucepan from the dish drainer, and took the lot over to the stove.

"Suit yourself." He lit the cigarette and then snapped on a miniature Lucite lamp sitting on the counter behind him. It sent a warm glow through the room. "And the whiskey is mine. Picked it up from the store today."

"Oh." She went about lighting the gas with a match and turned the blue flames down low. "I apologize for being snappish. It hasn't been a swell day for me."

"I assumed, from the discussion during cocktails." He indicated the direction of the parlor with his cigarette.

"Not my finest hour." She poured milk into the saucepan. "Would you care for a glass?"

"I'll stick with the whiskey." He poured another finger. "What happens if you can't finish the interview?"

"Oh, I've enough to write *an* article."

"An article, but not *the* article."

Her head bobbed as she stirred the milk. "Exactly. The magazine is supposed to send a photographer up this weekend. If I've been banned, he might very well be too. Then we'll have to rely upon the media shots that everyone has access to.

Makes the magazine look rather pedestrian."

"You know where Donna Morgan is staying. You could stake out her hotel. Hide behind the bushes and jump up like those paparazzi fellows with the flashbulbs."

She delivered a glance so withering it could melt an anvil. "That is *not* the type of magazine *Ladies' Lifestyle* aspires to be. We don't print unapproved photographs for our articles."

Walter picked up the tumbler to hide his grin at her pedantic comments.

Miss Winter returned her attention to the stove. A quick test with her finger verified the milk was warm enough, and she snapped off the burner.

"Mugs are in the upper cabinet to your left," Walter said.

Once the milk had been poured, and the saucepan left to cool on the stove, Miss Winter joined him at the table. She eyed the whiskey bottle.

"Take a jigger if you like," he offered.

She considered for a moment but shook her head. "Better not. It wouldn't be good to show up tomorrow morning smelling like a souse."

The pair sat in silence. The only sound was the occasional gust of wind that rattled the storm door, the tick of an antique Regulator clock on the wall, and the slight crackle of the burning tobacco as Walter sucked on the cigarette.

"I imagine that piece of paper is the reason you can't sleep." The girl held the mug with both hands just below her chin. Her red nail varnish shined beneath the glow of the lamplight.

"It's not what it looks like."

"It looks like a blackmail note." She sipped her milk.

"Would you believe me, if I told you I'd only done it once?"

With a tilt of her head, she invited Walter to elaborate.

Scrubbing his stubble, he headed into the miserable tale. "Connie and I hit a rough patch in our marriage. You see, two weeks after Pearl Harbor, all three of our boys signed up."

"Everyone was doing it." She lowered her mug. "Wait, you said *three* boys?"

"Mm-hm, George and David off to the Army. Jeffrey into the Navy. I have a weak ticker." He tapped his chest. "Childhood fever. I couldn't join up, but Connie was determined to do her part, and the war needed mathematicians. She got a government job at the university. Everything was bumping along just fine . . . until D-Day."

He took a moment to light a new cigarette with the old one before stubbing it out. Miss Winter remained quiet, patiently waiting for him to continue. "It was David. Our youngest."

She winced. "On the beaches?"

Walter shook his head. "Behind enemy lines. He was a paratrooper. His plane was shot to hell by anti-aircraft fire. Only two soldiers made it out the door in time."

Miss Winter put down her mug and poured a dollop of whiskey into it.

"While I grieved the loss, Connie started working day and night. She worked double and triple shifts, going at a manic pace. As if the end of the war relied on her shoulders. When she was home, her attitude toward me was angry . . . bitter. As if it was my fault David died. She grew thin and gaunt. I'd never seen that type of behavior from her. I had no idea how to fix it. And what did I do?" He threw his head back and blew a cloud of smoke at the white plaster ceiling. "Ignored it and spent more time at the office avoiding her."

"How did it happen?" She nodded at the paper.

"An unoriginal story. A business trip took me to New York City." He sipped the whiskey for courage. He'd never told another soul this story. "She was a charming blonde waitress working in the cocktail bar. I can't recall her name—Charity or Charlene—maybe," he mused tapping ash into the golden glass tray.

*Why did I lie?* He knew her name.

131

Linda.

Linda with her cherry red lips, and a silky red dress to match.

"I came home from New York to find the house a mess. Connie catatonic holding David's baseball mitt. I've never been so afraid in my life. She was rocking and humming. She hadn't showered in days. No idea when she last ate. Her office called not long after I'd arrived home. They were worried. She hadn't been to work since I left town."

"Did you talk about David?"

"Not then." He stared off into space absentmindedly smoking as the remembrance of finding his wife sitting on David's childhood bed played through his mind. Her hair was a wreck. Lines of mascara tracked her cheeks. A sour scent emanated from her pores. Unresponsive to his questions, or any noise for that matter. Just the rocking and off-key humming. Chills ran up his spine at the memory.

The clink of glass against glass brought him back to the present and the yellow kitchen. Miss Winter was pouring him more whiskey.

His brows rose.

"You look like you could use another," she explained.

He couldn't remember finishing the last finger, and this one went down the hatch in two gulps. The tumbler clanked against the tabletop when he finished.

"What did you do?"

"I called my mother who trained up from Hartford. She took one look at Connie and knew exactly what to do. She bathed my wife, wrapped her in a clean nightgown, fed her some soup, and read the Bible out loud until she fell asleep." He tapped the ash of his cigarette and took a drag.

"Connie slept for twenty hours straight while Mother cleaned up the house. She brought in a doctor, who diagnosed malnourishment with dehydration, and acute sleep deprivation. He wanted to admit her to the hospital. But between my mother and me, we convinced him to allow her to remain at home if she promised not to return to work for two weeks. *And* she had to start gaining weight. In those weeks, Mother made the most mouthwatering meals. I've no idea how she achieved it with the rationing, but she seemed to find a way."

"Connie recovered?"

"She improved after the first forty-eight hours." He shook his head in regret at the memory and placed the cigarette on the side of the ashtray. "Did you know, during the war, the Japanese used sleep deprivation as a form of torture on prisoners?" He reached for the pack, but Miss Winter slid it away from his grasp.

"Sounds like your mother arrived at just the right time." She tamped out what remained of the burning cigarette, the last bits of smoke curled above her head.

"You've no idea." He gave up on the cigarettes pushing the full ashtray aside. "Not only did she fatten up my wife, but somehow, she got her to talk about David's death so Connie could finally mourn."

Once again silence descended.

The girl sipped her milk, her pert gaze watched Walter as he fidgeted with the tumbler and stared into space remembering a different time and place. A time when David was still in this world.

"When did the letter arrive?" she asked softly.

His attention snapped back to her. "Six weeks ago. It came with photos."

"Where are they?"

"Burned them."

She nodded with understanding. "Is the cocktail waitress blackmailing you?"

"I'm not sure, but I don't believe so. As you can see the letter tells me to stay at the inn between the dates of February fifteenth to the twenty-fourth." His forefinger tapped the letter for emphasis. "I've been waiting for more information."

"You haven't figured out who sent the letter?"

"It isn't you, is it?"

"No." She gave a derisive snort. "What about the money? It asks for $5000."

"It's in the bottom of my suitcase."

She gurgled; milk shot onto the table. Coughing, she wiped her nose and mouth with the sleeve of her robe. "Don't you think that's—"

"Foolish?" He handed her a towel hanging from the sink.

She nodded mopping up the mess.

"Only a fool would've slept with that waitress." He sighed, "So, a fool, am I."

"You think it's one of the guests?"

Putting his palms together, Walter leaned forward and dropped his voice, "I *think* it might be Frank."

Brow furrowing, she replied with skepticism, "Mr. Wyler?"

"The inn needed a lot of work. I found out he asked Connie for a loan. In deference to her friendship with Irene, she gifted him a few hundred. Nothing big enough to cover all of this." He waved his hand around indicating the newly renovated kitchen. "I saw a past due bill sitting on the reception desk with a pile of mail. I think he might be underwater. But no one has approached me, yet. Until I receive more information, I can't say for sure who's putting on the black."

The pair mulled over the question when a new thought occurred to him. "You're not going to tell Connie, are you?"

She laughed. "Isn't it a little late to ask me that?"

"Well, you'd already seen the letter . . ." he said as a way of explanation for unloading such a secret.

Her head tilted and her eyes narrowed as she scrutinized him. "Do you love your wife?"

"Of *course*." He emphatically stated.

"And did you ever do it again?"

He held her gaze. "Absolutely not!"

She licked her lips and firmly placed the mug on the table.

"This is my thought on the matter, the sordid tale will hurt your wife, and I'm not sure it's a good idea to dredge up ancient history. I also don't feel it's my place to get in the middle of a marriage."

Relief spread through his limbs like a warm bath.

"But what are you going to do about the blackmailer?" she asked. "This could continue for years to come."

"I'll insist on the negatives."

"What if the blackmailer doesn't hand them over?"

He stared down at the empty tumbler and let out a deeply troubled sigh. "I suppose, then I'll have to tell Connie."

"Mm-hm. Take away his power."

"The thing I can't figure out, is *how* he got the photos."

"Obviously, whomever took the photos, was at the hotel the same time you were. Saw you with the cocktail waitress and took the photos for evidence to show your wife."

Walter grimaced.

"Or the waitress had a partner. Maybe the whole thing was a con job, and they targeted you. But it happened so long ago. Why bring it up now? Why sit on the evidence for fourteen years?" I mused.

"That's why I think it's Frank. He's gotten into debt and may not have the knowledge how to right the ship. I'd be happy to help him work out the finances if he'd put aside his pride and confide in me," Walter slurred the last part.

"Blackmail gets him quick cash. Which it sounds like he needs." Her chair scraped against the oak floors as she stood. "Until you hear from the blackmailer, there's nothing more you can do."

"Connie's my rock." His head drooped toward his chest. "Don't know what I'd do without her."

"Come on Mr. Sullivan. Time for bed, upsy daisy." She pulled Walter to his feet, and together they shuffled out of the kitchen.

# Chapter Twenty
## Ariadne

**Thursday**

The teeth-chattering bell of the alarm clock woke me at six. I flicked on the bedside lamp and stared up at the shadowed ceiling to orient myself. After leaving Walter at his door, I'd re-read the beginning of my article and made edits, drifting off to sleep long after midnight.

Yesterday's problems pushed their way to the front of my mind. Dread pooled in the pit of my stomach, as I stretched and sat up. A foggy frost covered the windows. Scraping a peephole with my nail, in the gray light, I saw a fresh blanket of snow covering the yard and became doubly glad I'd packed my fur-lined velveteen boots.

I made it down to the dining room, as Maria was placing a tray loaded with onion and pepper and potatoes into the chafing dishes on the buffet.

"Good morning," I said.

She stiffened and gave me a brief nod before turning back to the kitchen.

I didn't like being on the outs with the cook. After all, she was making meals for me. I didn't need a bout of food poisoning on top of everything else going on. "Mrs. Massey—"

The cook paused, a hand on the swinging door.

"I apologize if I've offended you. It was not my intention."

She rotated to face me, and said coldly, "I don't know what

you mean."

"I'm afraid you find me to be a bit . . . intrusive. Perhaps it's my journalistic training. It was truly an accident stumbling into your discussion with Mr. Wyler. I want you to know that I find your cooking quite delicious, and I-I think you're a great mother. You've raised an impressive young man."

The cook continued to stare at me.

Shifting my weight, I continued, "I don't wish to be at odds with you."

Her lashes came down shuttering tired eyes. After a deep breath, she reopened them. "Very well, Miss Winter." Her face relaxed. "Would you like a cup of coffee?"

"Please. And can you fill up a thermos for me? I have a feeling I'm going to need it." My stomach in knots, I was only able to swallow a piece of toast washed down with the coffee.

At five to seven, I went out to the front porch to await Aunt Ruby. A cold wind whipped through the air instantly chilling parts uncovered such as my face, ears, and hands. The pathway out to the street had already been cleared of snow, and someone, in a red plaid coat and a trapper hat was shoveling the sidewalk in front of the inn.

I called out a, "Hello." His head turned, and I recognized Johnny.

"Miss Winter. You're up and about early." He leaned against the shovel handle. "I haven't gotten to the driveway yet. Will you be taking the T-bird out in this mess?"

"My aunt is picking me up." I pulled on a pair of leather gloves and rubbed my hands together to warm them. The skies lightened turning tangerine with the rising sun.

"Be careful. I've salted the walk, but there are still slick spots.

Aunt Ruby's red and white Bel Air came into sight. I picked my way down the stairs and along the pathway. The car rolled over the fresh unplowed snow packing it down with a crunching noise. Once the car came to a halt Johnny opened the passenger door for me.

"Thank you, Mr. Wexler," I said climbing into the warm car.

Aunt Ruby had the heaters blasting away.

"Call me Johnny," he winked and leaned down to see inside. "Ruby, it's good to see you."

"Johnny." She nodded at him. "I see you're hard at it this fine morning."

Johnny's smile turned brittle, and he replied in a mocking manner, "We aim to please. Anything for the master."

She tsked, "I had hoped the two of you would have worked out your differences by now."

"Just as soon as he hands over my father's things that belong to me," he declared.

"Johnny," she said his name with a drawn-out sigh.

"Have a nice day, ladies. Drive safe."

The door shut with a thud. Aunt Ruby drove in contemplative silence. I didn't dare point out that I'd been correct about Johnny's animosity toward Frank.

When we arrived, Aunt Ruby shut off the engine and turned to me. "I'll speak to Donna first. Hopefully, then, she'll allow you to explain your side of the story."

"*My* side of the story!" I fumed. "I didn't *do* anything. What *is* my side of the story?"

"Exactly that. You kept your word, and it's not your fault the driver blabbed to that awful rag. Now, be careful getting out it's slippery."

Aunt Ruby's strategy didn't go exactly to plan. In answer to her imperious knock, the door was opened by Gaultier, the snooty Maldinian. His presence did not deter Aunt Ruby.

"I am here to do Miss Morgan's hair and makeup," she said and made to move past him.

Gaultier didn't budge.

She placed her case on the floor and indicated around her. "Am I to do Miss Morgan's hair in the hallway, then?"

He pointed at Aunt Ruby. "You may come in." The finger moved to me. "That one stays out."

Aunt Ruby pulled herself up to her five foot nine inches, which was closer to six feet in the heeled boots she wore. "*That* is *my* niece. You expect to leave my niece cooling her heels in the hallway? An innocent young girl, who could be accosted by any stranger roaming the halls?"

Gaultier flushed and cleared his throat. "The press is not allowed in with Miss Morgan."

"I see." Aunt Ruby picked up her case. "Then Miss Morgan can find someone else to do her hair and makeup. And good luck to her, because I know all the good salons in the area. And will be sure to tell them of the ill-treatment I have received."

I didn't want my aunt to lose a good job because of me. "Aunt Ruby, perhaps—"

"Perhaps nothing. Come along Ariadne. It is clear we are not wanted."

From beyond Gaultier, the soft but stern tones of Donna Morgan said, "Let them in."

We halted our retreat. Aunt Ruby stared at Gaultier who continued guarding the doorway. "Well?"

Gaultier turned his head and spoke French in hushed tones, "The reporter is not allowed."

"It is my room, and I say they are both allowed. I'm due on set within the hour. I cannot find a new hairdresser in the next forty-five minutes," she proclaimed also in French.

"I'll find you one—" he started.

"You'll do no such thing. The girl is not the one who spoke to the *Chronicle*. Now step aside and let them through!" she snapped.

Gaultier, his dome red and ears aflame, stepped aside and indicated we should enter.

"And Gaultier, please be so kind as to fetch me a fresh cup of coffee, and perhaps a dish of fruit." Donna stood in the middle of the small living area of the suite wearing a gray woolen skirt and a pink cashmere sweater set. Her hair was pinned up in curlers, and her beautiful features free of makeup.

Gaultier looked as though he wished to argue, but Donna dismissed him with a single, "thank you," and took her seat at the dressing table. The Maldinian finally left, closing the door with a crack that made me jump.

"Well, my dear, it seems you've hit your first road bump on the way to becoming a royal." Aunt Ruby placed her bag on the sofa and began removing bottles and tins. "How are you holding up?"

Donna sighed. "The House of Aaldenberg is up in arms, as you can imagine. Or perhaps it's that toad, Gaultier, who is up in arms."

"And what does the Prince have to say?" my aunt prodded.

"He brushed it off."

"It's not the first time his name has been in the papers," Ruby began rubbing lotion on Donna's face. "It won't be the last."

"No, it's not. I . . . we'd hoped the information wouldn't come out until after the wedding and movie release."

Upon closer inspection, I noticed the bags underneath her eyes. "Don't fret Miss Morgan. Everyone believes it to be a romantic gesture."

She gave a short tinkle of laughter. Aunt Ruby shot me a hard look.

I softened my tone, "But I am sorry our discussion was overheard by the driver and got into the papers. You can believe me when we discuss something 'off the record' it will *stay* off the record."

"I appreciate your discretion." Donna closed her eyes as my aunt rubbed on the heavy Max Factor pancake foundation used for stage and screen to keep the actors from looking washed out.

I shook my head. "It's my reputation and integrity on the line. I'll never get anywhere in this business if people think I can't keep my mouth shut."

She opened her eyes. "You'd best ask me your questions now. Gaultier will not allow you in the car today."

"Will I be able to come to the set?"

"I'm afraid not."

"Don't worry Ariadne." Aunt Ruby began brushing a hint of blush on Donna's cheeks. "The Tony Baldwin Band is being filmed at the Breakers tomorrow. They've asked me to help. You may come with me and meet the band members."

It sounded like the best deal I could get. "Very well." I sat in one of the armchairs, pulled out my notebook, and began firing questions at Donna.

# Chapter Twenty-One
# Frank

Frank stared dismally at the bill left by the flood remediation company. Just one more debt to pay. He entered the fee into the ledger book. Too much red. He'd gone over budget with the renovation costs, but figured he'd be able to make it up with the increase in nightly fees for the inn. What he hadn't counted on was a ten percent increase in his mother's care.

He'd reduced the inn's insurance bill by giving up some of the coverage to pay the difference in her fees. Flooding had been one of the coverages he'd given up. He knew it was a risk. However, the last hurricane to hit Rhode Island was Hurricane Carol four years ago. The newspapers had called it the "Storm of the Century." Frank figured they'd be safe for at least a decade, and by then he'd have added it back onto the insurance.

The reporter was supposed to check out on Sunday, and her room fees would pay the flood bill. Higginbottom's and Sullivan's bills would help pay for the outstanding electric bill, but they weren't supposed to check out until Tuesday.

Frank couldn't believe his bad luck lately. It's as though a gremlin was doing its level best to cause difficulties for him. The broken oven had cost him a night of dinner wages in parts. Now the flood. By chance, it happened in an empty room, and the remediation company did a good job drying it out to make it habitable for a weekend guest.

The ruined carpet in the green suite had been removed. Luckily the runner in the hallway dried without leaving stains or damaging the wood flooring beneath it. Still, the legs of the loveseat had been damaged, and he'd have to do something about getting some rugs down on the floors. Frank tapped his pencil against the ledger in thought. An ancient oriental rug, originally from the dining room, was in the cellar. He wrote a reminder note to have Johnny bring it up to the Green Suite.

On top of the oven and flood, had been the mouse incident. Paranoid of a shutdown by a health inspector, he'd had Johnny hide traps all over the house. So far, they'd caught nothing, but with this streak of bad luck, Frank was taking no chances. He planned to buy a house cat over the weekend. A homey cat would be good for the inn.

The ledger remained open, and Frank tallied up the outstanding debts one more time. So far, none of the guests requested deductions on their nightly fees for the nuisance of the flood. In part, because he'd kept the booze flowing. However, the way Cedric was going through the liquor, it was almost cheaper to offer a twenty percent reduction on their room rate—at least for the Higginbottoms.

The Higginbottoms.

Frank had been doing his level best to avoid them. The article in the *Chronicle* uncovered his lie about the investment. Another spot of bad luck. How was he to know the Prince of Maldinia was paying for the movie to be made? Everything his father had told him about movie making included investors, sometimes many of them.

All he needed was to hang on for a few more months and his fortunes to turn. The inn was booked solid from April through August. Those bookings would put him back on his feet, cover Cedric's loan, and make a dent in the other loans he'd taken out for the renovations.

A frigid wind blew into the foyer. The reporter shoved with a solid push to make sure the old wooden door shut properly.

Frank closed the outstanding bill inside the ledger. "Hello, Miss Winter. I'm surprised to see you back so early." He checked his watch. "It's not quite lunchtime."

"I've returned to do some writing," she replied dismissively. "I met your mailman at the box and offered to bring in your mail. Figured I'd save you a trip outside in this cold. Brr." She shivered. "It's the wind that gets to me." She placed the pile of envelopes on top of the closed ledger.

Smack on top sat a past-due notice from the electric company. Frank shifted it to the bottom.

"Have I any messages?" Miss Winter's eyes were wide, and her rosy cheeks enhanced her youthful looks.

"Yes, your editor phoned, again." He pulled the note from her room's cubby and handed it over. "Good morning, Mrs. Sullivan," he greeted his favorite guest as she came out of the parlor.

"Everything back in order with the guest room?" she asked.

"Yes, the suite has been put back to rights, and everything is dried out, thanks to your help. The flood company will retrieve the fans this afternoon," he replied absently flipping through the stack of the mail.

She nodded. "That's good to hear."

Frank paused his perusal to study his watch again. A 1926 Rolex Oyster once worn by his late father. The first watch of its kind, hermetically sealed to keep out water. One like it had crossed the English Channel on the wrist of the famous Mercedes Gleitze. He'd been thinking about giving the watch to Johnny.

His mother had been quite insistent on taking everything belonging to his father after his death. He'd come to realize that his mother had been bitter and, perhaps, behaved too harshly toward the Wexlers—especially Johnny. Considering he'd just rewritten his Will, Frank felt he should pass the watch over to Johnny. Not that he planned to go toes up any time soon, but the watch, and a few other items should be given to his half-brother.

*Perhaps if I hand over some of my father's possessions that I know Johnny wants, we could get past the hurt mother caused, and finally have the brotherly relationship I've always craved.*

Whenever they were in the same room, their interactions were rife with acerbic comments. Johnny would needle Frank. Frank would react with nastiness. He sighed. It was a vicious circle. With his mother packed away at the sanitorium, there was no reason Frank couldn't extend an olive branch to Johnny and clear the air.

On the other hand, he fingered the crystal face. He'd hate to do it, but he knew the watch would bring in enough money to keep things going, which included paying Johnny's salary. A job he'd offered at the urging of Ruby Winter. He had to admit, Johnny knew what he was doing when it came to construction, and he never would have gotten as good a foreman at the price he'd paid to his half-brother.

"Frank. Yoohoo!" Mrs. Sullivan waggled her fingers in front of his face.

He snapped out of his reverie and the words on the envelope in front of him came into focus. "There's a letter here for Mr. Sullivan."

"Thank you. I'll take it up to him. As I was saying, we're heading into Providence and will be gone with the Higginbottoms most of the afternoon."

"Will you be back for dinner?" Frank calculated the possible loss of revenue in his head.

"That's the plan. Walter would rather be back by dark before the roads refreeze. We'll be in time for cocktails. I'll phone if our plans change."

He relaxed. "I appreciate that."

Connie retreated up the curved staircase, opening the envelope in her hands. Mid-way up, she paused reading the missive. Her features furrowed with concern and confusion.

"Is anything wrong, Mrs. Sullivan?" the young lady asked.

Connie hastily stuffed the letter back into the envelope, and said with acidity, "It's nothing." She brushed past Johnny who was coming down the stairs.

"It didn't look like nothing," Miss Winter mumbled so only Frank could hear.

"The Green Suite is back in order," Johnny said tucking a red bandana in his back pocket. "Maria washed and dried the linens, and the room is set for a weekend guest."

"Good. If you'd kept an eye on the plumbers in the first place, this wouldn't have happened," Frank groused.

Johnny's cheeks suffused and his teeth snapped shut. Frank immediately regretted his words, knowing he'd been the one to insist on the cheaper plumbing crew. His concerns over the bills had made him edgy, and, as usual, he'd taken it out on Johnny.

Before Frank could formulate an apology, Miss Winter interjected, "I was wondering if you gentlemen could refer me to a place, where I could eat lunch? Perhaps find a bowl of clam chowder?"

Johnny turned and allowed that smarmy smile to come over his face. "Larry's Diner is only a few blocks away and serves a delicious bowl of chowder."

"I'm sure Miss Winter's tastes are a little more refined than Larry's Diner," Frank scoffed. "She'd be better off at Finn's Seafood."

"Oh, no," she decried. "I often find restaurants frequented by the locals tend to be much better than the tourist eateries. Besides, if Larry's Diner is just a few blocks away, I could walk there. No?"

"Exactly, Miss Winter." Johnny's teeth flashed. "Go right, walk two blocks to Church Street, and you'll see Larry's diagonally across the street on your left."

"Thank you. The roads are still a bit tricky with the slush, and I prefer to walk than drive Mother's car in this mess." She turned to Frank. "Is the phone booth working? Or is there a different phone extension I can use to call my editor? Preferably in a more private location." She glanced at the phone sitting at the reception desk.

"The electric company will be coming by this afternoon to inspect it. There's an extension in the kitchen—"

Johnny cut Frank off, "It won't be private. Maria's in there prepping for tonight's dinner. She said she's making Beef Wellington."

Frank frowned. "Beef Wellington?"

"She felt it was important to offer something special to the guests tonight considering all the, erm—" Johnny's eyes darted back and forth between Frank and Miss Winter. "—difficulties we've been experiencing."

"Never mind. I'm sure the diner has a pay phone I can use," she said.

Frank sighed. "No. I'll have this extension placed in the library for you. First, I have a few things to sort out here." He indicated the mail.

"Thank you. In the meantime, I'll go up to my room to freshen up. Should I come back down in about fifteen minutes?"

"Very well, I'll have it set up by then." Frank waited until she was on her way up the staircase before returning his attention to Johnny. "There's a floral Axminster rug in the cellar. Go fetch it, and I'll help you lay it down in the Green Suite after I've run the extension for Miss Winter."

"That would have been helpful to know *before* I replaced all the furniture," Johnny jibed.

"Well, you know it now. And I'll help," Frank replied in a dismissive tone looking down at the mail.

Johnny shuffled toward the back of the house, mumbling under his breath.

Frank sighed. He wished he and Johnny could be on better terms, but the man didn't make it easy for him.

Frank's finger came upon the life insurance policy he'd recently renewed making Edward the beneficiary. It was worth $10,000.

Oh, the irony. He was worth more dead than alive.

# Chapter Twenty-Two
## Ariadne

Raised voices came from the Sullivan's suite, though their exact words couldn't penetrate the thick walls. I wondered what was in the letter that upset Connie. Pretend as she might, her body language had spoken volumes when she read it.

I couldn't give it much more thought, as I had my own problems to deal with. Sighing, I locked my chamber door and retreated downstairs.

True to his word, Mr. Wyler placed the phone in the library by running an extra-long cord from the wall behind the reception desk. I carried the heavy black base, pacing back and forth in front of the snooker table, as far as the cord would allow.

Howard asked, "She spoke to you?"

A carved wooden cigarette box lay on the end table with a heavy silver lighter in need of polishing next to it. I flipped open the lid to find it filled with Chesterfields. Even though the lighter was deeply tarnished, someone kept it in good working order. Flame shot upward with one flick of my thumb. I sucked in the smoke allowing it to fill my lungs. "Yes. She's aware of who leaked the information. She knew it was not me. I reiterated my pledge to keep 'off the record' comments in confidence."

"Good. Stick with that upright, honorable pretense."

My lips pinched together. Slowly and evenly, I said, "It is *not* a pretense. My journalistic integrity is *everything*."

"Sure. That's what I meant. What about the Frenchie?" my editor said the last word with disdain. "Did he give you any trouble?"

"The Maldinian minister was dismissed from the future princess's room, and I continued the interview." I didn't feel the need to inform my boss that I was allowed into the room because my aunt threatened to walk off the job.

"Well then . . . erm," he cleared his throat, "Nicely done, Winter."

Mr. Bradley didn't often hand out compliments.

"Thank you, sir."

Howard plowed on to the next topic, "The photographer I planned to send up there, Whitey Gordon, has taken ill. Came down with chickenpox if you can believe it," he groused. "I'm sending Gavin Turnbull instead. You know him?"

Not only did I know Gavin; I'd go so far as to say, I favored him. With a disarming crooked smile, chocolatey eyes, and a crown of curly hair that the strongest pomade couldn't tame, Gavin was a favorite among the ladies. I guessed he was in his late twenties or early thirties, and was kind to everyone, including lowly assistants and those of us stuck at the copy desk. Unlike the arrogant Whitey Gordon—an ingenious photographer who believed himself to be a god among men and came with an attitude to prove it. I couldn't help the grin that spread across my face.

"Yes, I know Char—er, Mr. Turnbull." I leaned my hip against the pool table and pulled a blue ball out of the corner pocket.

"I'll have my assistant contact Miss Morgan's manager to confirm the Saturday photoshoot. I'd like you to grease the wheels for Turnbull once he arrives."

"You want me to attend the photoshoot? I, uh, hadn't planned . . . I mean, I thought I'd work on the article."

"There's plenty of time for that. I want you at that photo shoot to assist Turnbull!" his voice boomed across the lines.

"Yessir. I'll be there." I spun the ball across the table. It bounced noiselessly off the side and rolled to a stop in the middle of the green felt.

"And I want you back here on Monday morning. Understand?"

"Monday morning. I'll be there." I made a silent salute, the cigarette smoke curling above my head.

He hung up without a goodbye.

A whooshing sound escaped from the leather chair, that I despondently sank into to. Considering I'd been unceremoniously banned from the set today, and I had nothing else on the docket, left me plenty of time to work on the article. I didn't mind accompanying Gavin. I only hoped my presence wouldn't cause an issue. I couldn't imagine the mortification of being tossed out of the photo shoot in front of Gavin.

Tomorrow, Donna said she'd try to get me back on set. If she couldn't do so . . .

I cringed.

A feminine yelp and the phone being ripped out of my hand brought a halt to my ruminations. I raced to open the library doors to find Kitty Conrad splayed across the foyer floor, one shoe on, one shoe off.

I knelt to check on her. "Oh, my goodness! Are you okay? What happened?"

One of her kitten heels caught in the phone cord, causing her to trip, yanking the phone from my hands. What I couldn't understand was how it happened. Frank had run the telephone cord under the hallway runner, along the wall, and into the library.

"I-I don't know." She got up to her hands and knees.

"Kittikins!"

Kitty clenched her teeth at the exclamation.

Melvin galloped down the hall. "My god. What's happened, love?"

"Careful. Is your ankle twisted?" I asked softly.

She shook her head. "It's nothing, just a few bruises to my knees, and my ego."

Melvin and I each took an elbow and helped her rise. The hem of the brown dress, she'd worn on the first morning, hung down to her ankles.

"Oh dear, I'm afraid you've torn your frock. I have a travel mending kit if you need it."

"It's fine, I brought one," she brushed aside my offer.

Melvin bent to retrieve the wayward shoe. "What the devil is this?" He unwound it from the cord.

"The phone booth is out of service. Mr. Wyler pulled the extension into the library for me to use," I explained.

As if summoned, Frank came trotting down the stairs. "Has something happened? I thought I heard—" His gaze took in a rumpled Kitty, and Melvin on one knee assisting her into the heel.

"It's nothing, I'm just clumsy—" she stated.

Melvin rose to his feet, his face taut with anger. "As a matter of fact, there *is* something wrong. What on earth were you thinking stringing phone cord all over the place to leave it for my wife to trip on!" he snapped.

Frank's face suffused scarlet. "Well, I'm-I'm terribly sorry, Mr. Conrad. I ran the cords under the carpets to keep them out of the way. I didn't think—"

"That's right, you didn't think, and now my wife is hurt," Melvin accused.

Frank turned his attention to Kitty. "Oh, Mrs. Conrad allow me—"

"Melvin! It is no such thing," Kitty retorted wiping dust off her dress. "I've only torn a hem!"

While they argued. My gaze followed the line of the phone cord again. Kitty's heel caught on the cable near the library door. In other words, she'd been lurking right outside it. Having done plenty of my own lurking, I assumed Kitty had been eavesdropping on my conversation.

*Why?*

Cutting through the accusatory voices, I asked, "Was there something you were wanting, Mrs. Conrad?"

Everyone was silenced, including Kitty, and her gaze swept up to me. "Wanting?"

"You must have been by the library doors when you tripped. Were you looking for me?" I offered congenially with a smile, although I couldn't seem to help the narrowing of my own eyes.

She ducked her head and stuttered, "Er—no. I, um, well actually, I was looking for Frank. To-to, l-let him know . . . um . . . we would be eating dinner out tonight."

"We are?" Melvin asked.

"Why, yes. You said you were interested in trying one of the seafood restaurants in town," she said in waspish tones as if insulted that he questioned her.

"Of course!" Melvin's head bobbed. "I didn't realize we'd settled on tonight."

"I was hoping to ask Frank—" softening she turned to the innkeeper "—to recommend a place and make us reservations."

Frank drew himself up and looked down his hawklike nose. "Yes, of course. The Clarke Cooke House has some of the finest seafood in town. I'd be happy to make you a reservation."

"Then, it's settled." She gave one last swipe to her dress. "Melvin, you said I should go shopping while we were in Newport."

"Kittikins!" He gave one of his silly guffaws. "You didn't say anything, I didn't think you were interested or perhaps hadn't heard."

"Of course, I heard you," she spoke with impatience. "Now, I've torn my frock and would like to find a new one to wear to dinner."

"Let me get my coat," Melvin said in excited tones.

"Nonsense. Your taste is . . . too over the top when it comes to women's clothes. Always choosing flamboyant colors."

Melvin's face fell, but Kitty didn't seem to notice.

"I'll go alone. Or perhaps—" she swung around to me "— Miss Winter, you're home early today, would you like to accompany me?"

Taken aback at her abrupt invitation, my mouth dropped. "Uh . . . you want to go shopping . . . with me?"

"Yes, you *do* work for a fashion magazine, and your taste in clothing is impeccable. I adore that blue and green frock you're wearing. Very stylish." She indicated my royal blue pencil dress, topped by a matching plaid blue and Kelly-green collared jacket, with a wide green belt around my waist. Another set from The Wardrobe.

"If you're available. I'd like to take you to lunch. Then we can go shopping. Dot was raving about a boutique on Thames Street."

I couldn't figure out what Kitty was playing at. Was she telling the truth about her interest in my clothes? Her drab wardrobe could use a boost. Or had she been listening to my phone conversation with my editor and trying to cover it up? And if so, why? It's not like we'd been talking about national security secrets. Did she have an unexpressed interest in Donna Morgan's upcoming nuptials? Was she planning to pump me for information about the article in the *Chronicle*?

Or was she so desperate to get away from her husband she'd latched on to the closest female she could find?

My own curiosity being what it was, I determined to take her up on her offer, so *I* could pump *her* for information. Not to mention, the magazine was rather stingy with their per diem, it would be foolish to pass up a free meal. "Why that's very kind of you. I can spare a few hours to go shopping."

Her body relaxed. "Then it's settled. Melvin, you can drive us into town. I'll go change into a different dress and meet you here in ten minutes."

I nodded. "Very well."

Frank scratched his head, watching Melvin and his wife retreat to their room. "I truly thought the cords were safely under the carpets."

"As did I."

# Chapter Twenty-Three
# Kitty

Kitty thanked the stars Ariadne agreed to go shopping. She didn't really need another new outfit. She had plenty of others to choose from in her suitcase, and it would take, but a few minutes, to fix the rip in her brown dress.

However, she'd almost been caught eavesdropping on the reporter's phone conversation. She'd thought it had been Frank talking on the phone. She needed to know where he was. However, it wasn't Frank, instead, she'd found the girl talking to her editor about that silly article she was writing on Donna Morgan.

Goodness, Kitty couldn't understand what the hubbub was all about when it came to the private lives of movie people. The papers were making far too much about the entire thing.

She'd felt like a fool getting her heel caught on that stupid wire, only to have Miss Winter open the library doors, and find her face down on the floor. The sting of mortification crawled up her neck as she relived the incident in her mind.

She twisted in her seat. "How much longer will you be in Newport?"

Miss Winter stared out the side window watching the buildings go by. "I leave on Sunday. I have to be back in the office on Monday."

"What's it like working in New York City?"

The young woman's gaze shifted to pin Kitty. "Didn't you grow up there?"

"Well, y-yes, of c-course. In-in Brooklyn," she stammered. "We used to go into the city for the Broadway shows, or during the holidays. But I never worked in the city."

Miss Winter's brows wrinkled. "Crowded. Bustling. Full of energy."

"Always felt like an ant farm to me," Melvin interjected. "People coming and going. Hurry, hurry, hurry. Not a fan of the city myself. I'm a man who likes a slower pace. Just like my Kittikins. Right?" He pulled to a stop at the light and smiled at his wife.

"Well, I *could* do with a little bit more bustle than what Buffalo has to offer. And less snow," she stated baldly.

He let out one of his annoying laughs that put Kitty's teeth on edge. "You've got me there. More snow than we know what to do with."

"Must be why you're such a good driver in this snow," Ariadne commented.

"Aw, shucks. This is nothing. Only a couple of measly inches." Melvin's shoulders rose to his ears.

Kitty faced the front with a sigh. "My husband is correct. This is nothing compared to the blizzards we're subject to in Buffalo. I must wear boots from November until April at the earliest."

"I'll be sure to keep that in mind while we search for new clothing for you. We'll need to make sure they are made of warm fabrics."

"Pull up there." Kitty pointed to an open space in front of a green awning leading to a restaurant. "You like Italian?"

"Who doesn't like Italian!" Melvin chortled.

"Italian is fine." Miss Winter affirmed in her quiet way.

"There are three shops along this block I thought we could visit. Dottie mentioned them at breakfast the other day."

Melvin shifted the Buick into park, and a doorman dressed in a heavy black overcoat, red bowtie, and gray top hat came to open the car door for the ladies.

"Come back for us in two hours, Melvin," Kitty ordered pulling the seat forward to allow Miss Winter to climb out of the backseat.

He nodded and tapped his fedora with two fingers. "Two hours it is."

A few minutes later, the pair were seated in the bay window which overlooked the shoveled sidewalk. They'd both ordered and were waiting for the wine to arrive.

"I understand you were at the inn when the unfortunate flood happened yesterday," Kitty began.

Ariadne pulled her attention away from a woman walking her large, fluffy Newfoundland dog. She pegged Kitty with that intense emerald stare. "I was. Most unfortunate for Mr. Wyler. You were . . . in Providence?"

"We saw a small quartet concert, and went to the art museum," she replied airily. "I had to drag Melvin. But I refused to leave without visiting the museum."

"Are you a connoisseur of art, Mrs. Conrad?"

"I enjoy art. And please, call me Kitty," she reminded.

"I imagine you went to see the Metropolitan Museum of Art when you lived in Brooklyn." Miss Winter spread the napkin across her lap.

The server brought their wine glasses. Kitty waited for him to leave before responding, "It's my favorite museum of all time."

A soft smile spread across the young lady's features. "Mine too."

"Something we have in common." Kitty sipped her chianti before sending out another prod. "About the flood. Do you think it was Johnny's fault as Frank implied?"

Ariadne's eyes narrowed. "He didn't imply. He accused. And no. Mr. Wexler let it be known that Mr. Wyler chose substandard workers."

"Hm," Kitty glanced out the window. "Shame."

"Why are you so interested?"

Kitty felt her cheeks reddening. *Is that accusation in her voice?*

Luckily, the waiter arrived with a basket of bread. Kitty carefully placed a slice on her white scalloped plate and slathered it with butter. "Just curious, I suppose." She took a bite with the nonchalance of a trained English butler.

"Did you locate the Sullivan's room?"

The crusty bite stuck in her throat despite the thick spread of slippery animal fat. Her eyes watered. Kitty gulped the wine to get it down.

Ariadne watched her, like a specimen bug pinned to a corkboard.

Kitty cleared her throat. "I-I beg your pardon."

"Yesterday morning. You were looking for the Sullivan's room," the young lady clarified not taking her eyes off her tablemate.

Kitty rearranged the napkin on her lap. "Of course. Yes. I found Connie, and, um, we chatted. She's the . . . uh . . . the one who directed me to visit the museum in Providence."

A brow rose. "How kind of her."

Kitty did her best to divert the conversation onto safer ground. "I want to pick up some new makeup. Do you think you could give me some application tips? I like how you've drawn your eyeliner out from the corners. It seems to enhance your eyes."

Ariadne's gaze shifted, taking on a gleam as she swirled the ruby wine around in the bowl of the glass. "If you'd like."

"I would. Thank you."

"You might want to phone the inn and inform your husband we'll be a tad bit longer."

"Oh? How much?"

She squinted at Kitty. Tilted her head left and then right. "Tell him to pick us up at four-thirty."

"Four-thirty!"

"Four-thirty." She delivered with a curt nod.

Kitty sighed. "Very well. If you'll excuse me, I'll call and leave a message for him." Kitty walked to the back of the restaurant, past the bar where a pay phone hung. Maria answered, and she left a message with the cook.

On her way back to the table a loud voice halted her steps. "The lady with the mouse."

Kitty sucked in a breath. "I beg your pardon."

"You were in my shop a few days ago. Was your nephew pleased?"

Kitty's eyes widened in astonishment and her frantic gaze darted around the restaurant. She answered the gentleman in a low murmur. "Just fine. If you'll excuse me, my tablemate is waiting." Using every ounce of control, she glided back to her seat.

"Friend of yours?" Ariadne asked.

"Not at all. Mistaken identity." Kitty gulped at her wine and was relieved when the waiter arrived with their salads.

# Chapter Twenty-Four
## Melvin

Melvin pulled the laurel green Buick Special into an empty spot on the corner across the street from the address his wife had given him. The rosy neon sign in the window read *Bella Vida* in loopy curls. Bright pink chairs, the color of Pepto-Bismol, lined up across the front of the window like soldiers. The blinds were pulled to meet the tops of the chair backs, so Melvin couldn't see into the store.

He lit a cigarette and rotated the radio's tuning knob until he found a station playing *Stardust* by Artie Shaw. He tapped his fingers against the steering wheel as the clarinet wove a melancholy tapestry around him. He couldn't figure out people who enjoyed those rowdy new artists. That rock and roll. They had funny names like The Platters or The Chordettes. Sheb Wooley for heaven's sake. It suggested a sheep lost among the moors of Ireland.

*How, on earth, are you supposed to dance to that noise?*

Melvin rolled down the window to allow the cigarette smoke to escape. Kitty always complained about getting into a smoky car. She didn't care for a cold car either, so he kept the heater running while he waited. Melvin was glad Kitty had instigated this little shopping excursion with Miss Winter. He didn't know much about fashion, but he knew elegance when he saw it, and Miss Winter was class all the way.

Kitty had an aura of class about her when they met, lo those many years ago. Part of the reason he married her. He was on his way up in the vacuum business and knew he could use a classy lady at his side. She still wore the finest clothing manufacturers; Melvin saw to that. However, the years had not been as kind to Kitty as they had to others her age. Her hair was streaked gray, and she no longer bothered to style or curl it in the modern fashion the way she used to. Her face, which was once sunny, and plump, had a drawn look, her beautiful blue eyes had become sunken and often flashed with irritation.

Melvin blew out a puff of smoke. Too many miscarriages. At one time Kitty was desperate for a child. There had been four in all. After the last miscarriage—the one that almost killed her—Melvin put a stop to it. He couldn't stand the thought of losing her and moved into the guest bedroom.

At one point he'd suggested adoption, but Kitty had been in such a bad way afterward. When she shook her head, he didn't have the heart to push. He'd wanted a son to pass the business on to. When he realized, it wasn't going to happen, he invited one of his sister's sons to come to work for him after he graduated high school. Nathan had shown an aptitude for business. The kid would be ready to take over when Melvin retired.

Instead of staying home and keeping house, Kitty spent hours of her time volunteering at City Hospital. Her personality had turned harsh. Whether due to the miscarriages, or her work at the hospital, Melvin never knew. The beautiful girl he had fallen in love with was still there . . . on the inside. However, Melvin realized she'd sort of given up taking care of the outside.

Before, like the other ladies in the neighborhood, she'd gone to the salon weekly, to have her hair styled. Eventually, she cut back to every other week, and cut back again, until it was only once a month at the most.

"Why spend so much money on hair? All I do is pull it back into a bun," she'd snapped one day when he asked. "Getting fancy for the patients or the doctors is what the young nurses do. I'm too old for that. I haven't time for such nonsense. My job is to write Wills and letters to the families for the sick and dying. Sometimes their last letters. They don't care if I had my hair curled at the salon today."

Melvin couldn't or didn't want to argue with her. As far as he was concerned, Kitty was still lovely. However, this week in particular, when comparing her to her other school friends, her lack of maintenance seemed more noticeable. Not to mention the fact that Kitty had been acting strange since they arrived in Newport. Most secretive.

One morning, he saw her coming out of the side door of the kitchen like the help. He found a screwdriver and wrench from the toolbox he kept in the trunk in her pockets. And she'd been awfully snappish when he laughed and asked if she was doing a little car maintenance.

Thinking about repairs, he reached into his pocket and pulled out the golden bracelet that cow, Dottie, had stepped on. The one with the heart. His heart, he'd told Kitty when he gave it to her on their tenth anniversary. Thin golden links shimmered in the waning sunlight and looked delicate against his thick calloused fingers. She hadn't worn the bracelet in years and only brought it on the trip when he asked about it. Perhaps she'd realized the clasp was coming loose. If so, why hadn't she gotten it fixed? It's not as though Melvin was stingy with money. Kitty always had pocket money, and a Charga-plate in her name at the local Sattler's department store. In addition, the hospital paid her a small amount for the filing she did for them on Tuesdays and Thursdays.

He tossed the cigarette butt out the window as two ladies stepped through the door of *Bella Vida.*

Miss Winter pointed at the car.

Melvin didn't recognize the shorter woman with her. She wore a soft sage green swing coat with a matching fur beret, and tortoise shell sunglasses with green lenses. Her honey-brown hair curled beneath the brim, and she kept her head down as she picked her way through the dirty slush crossing the street. The women each carried three large shopping bags. Melvin surmised it was a salesgirl helping Miss Winter with the bags.

He was about to exit the car when, the stranger in green rapped on his half-closed window and said with an edge of irritation, "Melvin, you need to open the trunk."

The stranger was no stranger at all. He fumbled with the bracelet, almost dropping it. Clumsily, he turned off the ignition and came round back to where the ladies waited for him to unlock the trunk.

"I believe we've had a successful shopping trip, don't you?" Miss Winter said as she placed her bags in the trunk.

Kitty self-consciously played with one of her curls. "Well, we've certainly spent a lot of your money today, Melvin."

"No problem," he murmured.

Miss Winter climbed into the back seat, and his wife sat in front. She removed the new sunglasses, and Melvin couldn't help staring at her altered appearance.

The gray was gone from her hair, and the locks, trimmed above her shoulders, curled up around her ears and neck. Small bangs whispered across her forehead hiding the wrinkles. Her cheeks were pink with blusher, and she had done something to her eyes. They no longer seemed so sunken. They were ringed with dark liner, and the lashes seemed very long. The effect enhanced her cornflower blue peepers. Melvin couldn't remember the last time his wife had looked quite so . . . handsome.

She squinted. "Is that my bracelet?"

He blinked. "Uh . . . what?"

Miss Winter let out a snicker.

Kitty exhaled and pointed to the golden chain on the dashboard. "My bracelet."

He tore his gaze away and focused on the chain. "Why, yes, it is. I got it fixed at the jewelers while you were out."

Kitty took off a black leather glove and held out her hand.

Melvin clasped the bracelet around her thin wrist, the blue veins stood stark against her pale skin. "I had the jeweler put on a sturdier clasp and fix the bent charms."

"Very well." She put the glasses back in place and faced forward, then, as if remembering her manners, she murmured, "Thank you."

He cleared his throat. "You sure look mighty pretty, Kittikins."

She sniffed. "I can't see a darned thing out of these sunglasses. I don't know why I allowed you to talk me into them, Ariadne."

"The lady at the store said you could have them made with a prescription, if you take them to your eye doctor," Miss Winter softly explained.

"What a good idea. We'll do that when we return to Buffalo." Melvin declared, starting the car. The sunglasses were quite fetching, and he was determined to see his wife wearing them for years to come.

Kitty gave a half-shrug, and Melvin pulled away from the curb.

When they got back to the inn, Melvin offered to carry the shopping bags for the ladies. Kitty led the way up the front porch, but Melvin called out, "Miss Winter?"

The young lady turned pushing her sunglasses to the top of her head. "Do you need help?"

He replied in low tones, "Thank you for what you did today. My wife looks beautiful. I haven't seen Kitty so fetching, in well . . . it's been a long time."

She gave a soft smile. "It's my pleasure, Mr. Conrad. Wait until you see some of the new clothing we picked out. Suggest she wear the blue sheath dress out for dinner tonight."

# Chapter Twenty-Five
## Ariadne

I stepped into the foyer with Mr. Conrad at my heels. The chandelier was lit, its crystals created a kaleidoscope of light and shadow on the ceiling. The mouth-watering scents of seared onions, thyme, and beef hung in the air. Frank stood over a ledger book, his mouth agape and eyes riveted to the hallway where Kitty must have passed before I entered. Mr. Wexler, too, stood on the last step of the staircase, his hand on the rail, astonishment playing across his features.

"Gentlemen," Melvin spoke snapping Frank out of his incredulity.

The innkeeper cleared his throat and gave a brief nod. "Mr. Conrad."

"Did you place our dinner reservation?"

"Yes." Wyler flipped the ledger closed and picked up a scrap of paper beneath it. "You've got a seven-thirty seating at the Clarke Cooke House. I've written down the address for you."

"Very well." Melvin trudged down the hallway, the paper bags rasping against the walls as he went. A moment later we heard a door close.

The half-brothers rotated their gazes to me, as if I'd pulled them with a magnet.

Frank hooked a thumb over his right shoulder. "That *was* Mrs. Conrad. Correct?"

I allowed a tiny grin to tug at my lips. "What do you

think?"

Johnny clicked his tongue. "You did that in one afternoon?"

"Well, I had some help. Two lovely ladies at my aunt's salon, and a handful of shopgirls."

"Astonishing," Johnny murmured. "Did you learn that at the magazine?"

"Some. But mostly from my mother and Aunt Ruby. Two formidable ladies when it comes to the finer qualities of fashion and appearance." I tucked a lock behind my ear. "Now that I've had my fun, it's time to return to work. Have I any messages, Mr. Wyler?"

"As a matter of fact." Frank turned around and pulled a cluster of notes from the Rose Suite cubby. "A telegram, one hand-delivered letter, and two phone messages." Seeing my gaze drift to the Western Electric 500, back in its place at the reception desk, its cord tucked out of the way, Mr. Wyler imparted, "The phone booth is in working order if you need to make any more calls."

"Thank you." I took the papers. "Is it possible to have a tray of Mrs. Massey's Beef Wellington sent up to my room for dinner?"

His brows furrowed.

"I realize it's unusual." I flicked my wrist. "If it's not possible, perhaps I could order a carry-out nearby. Mr. Wexler, does your diner do that?"

Johnny nodded, "I've done it many nights—"

Frank cut across Johnny, "Don't be silly. Of course, I can send up a meal. Will you be wanting a glass of wine with that?"

"Not tonight. I'll be working. Better send up a pot of coffee with dinner, instead." Regretfully, I also declined the cocktails.

"Very well. I'll send Edward up with something before dinner service begins, around quarter to seven" He made a notation on a pad.

"That would be lovely. Thank you." I tucked the messages

into my handbag.

"Nice work on Mrs. Conrad, she's gone from dried-up prune to quite nice-looking. Mrs. Higginbottom will be beside herself," Johnny commented drily.

His belittling attitude of the older ladies surprised me. While I'd seen his cutting attitude toward Frank, he'd always been polite and proper when it came to the guests. After all, they were his bread and butter.

"Tut-tut, Mr. Wexler, you mustn't cast aspersions," I remonstrated. "One day you too will be as old as Mrs. Conrad, *if* you're lucky," I sang the last over my shoulder sashaying past him and glided up the stairs.

Wyler hissed something at his half-brother, though I didn't hear what. A moment later the front door slammed.

Back in my room, I flopped down upon the settee, slipped off my winter boots, and flung my arms out to the side closing my eyes. Once Kitty agreed to a new hairstyle, I'd found myself having fun dressing her up in clothing that fit, and colors to enhance her complexion rather than the brown and yellow detractors she seemed to favor. We'd spent an hour and a half shopping and two more at Aunt Ruby's salon. Although Aunt Ruby was at the movie set, the receptionist knew who I was when I called, and kindly fit Kitty onto the schedule.

I opened my eyes. The typewriter sat on a little table in front of the window with a half-typed sheet of paper in the roller standing at attention as if mocking me.

*Playtime is over. Back to the grindstone.*

I pulled the messages out of my handbag and spread them across the coffee table. The first phone message was from Howard written in Wyler's slanted scrawl:

*Morgan's Manager confirmed. The photoshoot is a go. Gavin has the location address. He will contact you with details.*

I breathed a quick sigh of relief that our photographer would be able to complete the shoot. The second missive was written in round cursive, making me think it had perhaps been Maria who took down the message. It simply read:

*Where are you? Call me. - Aunt Ruby*

The telegram was from Gavin Turnbull.

**Got a room at your hotel. Arriving late Friday. Photoshoot Saturday 9 sharp. Gavin**

So, Gavin would be relegated to the hapless Green Suite, next door to mine. I'll admit a slight tingle of excitement fluttered down my spine.

The hand-delivered letter came from Donna Morgan written in maroon ink.

*Dear Miss Winter,*
*I have arranged for you to come to the set on Friday. My scenes will be filmed at a new location. Please arrive at noon at the address listed at the bottom of this letter, and we will complete the interview over lunch. You may remain on set for the afternoon. However, I will not be available for any further discussion following lunch.*

*Yours Sincerely,*
*Donna Morgan*

I didn't recognize the address at the bottom—44 Ochre Point Avenue—and would have to look it up on the map. While the note sounded cordial, Donna made it clear this would be the last time she'd be able to speak with me.

I hoisted myself off the couch and made my way back downstairs to return Aunt Ruby's phone call.

# Chapter Twenty-Six
## Edward

Edward cautiously carried the tea trolley up the stairs and placed it to the side of the second-floor landing, out of the walking path. He'd heard Mrs. Conrad tripped over the phone cord earlier and didn't want to cause another accident. Then he jogged back down to the kitchen to gather the tray his mother had begrudgingly prepared for Miss Winter.

"I don't know why Frank agreed to this," she groused placing a pat of butter next to the dinner roll. Then she added a sprig of parsley on top of the beef and placed the plates on the floral metal tray. "We don't have room service here at the inn. I sincerely hope Frank charges extra for it."

"It's okay Mom." Edward didn't care. He was happy to carry a tray up for Miss Winter. She was pretty. He hadn't seen her this afternoon because he had basketball practice. As a matter of fact, he had a game Friday night, so he wasn't likely to see Miss Winter at all tomorrow.

Anne Cooper, a girl in his English class, would come to help serve like she usually did on Fridays when he had games. This time Mr. Wyler offered to work in the kitchen, so his mom could attend the game too. She'd prepare the dinner in advance and leave it warming on the stove, so all Mr. Wyler had to do was put it on the plates for Anne to serve. Mom often couldn't get away from the inn to see his games. He'd practiced extra hard today to make sure he would be ready to go up against the Trojans, their school's biggest rival.

Edward balanced the tray as he walked with measured steps to the front foyer. Good-natured laughter spilled out of the half-open doors of the library. "Don't worry Dottie, with practice, you'll get the hang of it," Mr. Conrad proclaimed.

Earlier, Edward had managed cocktail service in the library again. The older couples ended up congregating in there while Edward prepared their drink orders. As a lark, Mr. Conrad offered to teach the ladies how to play snooker. Meanwhile, Mr. Sullivan and Mr. Higginbottom settled in the leather chairs in the front window and delved into a discussion about rising golf star, Arnold Palmer.

When Mrs. Conrad first appeared in the doorway, the room had gone silent with shock. Mr. Conrad slipped his arm around his wife's waist and explained how she'd spent the afternoon with Miss Winter. "What do you think of my beautiful wife?"

Mr. Higginbottom and Mr. Sullivan observed how fine she looked.

Mrs. Sullivan commented, "Very nice, Kitty."

Everyone turned to Mrs. Higginbottom. After scrutinizing Mrs. Conrad like she was an exotic animal at the zoo, the lady remarked, "My goodness, I almost didn't recognize you. Definitely, a nice change from the dowdy dresses you normally wear."

Which Edward thought was a mean thing to say. The others must have too, because the room got quiet and uncomfortable. Edward was relieved when his mother called him to help in the kitchen.

Cautiously, as if carrying heirloom crystal, he climbed the stairs with the loaded tray, step by deliberate step. He reached the top without a single spill and placed it on the tea trolley. He took a moment to pat down his cowlick, before wheeling it to the Rose Suite.

"Good evening, Edward. Thank you for bringing my dinner." Miss Winter swung the door open and stepped aside to allow room for the cart. She wore a red turtleneck sweater with slim black pants and feathery pink bedroom mules.

"No problem." Edward wheeled the trolley past her.

Smoke suspended in a cloud above the room and Nat King Cole quietly crooned from the record player. A cigarette burned in the ashtray on the coffee table, and a fire merrily blazed in the hearth. The typewriter with a small pile of typed pages sat next to the ashtray, but the wastebasket held at least half a dozen balled-up pieces of paper with three more littering the floor next to it.

"Where would you like the tray?"

Miss Winter scratched her head. "Best put it near the fireplace. I'll pull up that bergère chair to eat." She pointed to the armchair with the padded back and seat.

Edward didn't know that chair had such a fancy name, but he tucked it into his brainbox, for future use. Maybe he'd impress some girl with it one day. "Looks like you've been busy." He wheeled the dinner over to the fireplace.

"I had a rough go for a while." She picked up the cigarette and indicated the trash. "But now the article is coming along swimmingly. How about you?"

"It's been swell." His head bounced. "I've got a game tomorrow night. Hey, maybe you'd like to come." The minute the words came out of his mouth, he wanted to pull them back in. A girl like her wouldn't waste her time at a high school basketball game.

She turned to blow the smoke away from him. "That's kind of you to invite me. A work colleague is arriving tomorrow, and I doubt, I'll be available."

He stuffed his hands into his pockets and stared down at his feet. "Yeah, sure. It was a dumb idea."

The clock on the mantle chimed the hour.

"Hey, what's your team called?"

"The Newport Knights," he mumbled.

"I'm sorry, I didn't catch that."

He drew his eyes upward and repeated it louder, "We're the Newport Knights."

"Well, even if I can't be there, you know I'll be rooting for you," she kindly said. "What position do you play?"

"Center." She nodded, but Edward could tell by the blank look in her eyes that she'd no idea what that meant. It was okay, many girls didn't. "I stand close to the basketball hoop, to make shots or assist other teammates do so. You know, to score points," he explained.

"That sounds grand." Changing the subject she asked, "Have you figured out a way to make more money for the internship?"

He lifted a shoulder. "My mom says not to worry. She's got it figured out."

"I'm glad to hear it." Miss Winter riffled through her handbag and pulled out a crisp bill. "Thanks again for bringing up dinner. Good luck tomorrow. Go Knights."

"No problem." He slipped the dollar bill into his pocket and bent to pick up the wads of paper on the floor. "Just leave the cart outside your door when you're finished. I'll fetch it after the dinner service." He tossed each piece into the wastebasket from the doorway, making every shot.

Her brows winged upward. "Impressive."

He grinned. "You don't know what you're missing."

A ripple of laughter followed as she closed the door behind him.

# Chapter Twenty-Seven
## Ariadne

### Friday

Friday morning, brought with it a partly cloudy sky. Like rays of hope, streaks of light broke through the clouds into my sitting area landing on the message Donna Morgan sent me. I stayed up past midnight writing and rewriting the article. I needed two more paragraphs to finish it, which I hoped to gain from today's final interview.

The little mantel clock chimed the top of the hour—9:00. Donna's letter told me to arrive at noon. Since I had the morning to myself and an almost completed article, I indulged in a long hot bath.

At quarter to ten, I entered an empty dining room to fill my plate with the dregs of the breakfast chafing dishes. The last hardboiled egg, the last piece French toast, and a bowl of fruit cocktail. I chose the table in front of the bay window.

Maria stuck her head out of the door. "I thought I heard someone in here."

I glanced sheepishly at my plate. "Sorry, I was up late last night."

"Would you like a cup of coffee?"

"If there's some left."

"I've always got coffee brewing," Maria airily replied. Humming a tune, she returned with the coffee pot. Maria's nonchalant attitude surprised me. She seemed almost buoyant.

She glanced at my plate and tsked. "Would you like me to fix you some eggs?"

"No. This will be fine." I cracked the eggshell with the back of my spoon. When she lingered, I commented, "You seem to be in a chipper mood. Your son mentioned you'll be going to see his game tonight. Are you excited?"

"Hm? Oh, yes. I enjoy seeing him play. Often, I'm unable to go," she replied with regret.

"But you will tonight."

"Wouldn't miss it for the world." She picked up a folded newspaper from the middle table. "Mr. Sullivan left behind his paper. Would you like to read while you eat?"

"Thank you." I pretended to read the *Boston Globe* while surreptitiously watching Maria out of the corner of my eye.

She closed off the Sterno cans and began removing the chaffing dish inserts, humming to herself as she went in and out of the swinging door. She carried the last bowl from the buffet, and I heard the clank of dishes being washed. Finishing my breakfast, I tucked the newspaper under my arm and rose.

"All done?" She chirruped directly behind me.

I jumped. "Yes. The French toast was delicious."

"Ah, *mi abuela's* secret ingredient."

I decided to take the bait. "Oh, and what is that?"

"If I told you, it wouldn't be a secret." She winked and emitted a giggle.

I didn't know how to respond, so I fell to pleasantries. "You have a nice day Mrs. Massey."

"It promises to be a good one!"

I'd never seen Mrs. Massey so chipper. She usually powered around the inn with a mildly irritated look of determination. I thought perhaps she'd discovered some way to cover Edward's summer camp fees, but I didn't dare open that intrusive line of inquiry again.

‡‡‡

The address Donna listed on her note turned out to be The Breakers Mansion. It was built by Cornelius Vanderbilt II in 1895. One of the largest mansions built along the waterfront during the Gilded Age. It boasted 70 rooms and was built in the Renaissance Revival style with a whopping $7 million price tag.

Donna invited me into her motorhome, which had been moved over from Kingscote. The caterer brought us chicken salads for lunch. With the uptight Mr. Gaultier gone, her attitude toward me noticeably relaxed. The fact that the article from the *Chronicle* only sought to increase the fervor and excitement over her coming nuptials, as well as the movie release may have also softened her outlook.

After Donna answered my final questions, I concluded the interview with, "My editor wanted to confirm tomorrow's photo shoot at nine."

She placed her fork and knife together on the plate and tapped the linen napkin against her lips. "The studio has obtained permission to use the mansion's Morning Room for the shoot."

"I'll let Gavin know." I made a note in my memo pad, then tucked it into my purse.

"If you'd like, you may stay for the musical rehearsal." Donna got to her feet, and I followed suit.

"It would be my pleasure to stay and watch rehearsals. Thank you." I gathered my things, and Donna ushered me out the door.

## Chapter Twenty-Eight
### Ariadne

That night, I returned to Ivy Tree Inn floating on air. Indeed, if my feet were swollen and sore, it had been a pleasure getting them that way. I'd made friends with Sammie Simone, the trombonist in Tony Baldwin's band, and got myself invited to the party they were hosting at their hotel.

"Pretty girls are always welcome to our parties," Baldwin had replied, wiping the sweat from his shiny forehead with a red bandana, when Sammie asked if I could join them. He grinned at me, his teeth gleaming bright against his coffee skin.

A few of the cast members attended the party, however Donna was not one of them. I danced with Tommy Tanner! He taught me the Charleston, and we had a bit of a harmless flirtation. If I hadn't had a crush on him before tonight, I certainly did now.

I pulled into a parking space next to Melvin's sedan and wondered if any of the guests would still be awake. Likely not, at half past midnight. The windows were dark and quiet. However, glancing up, I saw Frank's silhouette in the third-floor window. The curtain twitched closed.

The stuffy grouch was probably making sure I didn't bring home any late-night guests he could charge me for. He'd sounded quite put out when I called, as a courtesy, to inform him that I would not be eating dinner at the inn tonight. Granted, it had been quarter to seven when I rang up, but I thought he'd be relieved to have one less guest to serve considering Maria would be at Edward's basketball game.

Instead, he'd been short with me, almost to the point of rudeness.

Sconces burned low in the foyer and up the staircase lighting my way, I figured everyone would be tucked into bed and asleep. So as not to wake them, I tiptoed down the hall stepping over one of the squeaky areas.

Soft footfalls came from above, and I assumed Frank— assured that I wasn't sneaking any men into the house—would be heading to his bed.

The one good thing I can say about my repulsive pink room is that it had a modern record player and a dozen records to choose from. Kicking off my heels, I knelt and flipped through the stack. Not quite ready for the jazz-filled night to end, I chose a Duke Ellington record, and, in deference to my neighbors, I turned the sound down low.

Sammie hadn't wanted to see me go and jokingly pressed a half-drunk bottle of champagne into my hands. "A parting gift!" he exclaimed.

I sipped directly from the bottle as Ellington's piano wove an embroidery of notes surrounding me like a tuneful cocoon.

The record came to an end. The mantel clock struck one. I lay drowsing, curled up on the loveseat trying to motivate myself to move to bed.

*CRASH!*

I bolted upright. "*What was that?*"

I'd left my Keds beneath the coffee table and slipped into them before opening my door to investigate. A squeak and a rubbing sound came from the hallway. I found a switch and turned the low-burning sconces up high.

"Hello? Miss Winter? Are you all right?" Walter Sullivan, in a robe and slippers with his hair awry, stood in his doorway.

"It wasn't me," I answered. "I think it came from the top floor. Mr. Wyler's apartments."

"That was quite a bang. I'd better go up and check on him," he said. "Let me find my glasses first."

"What the devil was that noise?" I glanced over the balustrade to find Mr. Higginbottom halfway up the stairs in a state of deshabille.

"Sounds like it came from Mr. Wyler's apartment," I explained.

"It's probably nothing." Mr. Sullivan adjusted his glasses. "I'll go up and check."

For some reason, the words, "I'll come with you," came out of my mouth.

In retrospect, I wondered what would have happened if I'd simply returned to my room and let everyone else handle it.

"There's no need, Miss Winter," Walter replied.

"I insist." Determinedly, I followed him up the stairs.

Mr. Sullivan banged on Wyler's door. "Frank! Are you in there? Frank, open the door."

I knew he was in there, because I'd seen him half an hour ago, and I hadn't heard him come down the stairs. When Mr. Sullivan got no response, my concern turned to fear, and I joined the incessant knocking. "Mr. Wyler? Hello? Please open the door."

"Why isn't he answering?" Mr. Sullivan muttered under his breath.

I twisted the knob, and to our astonishment, the door swung into the room.

The apartment was steeped with beautiful antiques. Clearly, Mr. Wyler had chosen not to modernize the third floor. Instead, he kept the charming historical aspects of its original building era—like the handmade tile around the fireplace and walnut paneling. The cushioned couch, oval coffee table, and modern television set were a few items that seemed out of place among the older pieces. Also, the little wooden A-frame stepstool parked in the middle of the room.

Our innkeeper lay stretched peacefully on the floor of his main living area. If the rug hadn't had a cream background, we might not have noticed the blood seeping from a wound on the back of his head. The delicate Chinese rug would never come clean from that stain.

"He must have fallen." Mr. Sullivan crouched next to the innkeeper and shook his shoulder. "Frank. Hey Frank! Wake up."

When the innkeeper gave no response, Mr. Sullivan placed his fingers against Frank's wrist. "This isn't good. I'm not feeling a pulse. I'd better call for a doctor." His knees cracked as he rose. "Are you quite all right Miss Winter?"

Absently, I nodded, but something was out of place. My mind seemed sluggish as if wading through a pool of molasses—probably due to the champagne. "This is wrong."

"It *is* a bit gruesome," he acknowledged. "Why don't you return to your room? Or go back to mine and Connie can look after you. Cedric and I will take care of this. Call him up for me, will you?" He strode to the telephone table and picked up the handset. "Operator, hello? Put me through to the hospital emergency line. There's been an accident."

Granted, the greasy lump in my gut could be attributed to the ghastly scene, but that wasn't it. Just as Aunt Ruby once said, not much got past me, and something about the body didn't add up.

The brass chandelier hanging from the vaulted ceiling must have been at least ten feet. I couldn't imagine the little stepstool would have given him enough height to reach the chandelier.

*Did he lose his balance and hit his head? On what?*

I could find no bulb—new or burnt out in his hand, on the floor, or missing from the burning chandelier. The coffee table wasn't near his body, but I checked the smooth rounded edges of the wood for damage or blood.

*Did he hit his head on the hard floor or perhaps the little ladder?* I paced the space scrutinizing it. The room took up the area of my small sitting area and bedroom combined.

Walter finished his phone conversation and hung up. "They're sending an ambulance." He strode to the open door and called down the stairwell, "Cedric! Frank fell off a stepstool. It doesn't look good. I've called for an ambulance. They're on their way. Unlock the front door, will you?"

When he returned to the room, I spoke in a subdued voice, "Call the police, Mr. Sullivan."

"I say, Miss Winter! No need to be dramatic. I don't think we need the police for a slip and fall."

"That's the problem. I don't believe this was a mere slip and fall."

"What do you mean?" he blustered pulling a pack of Winstons from his robe pocket.

"Please don't light that," I implored pointing at the cigarette he'd tapped out.

"Look here, I know Frank wasn't a smoker, but . . . well . . ."

I shook my head.

He harrumphed jamming the pack back in his pocket.

"That's the rub." Though my clothes still smelled of booze and cigarettes from the party, there lingered a scent of smoke that came from inside the room.

I sniffed. "Do you smell that?"

Mr. Sullivan's nose wrinkled as he drew in a deep breath. Once. Twice. "Perhaps," he replied, though his features remained doubtful.

"As you say, Wyler wasn't a smoker, but someone *has* been smoking." I strode over to the cold fireplace and crouched down.

There it was. One single butt.

I picked it up and spun around. "Ha!"

Walter showed a distinct lack of awe in his demeanor. "So? Maybe Frank broke his rule and lit up. Plenty of folks claiming to be non-smokers light up occasionally."

"It's a Chesterfield." It had been smoked down to the filter. However, since it was my own brand, I identified what was left of the tiny script just above the filter.

182

"There's an entire box of Chesterfields in the library. Probably snitched one on his way upstairs," Walter explained.

Tossing the butt back into the hearth, I dusted my hands and got to my feet. "Do you know if Mr. Wyler had a guest up here tonight?"

"Not that I know of. Let me think." He furrowed his brow in concentration. "The Conrads turned in early, before nine. We played bridge with the Higginbottoms until nine-thirty, and Dottie and Connie decided to retire. The girl helping Frank with the dinner service must have left, because Frank came out of the kitchen and chatted us up for a bit. Then Edward and his mother arrived home full of pep because his team won the game. He gave us the play-by-play, until his mother reigned in his exuberance, and they headed to their quarters above the garage."

"What time was that?"

He scratched his stubble. "No later than ten."

"Did you go to bed then too?"

"No. Cedric had a bottle of port he wanted to open."

"So, it was just you and Cedric? Drinking the port?"

"Yes. Cockburn's. Have you ever had port? No? It's a fortified wine, and Cedric's was a very nice one. A fifty-one vintage, I believe." Sullivan explained.

"Did Frank stay up with you?"

He swayed his head from side to side. "Frank made his rounds locking the inn. Then he went to his apartment."

"How late did you and Mr. Higginbottom stay up?"

"Oh, not too late. Connie was in bed. She'd fallen asleep with a book on her lap. I changed, brushed my teeth, and I was in bed when the hall clock chimed eleven."

As I took another turn around the room, the gears in my brain finally began clicking. "I saw him in the window half an hour ago."

My feet paused in front of the fireplace. A black and white framed photo of a middle-aged woman wearing Victory rolls sat

183

in the center of the mantel along with three Hummel figurines. A tall pair of silver candle holders, empty of candles, sat on the left-hand side of the mantel. Dust covered the mantel and the bric-a-brac, except for an area on the right-hand side.

"Something with a round base was sitting here, on the mantel."

"So? Maybe it was a vase with flowers that died, and Frank threw them out," Mr. Sullivan rationalized.

I paced over to the innkeeper. "Notice how perfectly stretched out the body is? A little too perfect if you ask me. When a person falls, especially if they fall off a chair or stepstool—" I indicated said piece "—they don't usually land with their legs out straight and arms at the side. His positioning is too peaceful."

Doubt flickered across Sullivan's features.

I chewed my bottom lip staring at Frank's body.

*It must be done.*

With a cringe and silent apology to the heavens, I crouched down and pushed the innkeeper's upper body to the side. His blood-matted hair peeled off the sticky rug, and I smelled a distinct metallic tang in the air. Gagging, I slammed my eyes shut, and breathed deep, before reopening them.

"I say, Miss Winter, what are you doing?" Sullivan cried in dismay, "I don't think you should be doing that."

There was a definitive indentation where the skull had been crushed. With no blood on the ladder and no furniture nearby, I could not determine what made the gash. Gently, I allowed the body to roll back in place and got to my feet to face Walter's disgust and annoyance.

"That's quite unwomanly of you, Miss Winter," he chastised.

"It's only been minutes since we heard the crash. Why is the blood already congealing? And his face is cold to the touch." My troubled gaze stared at the body, and I whispered, "I think he's been dead for a while." My hands shook, and an unexpected wave of nausea washed over me.

"You're being hysterical," he bluntly replied.

Balling up my fists, I swallowed down the sick feeling. In firm but calm tones, I uttered, "Mr. Sullivan, I am not hysterical. Furthermore, I believe our innkeeper may have met with foul play. Either way, the police must be called to investigate further. Now, shall I phone the police, or will you?"

Walter adjusted his glasses and cleared his throat. "I suppose it can't hurt to call the authorities." He picked up the handset. "Operator, get me the police."

"What are you doing?" Connie's rough smoker tones asked from the doorway. Her hair had been rolled in pink curlers and wrapped in a blue scarf. She wore a long yellow chenille robe with black slippers.

"Checking to see if the windows are locked," I answered.

"What on earth for?" She caught sight of Frank and the blood-stained carpet. "Oh dear, Frank's looking a little gray and that's quite a bit of blood."

Mr. Sullivan hung up the phone. "The police are on the way."

Connie straightened. "Should've told them to bring a hearse."

My fingers paused their search of the window latches. "Shh, did you hear that?" On cat feet, I darted to the open apartment door and cocked an ear.

"Hear what?" Connie asked at my shoulder.

"That squeaking." I whispered, but the sound had stopped again. "I heard it earlier."

"Probably another mouse," Mr. Sullivan suggested.

I strode back over to the window, where I'd seen Wyler when I returned tonight. The scent of cigarettes was strong, and, as I twitched aside the curtain, another butt fell at my feet. "Were any of the staff up here this evening?"

Sullivan frowned and rubbed his unshaven chin in thought. "I told you Maria and her son went to their apartment around ten. The kitchen assistant was gone by nine-thirty."

"What about Johnny?" I asked.

"Oh, Johnny left before four," Connie asserted.

"You're sure?"

The pair nodded in unison.

"Connie and I had a brief conversation with him. Said he had to drive to Providence to buy a part for the water heater in the garage apartment. He'd been working on it most of the day."

"Pawtucket," his wife corrected, "he said Pawtucket, not Providence."

I stared out the window where I'd seen Mr. Wyler standing. "Did Johnny Wexler return to the inn tonight?"

"No. Not that I recall. Connie, do you remember seeing him?"

She gave a negative shake of her head.

"He must not have returned. I didn't see his truck parked in its usual spot." Touching the butt with my toe, I pondered the clues around me.

*Was that crash our innkeeper falling off the little A-frame? It didn't sound like a body thudding to the floor. And why is the blood already congealed? If there was someone else up here in Frank's apartment, where was that person now? How did they leave without going past Walter and me in the main stairwell?*

My ears perked up. "There it is again."

I dashed across the room, and down the hallway that led to the bedroom. It held a four-poster bed still made up, with a pair of pajamas neatly folded at the foot of it. A mahogany chest of drawers was on the wall opposite the bed. Matching bedside tables with matching lamps, which burned low, flanked the bed. My mind ticked off each piece of furniture.

The rubbing sounded again, only now it was behind me. I retraced my steps to the hallway bathroom. A flick of my wrist, and the fluorescent light spasmodically flickered, casting erratic shadows across the room. It came to life burning a weak but steady glow, and the rubbing sound stopped. As did my heart.

Smeared in blood across the mirror was a message.

# *PAY UP OR ELSE!*

I gasped a lungful of breath.

"What's wrong?" Connie came to investigate.

I pointed.

"Oh my." She put a hand to her mouth.

"Do you think it's *his* blood?" I whispered the last part.

She went up close to the mirror and squinted. "Not blood. Lipstick. Red Velvet by Bésame if I had to guess."

I peered closer and realized my mind had jumped to conclusions. Connie was correct. Before I could ask her how she knew the exact shade, raised voices drew our attention back to the living room.

# Chapter Twenty-Nine
## Ariadne

Mr. Conrad, still in his robe and slippers, led two men, wheeling a stretcher cot low to the ground, into the apartment.

The younger attendant wearing a plaid flannel jacket over his white uniform remained next to the stretcher as if waiting for directions from his associate. His round cheeks were red and chapped. He didn't look much older than Edward.

The gray-haired, senior attendant bent over the patient and used his stethoscope to check the patient's heartbeat. When he couldn't find one, he pressed two fingers against Wyler's throat.

We remained silent, as the attendant came to the same conclusion that Walter and I had already reached.

Finally, he wrapped the stethoscope around his neck. The crow's feet around his eyes drooped as he delivered the bad news, "I'm afraid this man's dead. There is nothing we can do for him." He rolled Wyler to the side to examine the injury to the back of his head.

"I'll be damned." Melvin scratched his cheek, his face somber.

The elder attendant and Melvin straightened as one.

"He musta fallen off the stool and busted his head. Eh, Mr. Thompson?" the young man said with a nasally Boston inflection.

Mr. Thompson surveyed the room with a skeptical eye. "Did any of you see him fall?" He glanced at Walter and

Melvin who each shook their heads.

Connie pronounced baldly, "No, but we heard a crash."

"Who found him?" Mr. Thompson asked.

"I did," Walter replied.

"We did," I corrected stepping full into the room.

Melvin plopped a hand on his bald head, and yelped, "Miss Winter! I didn't see you there!"

I pointed to the dead body. "He was lying just like that when Mr. Sullivan and I arrived."

Walter opened his mouth, then thought better of it, and closed it.

Thompson's face tightened "Well, Timmons—" he looked to his colleague "—there's nothing more we can do here."

"Now wait just a minute." Connie stepped into the doorway and placed her palm forward in a stop motion. "Where do you think you're going? The police will need you to take the body. We can't stay here with a-a corpse."

Thompson gave a negative head motion. "Ma'am, the police will call the coroner to come pick up the body. We only take the live ones. Step aside, if you please." He grabbed one end of the stretcher. "Come on, Timmons."

Taken aback, Connie moved to allow them to pass.

Ready to leave the disturbing scene, I followed the pair into the hallway planning to wait for the police on the main level.

However, the ambulance attendants halted at the top of the stairs. "Just a minute, Timmons. Someone is coming up."

I didn't need to peer over the balustrade to know who it was. He was huffing like a steam engine as he chugged up the stairs.

An exceptionally tall police officer trailed behind Cedric at a forced leisurely pace—his boots striking each tread with a distinctive click. The older man made it to the landing and reached a hand against the wall, placing the other one against his chest as he labored to catch his breath.

The police officer moved past his stout figure but paused in front of ambulance attendants. "Well?"

"Nothing we can do. He's all yours," Mr. Thompson replied.

The officer removed his campaign-style hat and dusted the snow off the wide brim. "Dead?"

Thompson gave a sharp nod. "Can't be more than a few hours. The body is still flexible. Rigor mortis hasn't set in."

Cedric spotted the empty stretcher and plopped his ample figure down upon it wheezing like a bagpipe running out of air.

The officer entered the apartment with a grim demeanor. His six-foot-three frame would have been imposing enough, but wearing the distinctive black, Rhode Island State Police uniform, with the brown leather utility belt, and matching knee-high boots, his presence was nothing less than daunting.

I leaned against the door jamb as he prowled the room.

His steely gray eyes took in the body, stepstool, and surrounding furniture. He squatted down, tilted his head, and placed two fingers to Wyler's throat. When he didn't find a pulse, he rolled him to the side to see the injury to the back of his head. "Who moved him into this position?"

"No one. He was like that when Mr. Sullivan and I arrived," I stated.

The officer pinned me with his gaze "Who are you?"

I lifted my chin. "Ariadne Winter. I'm a guest."

Plopping the hat back on his head, the officer rose to his full height. "Were any of you in here when this happened?" His questioning gaze encompassed the room.

We murmured in the negative.

"There was a crash. We heard a crash," Connie asserted, as she'd done for the ambulance attendants.

The officer paced purposefully through the room, and eventually down the hallway to the bedroom and bathroom, where I'd left the lights burning. He stopped cold in front of the bathroom doorway.

Connie and I exchanged a look but remained silent.

He disappeared into the bathroom, momentarily out of my view, only to reemerge, and return to the living room with purposeful strides. "All of you, please go down to the main level, and await me in the front room. You—" his long finger speared Walter "—what's your name?"

Walter stiffened. "It's Sullivan. Walter Sullivan."

"When you get downstairs, ask my partner, Officer Webster, to phone Detective Kingsley. Tell him he needs to see this."

# Chapter Thirty
## Ariadne

"I don't know how you can stand it, Connie. My nerves are shattered, simply shattered." Dottie, in a luxurious red velvet robe with black fur cuffs and collar, draped herself across the sofa like a yearning lover in a Shakespearean tragedy. In one hand she held a bottle of sherry—filched from the kitchen.

Her husband laid his ample figure across from her on the other sofa, still recovering from his descent from the third floor with the help of young Timmons—who fled the premises with a look of relief.

At the request of Officer Webster, we gathered in the parlor to await further instructions, while he joined his colleague on the top floor. The Higginbottom's positions relegated the rest of us to take up random chairs around the room. We were a motley bunch gathered in the parlor. Everyone was dressed in their bedclothes except for me and, to my surprise, Kitty Conrad.

Kitty wore her new sage coat over top of black wool trousers and a beige sweater. Her features were rosy with cold, and she sat across from Connie in a pair of chairs by the French doors that led to the front porch. Melvin had pulled up a side chair next to Kitty, while Walter smoked and paced the room. I took up a straight-back slipper chair that provided me a view of the entire assemblage.

Cedric reached toward his wife. "It was best you didn't see him, my darling. I'll never forget those unstaring blue eyes."

*Unstaring eyes?* I knew Wyler's eyes had been closed and was certain Cedric couldn't have been able to see more than his shoes from the hallway gurney.

"Oh, Ceddie! How could you! That is the only thing, I'll be able to think about now." Dot dramatically threw an arm across her face.

"Come, now! It was no such thing. His eyes are brown, not blue, and they were closed," Connie snapped, for once her taciturn composure shaken with irritation. She'd retrieved her fur stole before joining us in the parlor and pulled it tighter around her shoulders.

Cedric sputtered in defense.

The fire had died hours ago, and the room turned frigid. I longed for my robe or winter coat and envied the other ladies wearing their extra covering. Hugging my arms around my waist, I clamped my teeth tight to keep them from chattering. Perhaps it wasn't the cold that had me shivering. The sight of a dead body, coupled with the realization that one of this crew must have killed the innkeeper, may have been the cause of my trembling reaction.

"For the love of Pete, it is categorically freezing in here. Miss Winter's lips are blue. Someone light the fire before we turn into popsicles," Connie demanded.

Walter paused his pacing. "Good lord, Miss Winter, why didn't you say something!"

Always the helper, Melvin Conrad jumped to his feet. "I'll start the fire."

"Here now, Cedric, move off the blanket. Miss Winter needs it." Walter tugged at a green hand-knit afghan throw draped across the back of the sofa. Cedric levered his walrus-like body into a sitting position allowing Walter to pull it off. "Here you go."

I thanked him but nearly jumped out of my skin when a voice rang out above my shoulder.

"*Dios mío!* What is going on? What are you doing up?"

Maria stood in the dining room doorway. Her hair was braided in a thick plait down her back, and she wore a man's fleece-lined coat over her flannel nightgown. "Is that my cooking sherry?"

Dot groaned in response.

"What are you doing up?" I asked through chattering teeth.

She glanced down at me. "Looking for Edward. I thought I heard a popping noise. It woke me up. I went to check on Edward and found his bedroom door open. When I saw the lights on in the house, I assumed he'd come over here to find something to eat. The kitchen door was left unlocked."

The front door opened, and our attention swiveled to the foyer. In walked Edward fully dressed and bundled in his winter gear dusting snowflakes from his shoulders. "I saw the police car. What's happened."

"Edward! What are you doing up?" his mother demanded, stepping further into the room.

Edward's mouth dropped. "Mom! I-I didn't see you there."

"Where have you been? Do not tell me you went over to that party at Dickie Johnson's house."

He stared down at his feet scratching the back of his head. "Shucks, Mom. The whole team went."

"And decided to sneak out, after I told you, no?"

Edward didn't respond.

The fire crackled to life under Melvin's capable hands, but our attention remained riveted on mother and son.

"How did you get there? Did that boy, C.J. drive you? Or was it Johnny? I thought I heard his great rattling truck. Did Johnny bring you home?"

"Naw. I walked," he mumbled with a half-shrug.

She sucked in a breath. "His house is at least five miles away, and it's ten below out there!"

He rolled his eyes. "It's only about three miles. I was fine."

I pitied Edward. It wasn't that long ago my parents had forbidden me from attending a high school graduation party hosted by a boy my mother deemed a "rabble-rouser." Instead, she forced me to attend dinner with a "nice" college boy she'd dug up from the country club. He had a perpetually runny nose and smelled of onions.

Maria stood like an avenging angel, with arms akimbo, staring up at her handsome son who outweighed her by at least two stones, and pronounced, "Edward Martin Massey, you are grounded."

"But Mo-om—"

We weren't to know what Edward planned to beg from his mother, as the two police officers came down the stairs at that moment.

Abject fear suffused his features, Edward hissed at his mother, "Did you phone the police?"

She shook her head in confusion.

"Are all the guests accounted for?" The tall officer asked the room at large.

"This is everyone," Walter affirmed.

"I'm Sergeant Carmichael and this is my partner, Officer Webster."

"Walter Sullivan." He shook hands with each officer, then he worked his way around the room introducing the lot of us.

"This is Mr. and Mrs. Cedric Higginbottom. In front of the fire is Melvin Conrad, and that's his wife, Mrs. Conrad in the green coat. Sitting next to Mrs. Conrad is my wife, whom you met when you arrived tonight, along with Miss Ariadne Winter. This is Maria Massey, the cook, and her son, Edward."

"Detective Kingsley is on his way," stated Officer Webster. "In the meantime, Sergeant Carmichael and I will begin by obtaining all of your statements."

"Statements? What for?" Maria asked in fadeaway tones.

Dottie righted herself plunking the sherry bottle on the coffee table. "I can tell you my statement, Cedric and I have been in bed since nine o'clock." She pushed to her feet. "Now, if you don't mind, this has been quite traumatic for me. I'm awfully tired and would like to return to my room."

"As would I!" Kitty proclaimed also rising to her feet. "I understand a man died, but can't these, statements, wait until morning?"

Carmichael's imposing figure stepped forward. "Ladies and gentlemen, a man hasn't just died, he's been murdered," he paused, and Maria's gasp filled the room. "We will *not* be waiting until morning."

Melvin's head snapped up. "Murder? What's this? I thought he fell."

"Murder? *Dios mío.*" Maria crossed herself. "Who? Who is dead? It's not-not Frank?" Her eyes darted frantically around the room.

When no one said anything, Connie's deep tones answered her question. "I'm afraid so, Maria."

"No-oo!" she wailed, crumpled into her son's chest, and commenced sobbing. He buried his face into her hair and held tight.

It occurred to me, that for a houseful of people claiming to be close friends with Frank and his mother, only Maria and Edward showed sorrow at his death. Once Maria's wailing began, the room became thick with voices running over top of each other.

Melvin rushed over to soothe the mother and son by proffering his handkerchief.

Meanwhile, Cedric tried to argue with the officers. "See here! The ladies' nerves are—"

"Shattered! Simply shattered!" cried Dottie, once again sinking onto the couch.

"I *could* use some rest," Kitty proclaimed rising from her chair. "I haven't been sleeping well."

Connie, stoic as always declared in rough tones, "I am fine. I'll answer any of your questions officers. I have nothing to hide. And I've some questions of my own." She cast a wary gaze across the assemblage, scrutinizing everyone with narrowed, suspicious eyes. Her gaze paused momentarily on Kitty and then Dottie.

Connie's little dig only sought to increase the noise. The room erupted into chaos. Maria's wailing intensified, and the guests began arguing in earnest.

"Are you implying *I* had something to do with his death?" Kitty screeched at Connie.

"I imply no such thing. But I am wondering what you are doing fully dressed, in the middle of the night," Connie drawled.

"How dare you!" Kitty stormed across the room to the hearth.

"There was no reason for me to wish the man ill," Cedric pronounced.

Dot sat up again and waved her hand in the air. "Yes! Ceddie and I cared for poor Frank. We wouldn't hurt him. We have *nothing* to do with his death."

Kitty spun around, her face a sour mask. "What about the money?"

The color drained from Cedric's face while his wife turned a mottled shade of puce. "Why you little—"

"You think you're the only one Frank came to begging for money? I wasn't foolish enough to write him a check," Kitty said in a particularly nasty tone.

Melvin's mouth dropped. "Kitty?"

I recalled the message written on the bathroom mirror, and my gaze locked onto Connie's profile.

She didn't notice. With an assessing stare, she watched Kitty and Dot.

"Hello? What's all this?" A deep baritone voice rose above the fray. Standing behind the police officers, his coat and fedora sprinkled with snow, and a valise in his right hand, stood one of the most beautiful sights I'd ever seen.

I'd completely forgotten he was supposed to arrive. Without thinking, I leaped from my chair and rushed pell-mell, dodging around Walter Sullivan, past the Massey's, toward the one man I knew who couldn't have been involved in Frank Wyler's death. "Gavin!"

His eyes alighted on me, and a welcome smile drew across his face. "Ariadne! You're still up!"

His features quickly turned to surprise, as I threw my arms around his neck and cried, "Thank goodness, you've arrived!"

"There, there, now." He folded his unencumbered hand around my waist. "Didn't you get my telegram? It said I'd be late. Although, I expected to be here sooner than this. The blooming tracks froze up, and the train is running hours behind," his deep voice rumbled in my ear.

Sergeant Carmichael let out a piercing whistle which silenced the cacophony of voices. "That's enough!" he bellowed.

Coming back to reality, I peeled myself off Gavin. He retained a loose hold around my waist, which I didn't object to, regardless of the fact the dampness on his coat had begun to seep into my clothes.

The only sound was Maria, as she quietly wept into Melvin's hankie.

"All of you. Take. A. Seat." Carmichael pointed to those of us standing, which was everyone except Dottie.

Cedric plopped down on the sofa. Walter took Kitty's prior seat, next to his wife, while Kitty retreated to sit at the card table. Melvin assisted Edward in leading his sniffling mother to the card table as well and they made up a foursome.

While the guests were following the Sergeant's directions, I assisted Gavin in removing his hat and coat whispering, "The innkeeper has been murdered."

"Murdered! You don't say," Gavin replied in hushed tones. "How?"

"Someone struck him with something heavy on the back of the head and did a poor job staging it to look like an accident." I glanced over my shoulder to make sure the police were still occupied with the others, and added, "The murderer left a threat on the mirror in blood-red lipstick."

"Jiminy Christmas. Who do you think did it?" He followed my gaze, which swept the room of suspects. "Hoo-boy." He took my elbow and guided me into the parlor.

"You there, what's wrong with you? Stop all that moaning and sit up. This isn't your bedroom." Sergeant Carmichael admonished Dottie. "And you, you're her husband, make her stop these histrionics. Can't stand an over-emotional woman. Move next to her, and allow the two lovebirds to sit together," he directed to Cedric who levered himself up with cracking knees to relocate to the sofa his wife occupied.

I didn't bother to correct the officer's assumption. My behavior was certainly not that of a coworker.

"Come, dearest." Gavin seemed to enjoy the officer's incorrect assumption. He allowed a mischievous grin to light his face and took my hand in his. "Good lord, Ariadne! Your hands are freezing. Come over next to the fire and warm up."

I held them toward the licking flames welcoming the searing heat. The front door swept open once again and ushered in a colored man wearing a snow dusted overcoat.

"Kingsley! It's about time," Officer Webster admonished. "What took you so long!"

"Officer Webster." The newcomer nodded in acknowledgment. "Where is the body?"

"Top floor," Carmichael answered.

The detective removed his leather gloves and gave a great yawn. "Is there any coffee to be had?"

"I-I can make some coffee," Maria timidly offered.

"It would be much appreciated, Ma'am." The detective took off his trilby hat dropping the gloves inside. "Sergeant Carmichael, what have you got for me?"

"Looks like the victim was bludgeoned to death. Webster and I were about to get statements from the suspects."

The Sergeant's aspersions sent the room into another uproar.

# Chapter Thirty-One
## *Ariadne*

The hall clock chimed thrice. I yawned and took another sip of the strong coffee Maria had doled out to everyone. Although her employer was dead, she couldn't stop playing caretaker to the guests. Wincing with disgust as the cold coffee hit my tongue, I replaced the cup on the table and sighed.

Sergeant Carmichael, the coroner, a photographer, and Detective Kingsley had spent at least an hour in Wyler's apartment investigating the crime scene. Meanwhile, we were left cooling our heels under the watchful eye of Officer Webster.

After the coroner wheeled the body into the back of his vehicle, Detective Kingsley directed Sergeant Carmichael to search for footprints around the house. Upon reporting his findings to the detective, Carmichael left telling Webster to ride back to the station with Kingsley. Webster seemed none too keen on that. I heard him mumble a rude epithet about negros under his breath which also brought into question Kingsley's skills as a detective.

Carmichael shut him down. "He's the best detective on the force. Do your job, Webster."

Officer Webster begrudgingly followed orders to keep us quiet, and from leaving the parlor, until we'd been dismissed by the detective.

Talk about an awkward silence. No one wished to speak in front of the officer, so the room remained subdued, only broken when Maria offered more coffee. Suspicious, uneasy glances continually darted about. It was difficult to determine whether the anxious faces of the guests were due to guilt, or fear, or some of both. Between Gavin, the fire, and Maria's hot coffee, my body finally warmed to normal.

The parlor dwindled to three people, and I was the only one awake. Our warden snored quietly with his chin to his chest, in a wooden chair guarding the threshold that led to the foyer. Gavin, bless the man, remained by my side on the sofa. Despite the fact he'd been dismissed by Kingsley rather quickly when Sergeant Carmichael explained to the detective that my colleague arrived *after* the murder had been committed. The poor man's head lolled against the back of the sofa, with his hands crossed over his stomach, and his feet on the coffee table.

The pocket doors slid apart.

Melvin exited and murmured, "You're up next, Miss Winter."

"Thank you, Mr. Conrad." I pushed to my feet.

Gavin jerked awake slurring, "Whass happening?"

"It's my turn with the detective. Why don't you go to your room and hit the hay."

He rubbed his eyes. "I'm coming with you."

"I'll be fine. Don't forget, you have an appointment with Donna Morgan at nine."

"I insist. Howard would never forgive me if something happened to you."

The ghost of a laugh slipped between my lips.

Gavin stretched his arms above his head. "I'm not joking. He specifically told me to watch out for you. I'll never hear the end of it if you are sent off to the pokey."

It made sense, considering Howard believed *Look* would get the Donna Morgan interview if I didn't deliver. I was the goose laying his precious golden egg.

"If you insist." I held out my hand to help Gavin to his feet.

Spotting a pad and pencil at the game table, I took a quick detour before making my way to the dining room. Details of the past week swirled in my head, but the coffee and lack of sleep left my brain unfocused. Try as I might; I couldn't create coherent connections. Writing down my thoughts would be a good start.

I yawned. So would a solid eight hours of sleep.

Kingsly's shirt sleeves were pushed up past his elbows revealing a deep scar slashed across his left forearm. He sat at the larger table in the middle of the room. A small notebook was in front of him. "Mister . . ." He flipped through his notes.

"Turnbull," Gavin supplied.

The detective looked above the black-rimmed reading glasses perched on his nose. "Right. I've got enough from you. You're free to leave."

Gavin pulled out a chair for me and then took the one to my left. "Nonetheless, I'll be staying."

"I don't think you understand, you're not required. Please leave," the detective replied in dulcet tones.

Gavin's face flushed with anger. Before he could retort, I laid my pad and pencil on the table and coolly explained, "Detective Kingsley, I don't think *you* understand."

The detective's golden-brown eyes swiveled to me, and he removed the glasses.

"You see, my father is a lawyer, and he once told me, 'Ariadne, if you're ever questioned by the police, request a lawyer.' Apparently, there are laws about representation."

"That applies when you're arrested. I'm only gathering statements," Kingsley explained.

"Then you won't mind if my co-worker remains with us . . . since you're 'only' gathering my statement." I crossed my hands together on the table and calmly waited for him to begin.

"I prefer to do it one-on-one. As you may have noticed, I interviewed the married couples separately."

"But Miss Winter is not an old married lady. She's quite

young, and attractive, as you can see." Gavin pointed out. "It's three in the morning, and it would be most improper for me to leave her alone with a strange man."

I could have handled the detective on my own, but I had to admit, Gavin's protectiveness made a warm gooey feeling spread through the pit of my stomach. I realized; I *wanted* him to stay. "If you wish for a statement from me, then you must allow Mr. Turnbull to remain."

"Very well," the detective sighed and slid his glasses in place. "Name and occupation."

"Ariadne Winter. Journalist."

His gaze flicked up from the notebook. "I understand you work at *Ladies' Lifestyle Magazine*, with Mr. Turnbull. Yes?"

"Correct."

"Tell me your whereabouts this evening, Miss Winter."

Succinctly, I ran down my timeline. Returned home at half past twelve. Listened to a record. Heard the crash at one.

Detective Kingsley paused his scribbling to glance up at me. "You're sure it was one o'clock?"

"Very. I heard the little clock on the mantel in my sitting room chime one. The crash happened only moments later."

"You said you were listening to a record. What were you listening to?"

*Ah, very good detective. Making sure to get the little details, after all, they are the ones that matter.* "Duke Ellington."

Kingsley wrote that down. "And how did you know the victim?"

"I didn't. I'd only met the man upon my arrival Monday evening."

He pulled his glasses to his nose and peered at me above them. "You've never met the man before Monday?"

I shook my head.

"The cook is under the impression, that your family has a long-standing relationship with the victim."

"She is mistaken," I calmly replied writing that information down before continuing, "It is true, my Aunt Ruby is known . . . I'm sorry, *was* known to Mr. Wyler. I never met the man before my arrival. It is she who booked a room for me here, at the inn."

"I see, and your aunt is?"

"Ruby Winter. She owns—"

"*Bella Vida,*" he supplied.

I rested my chin on my fist. "So, you've heard of her."

*Bella Vida* was the only salon in town that employed a colored hairstylist—Alvita. She supplied services to colored women from Newport to Portsmouth. Twice a week, Alvita came over from Providence, where the largest portion of Rhode Island's small colored population lived. When Aunt Ruby hired Alvita, she told any of her clients who might be squeamish about having their haircut in the same salon as other colored women, they could either plan to have their hair done on other days of the week or find another hair salon.

"Newport is a small town." He cleared his throat. "You said you heard the crash at one. Then what happened?"

"I popped my head out of my room and found Mr. Sullivan in the hallway. We realized the noise came from Frank's apartment. It was so loud, it woke Mr. Higginbottom. I remember he was on the stairs and asked what happened."

"So, Mr. Sullivan was outside his room, as was Mr. Higginbottom?"

I thought about that for a moment and made a note on my pad before responding, "Yes. That is correct."

"Aside from Mr. Higginbottom, did you hear anything outside your door before or after this crashing sound?"

I shook my head.

It was a knotty problem that kept me going in circles. Not only couldn't I determine who did the murder—there were so many suspects—but *how* he or she got out of the apartment. The stairs and the hallways creaked like the rusty hinges of a forgotten gate. I would have heard footsteps, especially those of someone trying to make a quick getaway. Mr. Sullivan did not seem out of breath when we met in the hallway, but he may be spryer than I gave him credit. I'd witnessed the effort it took Cedric to climb those stairs. There was no way he could have made it past my room in the time it took me to put on my sneakers and open the door.

*Had I been deeper asleep on the couch than I'd thought?* After all, there had been the champagne.

*Or . . . was the murderer hiding in the room when Walter and I arrived?* I shivered at the thought.

*Did he or she go out the window?* I shook the thought away, remembering how I'd checked all the window locks.

Realization hit. I didn't have a chance to check Frank's bedroom. A picture of Kitty, pink-cheeked sitting in her new coat, rose to mind.

"Now it's my turn," I announced.

"I beg your pardon?" Kingsley frowned in confusion.

"I've answered your questions. Now it's my turn. You must answer one of mine."

A smirk crossed his features, and his gaze returned to the pad. "That's not how this works."

"Very well." I pushed my chair back and rose from my seat.

Gavin jumped up.

"Where do you think you're going?" Kingsley asked, whipping off his glasses.

"I've finished my statement."

His lips flattened and his nostrils flared. "I'm not done with you."

"Then arrest me." I offered both of my hands.

Gavin choked out, "Here now, Ariadne—"

When Kingsley didn't move to get out his cuffs, I continued, "You can't. Can you? You haven't enough information, or-or evidence!" I snapped my fingers. "Yes, that's it, you haven't enough evidence against me."

"I know you touched the body," he threw out.

His accusation gave me pause. Walter would, of course, have told the detective of my—what did he call it? Unwomanly behavior?

It only took a moment to scramble a comeback, "So did the ambulance attendants. So did Sergeant Carmichael. Are you arresting them?"

His mouth worked in frustration until, he barked, "Sit down!"

"I say, Detective, there's no need to raise your voice like that," Gavin chided. "This is a hotel, not a dirty prison! I expect more gentlemanly behavior from a lawman to a young lady."

"It's okay, Gavin. It's late and we're all tired." I didn't want to make an enemy of him. "Right, Detective Kingsley?"

"As you say." Deflated, the investigator looked away and scrubbed his face with a hand. "Please. Sit," he invited a little more cordial.

I lowered my bottom to the seat and leaned forward on my elbows. "Here's the deal, Detective Kingsley, I have information. Information *you* need for this investigation, but I'm also a reporter. This case could be my break to get me onto an investigative beat at a newspaper, where I want to be."

I needed his help to solve this case, and, while a white man would be dismissive of me, I hoped a colored man who fought against his own societal prejudices, might be more willing to take me seriously.

Shock played across Gavin's features as he fumbled to retake his seat.

The detective ruminated over my words. "Okay, Miss Winter. I'll answer your question if I feel it won't compromise my investigation," he replied in conciliatory tones.

I could tell he was humoring me. I didn't care. "Did you or Sergeant Carmichael search the entire apartment?"

"Sergeant Carmichael did so."

"I'm assuming he did not find the murderer hiding in the closet or beneath the bed."

A quick headshake. "He did not."

"Why was Kitty Conrad dressed in her outerwear?"

The right side of his lip lifted. "She said she's an insomniac, and, sometimes, it helps her to go for walks."

I tapped my pencil against the pad. "Kitty was not in the room with Mr. Conrad when the crash happened?"

"Correct. According to Mrs. Conrad, she'd been walking around the garden. She claims to have heard you arrive home around twelve-thirty. She dressed and left the house not long afterward."

"Did she witness anyone else lurking around the house?" I prodded.

"No. Although—" he checked his notes "—she said, she thought she heard an animal run past the garage."

"Have you found the murder weapon?" I pelted questions at the detective.

"I'm not going to answer that question."

I jotted on my pad—*has not found the murder weapon.*

The glasses returned to their place. "Now, I've answered your questions, Miss Winter. What is this information you have that I need?"

"When I returned to Ivy Tree, I saw Mr. Wyler in his window. The one above my own. And when I got to my room, I heard his footsteps above me."

Detective Kingsley rubbed the stubble on his chin. "This was at twelve-thirty?"

"Yes. I saw his silhouette in the window, watching me enter. Therefore, the murder must have been committed between twelve-thirty and one. Probably closer to twelve-thirty."

His brows rose high causing his forehead to wrinkle like my mother's Shar-pei. "Why do you say that?"

"The blood . . . it had already congealed. Become sticky," I clarified. "By the time Mr. Sullivan and I found him."

Kingsley pursed his lips together. "You don't believe the crash you heard was the murder itself?"

I rotated my head from side to side. "I think the crash we heard was the murderer leaving." Tapping my nails against the table, I stared past his left shoulder into the darkness of the window beyond. "But how? If he didn't come down the main stairwell, how did he get past me?"

Gavin who'd watched our exchange in silence suggested, "Maybe he climbed out a window and went down the drainpipe." He yawned causing the detective to follow suit.

"Yes." Wide-eyed, I leaned forward. "There is a trellis going up the chimney wall. Maybe the murderer dropped onto the porch roof and climbed down? Did Sergeant Carmichael find any footprints near a drainpipe or the trellis?"

"No. With the snowfall . . ." Kingsley trailed off.

"Oh." I deflated back into my seat recalling how everyone who'd entered came in with a dusting of snow. "Of course. The snow would have covered the tracks and muffled a retreat off the roof."

"All the windows were locked from the inside."

I knew the living rooms windows were locked and asked for clarification purposes, "Even the ones in the bedroom?"

"All of them." Kingsley closed his notebook. "It's late. You're free to go."

I gathered my things and rose.

"Don't leave town, Miss Winter." He used his notebook to point at me. "I may have more questions for you."

"Wouldn't dream of it. Come on, Gavin." I hooked my arm through his elbow, and we swung around. "Let's go find your room key." My gaze caught sight of something that brought me to a standstill.

"Ariadne?" Gavin tugged at my hand.

"Detective," my voice came out high and pitchy, "Is that . . . blood?" I pointed to the painted white frame of the swinging door.

Kingsley peered at the stain turning his head this way and that. He touched it with the erasure of his pencil. Then, he straightened. "You know, Miss Winter, I believe you are correct." In a raised voice, he called, "Officer Webster, I need you in here!"

‡‡‡

Eventually, we retrieved Gavin's room key from the cubby behind the reception desk, and I showed him to the Green Suite. At the door, he asked, "Do you actually wish to be an investigative reporter?"

"Of course. I want to uncover political corruption, global injustice, fight for the little guy."

His face twisted and he asked wryly, "What are you doing at a fashion magazine?"

As an answer, I posed a question back at him, "How many female journalists do you know?"

He scratched his head.

"How many are investigative reporters?"

He shrugged.

"If I can solve this murder, it may be my ticket into that world."

"Well, good luck to you." He covered another yawn. "I'll knock on your door at nine. We'll have breakfast before we leave."

"Nine?" I pursed my lips. "I thought the photoshoot was at nine."

"Didn't I tell you? No? I suppose there hasn't been time. *Her royal highness requested we move it to ten,*" he said with an exaggerated snobby English accent. "Howard got a message to me before I left New York."

I rubbed my eyes. "I, for one, am glad it's been delayed. I need the sleep."

Sadly, sleep didn't come. My brain whirled in circles. I

210

tossed and turned alternately pulling at the counterpane and throwing it off. When the mantel clock chimed four, I gave up, turned on the light, and retrieved my pilfered pad and pencil.

# Chapter Thirty-Two
## Ariadne

### Saturday

"Coming!" I croaked rolling off the divan and onto the floor, bashing my knee against the coffee table on the way down. Whimpering, I crawled on all fours and used the doorknob to pull myself to my feet before flinging it open.

"What's wrong?" I rubbed my eyes.

Blinking to clear my vision, I found Gavin in a natty navy-blue suit with a red plaid ascot, hair swooshed into perfect chaos, and smelling delectably of woody moss and citrus. Only his bloodshot eyes betrayed any lack of sleep. Conversely, I stood in the doorway with my robe opened to reveal my pajamas, no makeup, and my hair still twisted into pin curls beneath a purple headscarf.

He squinted at me. "Ariadne, are you ill?"

"You said nine." I checked my wrist, but my watch wasn't there. Behind me, the clock began to chime. Nine on the dot. "Oh."

"What's going on?" He stepped around me taking in the notes splayed across the coffee table, balled-up pieces littering the floor, and general disorder. The curtains were drawn shut, but the standing lamp threw a puddle of light across the loveseat. "What *is* this? Have you been awake all night?"

"Um, think I fell asleep about four-thirty," I murmured with a yawn.

He picked up one of the notes. "C. Higginbottom. Five

grand."

I took it from him and placed it back on the table. "Don't mess it up. I've organized them."

Putting his hands on his hips, he harumphed. "You weren't kidding when you said you wanted to solve this murder."

"Nope."

He scratched his chin "I suppose, I'd best leave you to it then."

"Can you take care of the photo shoot on your own?" I couldn't help the yawn that escaped.

He delivered a wry smile. "Unlike the almighty Whitey Gordon, it is unusual for me to have an assistant on assignments. I don't rank high enough at *Ladies' Lifestyle* to necessitate one. I was surprised when Howard said you'd accompany me."

"You usually don't do photoshoots of the future Princess of Maldinia, either," the thoughtless comment popped out. Immediately, I wanted to chop off my tongue.

Gavin didn't take the slightest heed, instead, he chuckled, "Very true. I imagine Howard assigned you to accompany me because you have a car, and it'll save the magazine cab fare."

*Sounds like Howard. Always pinching pennies, regardless of the fact Ladies' Lifestyle has the largest circulation in the nation.*

"Would you mind terribly, giving me ten minutes to dress?"

"You still want to come?"

"No, I want to judge the mood of the other guests at breakfast." My stomach growled like a bear in an empty cave.

Gavin's eyes rounded.

I could've pretended not to have heard it, but the noise practically bounced off the walls. "Also, I need to eat."

"Ten minutes," he stated sharply like a drill sergeant giving orders. He softened the demand by ending it with that dimpled grin that made my stomach flutter.

Or maybe it was just hunger pangs.

"I'll be back." His scent wafted past me.

The flutter rippled again. Emitting a sigh, I set about removing the bobby pins from my hair.

Twelve minutes later, I knocked on Gavin's door fully dressed in my warmest wool suit. It had a forest-green jacket with black piping and a velveteen collar. The matching skirt came down to my shins. My makeup took a bit of finessing, but I'd done a decent job of hiding the dark circles beneath my eyes and pinched my cheeks to make them bloom like a June poppy. "Shall we go down?"

He did a double take, then peered around me, past each of my shoulders.

"What are you looking for?" I glanced behind me. Nothing there.

"Where is Ariadne Winter?" He leaned back on his heels and squinted at me. "What have you done with her."

"What the devil are you talking about?" I snapped with impatience.

"There is no way, the Calamity Jane I saw ten minutes ago, is the same woman standing in front of me now. You must be an alien replacement," he joked.

"Quit fooling around." I swatted his shoulder with the envelope I had in my hand. "I'm starving. Let's go."

On our way down the stairs, I handed him the letter. "Here."

"What's this? You need me to mail it?"

"No. I need a favor. I'm giving you my car for the photo shoot, but it comes with conditions."

"And those would be?"

"I need you to deliver this article to the metro editor at a local newspaper. I've written down the address. It's on your way to the venue.

When he didn't answer immediately, I put my hands together, fluttered my lashes, and entreated, "Please."

214

He flipped them over. "*The Gazette.* Is this about last night's murder?"

"A simple article stating the facts. They may have already got a reporter on it. But if not . . ." I gave a half shrug.

"What about the magazine?"

"There is nothing in my contract that states, I cannot moonlight for other papers. As long as it's not in direct competition with the magazine." Being my father's daughter, I'd read the employment agreement backward and forward before signing it. "I doubt Howard could argue these local newspapers compete with a national ladies fashion journal." I grimaced. "Besides, it's not as though we report on homicides."

Gavin tucked the envelope into an inside pocket. "I'll let you know what they say."

To my relief, the scent of fresh coffee and sausage grease assailed my nostrils as soon as we hit the bottom step. With Frank dead, it occurred to me Maria might decide to take to her bed for the day, leaving the guests to fend for themselves. I wouldn't have blamed her one bit. It's certainly what Dottie Higginbottom would have done in the cook's position.

Maria was made of sterner stuff.

Gavin rubbed his hands together. "Smells divine. Nothing like a hearty breakfast to clear out the cobwebs from a sleepless night, eh?" he announced to the occupants in the room, which consisted of Melvin, sitting by himself in front of the windows. Both the Sullivans, at one of the tables by the pocket doors, and Cedric alone at a table across from the Sullivans.

The breakfast room assemblage didn't surprise me. Dottie would be likely to remain abed until noon, and if Kitty suffered insomnia, she would be as exhausted as me. Whereas Connie would be like Maria, and not allow loss of sleep to bar her from plowing forward with the day like a lieutenant leading his troops into battle.

Edward must have heard our arrival, because he propelled into the room, the swinging door swishing back and forth behind him. "Good morning, Miss Winter."

"Hello, Edward. I don't think you were formally introduced last night, this is Mr. Turnbull."

"I figured." Edward executed a short little bow and indicated the buffet. "Mom made pancakes with cherry compote and sausages. Also, hard-boiled eggs. Coffee?"

We spoke in subdued tones, like the ones people used at a golf tournament.

"Rather slim pickings this morning," Cedric grumbled cracking one of the three eggs he'd piled onto his plate.

Edward stiffened and his neck turned red.

Gavin jovially said, "Sounds like a fine meal. Pancakes are my favorite. I'll have a coffee, black."

My stomach was a little queasy from the gallon of coffee I'd polished off a few hours ago, so I opted for tea.

Gavin and I filled our plates and took seats at the center table beneath the sparkling chandelier. The room remained quiet, except for the scraping of forks and knives against the china. Guests' faces were drawn with fatigue. My own eyes burned gritty from lack of sleep, but I wasn't ready to throw in the towel just yet.

Edward returned with our hot drinks.

"How is your mother holding up?" I asked, stirring a spoonful of sugar into the cup. "I understand she and Mr. Wyler have been friends for a long time."

"Yeah. She's taking it pretty hard." He glanced over his shoulder.

"Has Johnny, erm, Mr. Wexler shown up yet? Has he been told about Frank?" For some reason, I whispered the last part.

"Yes. He came to shovel the walkways early this morning. Mom spoke to him."

What I wouldn't give to have been there to see how Johnny reacted, when Maria revealed the news.

The tinkling crash of glass shattering met our ears followed by a spate of Spanish.

Edward rushed into the kitchen. "Mom! Are you okay?"

Her answer was muffled by the door swinging shut.

I jumped up and followed him. The kitchen smelled of coffee intermingled with a crisp, sweet, alcoholic aroma. Maria knelt on the floor scooping up the remnants of the broken sherry bottle.

"What do you want?" she snapped her red puffy eyes glaring at me.

"I heard the crash and wanted to make sure you were all right," I said.

"The *gordita*, that Dottie woman, she left the sherry in the wrong cupboard. There was not enough space," the cook replied. "When I opened the cabinet, out it fell. Crash. *Estúpida*," Maria groused.

I bit my lip to keep from smiling. I'd taken a few years of Spanish in high school and knew the words for chubby and stupid. Edward came out of the butler's pantry with a broom and dustpan in hand and began to sweep up the broken glass.

Getting to her feet, she dumped the broken glass into the trash. "Ow!" She made a hissing sound between her teeth, and a drop of red bubbled up on her ring finger.

At the same moment, Maria spun around to go to the sink, the back door opened, and in walked Johnny.

He caught Maria by her forearms before she bashed into him. "Whoa, there!" He wore a light gray barn coat, and wet galoshes.

"Sorry, Johnny." Maria extricated herself, and hurried to the sink, as the blood was now running down her hand.

He took in Edward brooming up glass, and Maria's blood running beneath the water. "Is it deep?"

"No, but it stings."

Then, in a déjà vu, Johnny retrieved the first aid kit and bandaged up Maria's finger, much like he did on the night Edward received a cut.

Dot took that moment to stick her head in through the kitchen door. "If it's not too much trouble, I'd like a cup of coffee," she said in haughty tones completely uninterested in the goings on of the kitchen occupants.

My jaw dropped at her attitude, while Johnny delivered a look of pure disdain.

Before Maria could utter whatever reply was on the tip of her tongue, Edward spun around, with the dustpan full of glass and remnants of the sherry to answer, "I'll be right out with it, Mrs. Higginbottom."

Perhaps it was the lack of sleep, or maybe I was finished with Dottie's self-centered attitude, but I couldn't let it pass.

"Dottie," I said sweetly, "It would seem the sherry bottle you borrowed last night was put back precariously, and fell out of the cupboard, causing Maria to receive a nasty cut." I indicated Maria's bandaged finger.

"Humph. *I* didn't bother to put it away. *I* left the sherry in the parlor. Furthermore, the *staff* should be thanking *me*." She sniffed, stepping fully into the kitchen.

Johnny and Maria shared a confused glance but said nothing.

I took the bait on their behalf. "What can you mean?"

"When I came into the kitchen last night *someone*—" she glared pointedly at Maria and then her son "—left the back door wide open. There was a small pile of snow gathering, and I shut it. Who knows what kind of creature could have wandered in from the cold? More rats? Why even a raccoon?" She waved her hand in the air. "Geraldine Sandhurst had a raccoon enter through an open window. It ransacked the entire kitchen." Her head bobbed in self-righteous justification.

Edward's face reflected a state of confusion. Maria seemed affronted by Dot's remarks, while Johnny delivered a hard stare with drawn brows and locked jaw. Dottie appeared oblivious to their reactions as if waiting for their gratitude to be verbalized.

"Dear me." I put a hand on my chest. "I suppose it *was* a good thing you came in to tipple the sherry when you did. How kind of you to close the door."

The woman had the grace to blush. "Yes . . . well . . . it was a most upsetting evening. I needed something to calm my nerves. I am a *very sensitive* person."

*More like high-strung.* "I hadn't noticed," I remarked sweetly.

Dottie pursed her lips together as if she couldn't decide whether I was being serious or sarcastic. "It's not easy," she mumbled.

"I'll fetch your coffee right away, Mrs. Higginbottom," Edward reassured the patronizing guest, and she flounced out of the kitchen.

The moment she left, Maria hissed, "Edward did you leave the back door open when you snuck out last night?"

"Don't look at me. I didn't come into the big house at all. I went out through the alley," he said referring to the back passageway behind the garage.

Johnny transferred that hard stare to Edward.

"That's a dangerous alley. You shouldn't be walking it at night," the handyman reproved in edgy tones. "There are all sorts of rusty scrap metal pieces lying around. You could have tripped and gotten hurt."

"Yeah, a truck was blocking the Church Street side, so I went the long way around. It was no big deal." He took the broom back to the pantry.

"Perhaps Kitty went out the kitchen door and didn't close it all the way." The adults' eyes swiveled to me.

"What?" Johnny said in a funny high voice, then cleared his throat and repeated, "What do you mean?"

"She suffers from insomnia. Apparently, she took a walk in the garden last night. I've noticed if that door isn't closed properly, it can blow open."

Maria rolled her eyes. "*Dios mío.* It was ten below last

night. Does the woman have a death wish?"

"It wasn't that bad." Edward scoffed while pouring coffee from the percolator into a cup. He put it on a tray along with a miniature sugar bowl and matching creamer.

Maria opened her mouth, probably to scold her son again, but I hurried to say, "To each his own, I suppose. While I'm here, I wanted to thank you for making breakfast this morning, Mrs. Massey. With everything that's happened . . ." I made a flapping motion with my hand. "It's kind of you to take care of us."

"Of course, it is my job. Anyone would have done it," she asserted.

From across the room, I looked her square in the eyes. "I beg to disagree. Not everyone would have soldiered on, the way you have."

"Yeah, not Mrs. Higginbottom," Edward snorted.

"*Edward!*" she scolded.

"He's right," Johnny put in.

I grinned along with Edward. "Your actions are commendable, and I thank you."

Maria stared down at her feet shuffling them around. "You're welcome."

"I am sorry for your loss. All of you." My gaze landed on Johnny. "Especially you, Johnny. I realize you had your disagreements with your brother, but he was family after all."

Edward frowned, and Maria's black gaze turned watery, Johnny didn't meet my eyes, instead, he glanced down and chewed his thumbnail. "Thanks," he mumbled.

Edward shuffled past me. "I'd best bring Mrs. Higginbottom her coffee."

Johnny turned to pour a cup of coffee. "I've shoveled the walk and parking lot."

"Did much snow fall last night?" I asked.

"Only a few inches. You shouldn't have any problems getting your car out today." He took his first sip of coffee.

"Johnny! You've got blood on your elbow."

"Where?" He moved his elbow this way and that, trying to take a gander at it. "I don't see it."

"On the backside." She pointed to an area impossible to be seen by the wearer. "Leave your coat on one of the chairs. I'll clean it after breakfast."

"No need, I can take care of it," Johnny said rather sharply.

"Nonsense. It's my blood." she insisted, clucking over him. "Now sit down, and I'll make you some eggs and sausage."

Edward returned from delivering Dottie's drink. He held the door for me, as I slipped past him into the dining area. Melvin and Connie were gone, and Walter sat by himself. Now Cedric had Dottie at his table, both had freshly piled plates of food in front of them.

"Everything okay?" Gavin asked as I sat down. He hadn't waited for me. He'd worked his way through the meal and was down to his hard-boiled egg. Liberally, he dusted it with salt before taking a bite.

"It's fine. Just a little broken glass. No big deal." I continued in a louder voice, "I was thanking our hostess for fixing our breakfast. She must be devastated by the death of her friend."

I couldn't see Higginbottoms' expressions, but I did see Walter glance up from his newspaper and frown as if the thought had not occurred to him.

Gavin swallowed his egg and checked his watch. "I'll be sure to convey my appreciation when I return. Right now, I'd best high tail it out of here. I don't wish to keep the Princess waiting." He wiped his mouth, dropped the linen napkin on the empty plate, and pushed back his chair.

"Be sure to eat lunch while you're out. The inn only serves breakfast and dinner," I explained.

"Shall I bring something back for you?"

"That would be lovely."

Walter exited not long after Gavin, and, to my surprise, the room remained silent. Only the sounds of Dottie and Cedric's mastication and murmurs from the kitchen could be heard. I'd expected Dottie, at least, would be jabbering about last night's murder. Perhaps my stinging comments *had* hit their mark.

The kitchen door swung open to expel the handyman. With a fork raised halfway to my mouth, I observed Johnny's eyes dart about the room taking in the occupants, the sideboard, and tables—as he searched for something. His gaze collided with my inquisitive one. Abruptly, he stiffened, gave me a brief nod, and went on his way.

I finished and returned upstairs. The shadowed hallway leading to the Sullivans' room drew me toward it. The plaque on their door read *Blue Suite.* I heard murmurings of conversation and raised my hand to knock, before thinking better of it. Instead, I turned back toward the Rose Suite, but something I hadn't noticed before paused my steps.

An unmarked door—practically hidden in the darkened hall.

"What do we have here?" I whispered to myself.

*A bathroom? A hidden staircase? A secret room to hide Irene who wasn't at the sanitorium at all?* My thoughts spun outlandish theories.

Imagine my surprise when, expecting to encounter resistance, the knob turned easily beneath my hand. I steadied myself to meet, head-on, whatever lived behind the door.

The hinges creaked, the door swung inward, and the wintery light from a single window revealed nothing more exciting than a long narrow closet. One side was lined with shelves filled with sheets and towels. The other side housed buckets, mop, vacuum, and other sundry cleaning items.

"What are you doing!"

I nearly jumped out of my skin. Spinning, I put a hand to my pounding heart to find Johnny in the hallway. Due to the low lighting, I had difficulty reading his features, but his tone sounded harsh to my ears.

"Oh, Johnny. I didn't hear you. I-I was looking for, um, fresh towels," I reached in and grabbed a pink fluffy towel. "I believe these go with the Rose Suite?"

"Maria is in charge of keeping track of the linens," he said in a hard voice.

My brows furrowed and the hairs rose on the back of my neck. I couldn't fathom what was making Johnny so tetchy about a linen closet.

His muscles tensed, and he seemed to purposely remain standing in the shadows looming like an intimidating vulture. His voice grated out, "Normally guests ask—"

I cut him off, "Yes, normally, I would have asked Frank or Maria. However, today is *not* a normal day. I figured Maria would be preoccupied and didn't want to bother her with something so trivial. I'll be sure to let her know, I've taken one." I stepped past him out of the uncomfortably enclosed space.

He leaned in to close the door behind me, and the sun lit his scowling features. His gaze scanned the room as if making sure everything was in its proper place.

*Does he think I'm here to steal the linens?*

"Don't worry about it. I'll let Maria know. Is there anything else you need, Ariadne?" While his question sounded solicitous, it held an underlying edge, and he'd called me by my first name.

"No." I returned to my room post haste, flipped the lock with a resolute snap, and released a shaky breath.

The cloudy, sleep-deprived, detachment that carried me through breakfast disappeared during my encounter with Johnny. It left behind a pounding headache. My fingers had to fish all the way to the bottom of my train case to locate a small tin of aspirin. I shook the yellow container. To my relief, the sound of tablets clinked. Taking three, I laid down on my bed with a cool washcloth over my eyes to rest for a few minutes.

# Chapter Thirty-Three
## Ariadne

Once again, I was awakened by a persistent tapping at my door. I put my feet on the floor and shook my head to loosen the cobwebs.

"Ariadne? Are you in there?" Gavin's voice penetrated the heavy wood.

"Coming!" My watch read half past one. I yawned, straightened my skirt, and slipped on my Keds. "How did the photo shoot go?"

He grinned from ear to ear and slapped a hand to his chest. "She stole my heart. If she wasn't marrying the Prince, I'd throw my hat in the ring for her hand."

"She is a beauty, I'll give you that," I said drily.

"Even more ethereal in person than on film." He tossed his head to dislodge the lock of hair that had fallen into his eyes and swept into my room carrying a brown paper sack. "Sheesh, it's dark in here." A moment later the clank of curtain rings against the metal rod rent the air, and the weak winter sun inundated my sitting room. "That's better. Now, where to put this?"

I could see the mental debate that went on in his head as he approached the note-laden coffee table. "Don't even think about it! Put it over here on the side table." I swept away a book and the empty bottle of bubbly.

"Oh! I almost forgot." Gavin reached into an interior coat pocket and pulled out an envelope. "The *Gazette* paid six dollars for your article."

My mouth O'd and, and gripping the envelope with both hands, I held it to my breast. "My first investigative article!" I squealed.

Gavin chuckled. "*The Gazette* said they would put it out in their evening paper. The editor wanted to know if you were local. It sounded like he might want to offer you more work, but I told him you were a New Yorker through and through."

"Yes, but, if I could get my foot in the door at a local paper like *The Gazette*," I mused.

"Forget it. *The Gazette* is small time. You work at a national magazine, once the article on Donna Morgan comes out in *Ladies' Lifestyle*, you'll be set. If you solve this case, I'm certain one of the Manhattan papers will want you."

My mouth twisted with skepticism. "You really think so?"

"You betcha. I read the article you gave me." My face fell and he put his hands up defensively, "Hey don't give me that look. I had to make sure, what I was endorsing was on the level. As a matter of fact, it was better than good." He brushed aside that stray strand of hair falling onto his forehead. "You're a top-notch writer, Ariadne."

My face heated with pleasure. I wanted Gavin to think I was good at my job. Heck, I wanted everyone to think I was a good writer, but, hearing it from Gavin gave me an unexpected shiver of delight.

"Um, thanks." I rolled my lips inward to keep from grinning like a loon. "What's in the bag?"

Gavin stared at me for an extra moment before transferring his attention to the bag on the table. "Lunch! I found a deli not far from here. I hope you like pastrami on rye. Have you got a bottle opener?"

Relieved to occupy myself with a task, I extracted a Swiss Army knife from my handbag.

"Aren't you full of surprises?" He pulled two bottles of Coca-Cola from the sack, handily opened them, and passed one to me. The wax paper-wrapped sandwiches were next. The smoky, peppery scent of the pastrami had my mouth watering. "Have you gotten any further with the investigation?"

Grimacing, I replied sheepishly, "I fell asleep."

"Want some help?"

"I'd love it."

He winked and pulled a roll of Cellophane tape out of his coat pocket. "Nicked this from the reception desk. Doesn't seem as though anyone is working it. The phone was ringing off the hook when I arrived."

"What am I supposed to do with tape?"

"Hm." His gaze roamed the room, planting itself on a painting in shades of oranges and reds with two blue circles and a black stripe. It was on the wall above the record player. "We need to move this out of the way."

I couldn't argue with that sentiment. It was a poor example of abstract expressionism. With the painting put aside, he tossed me the roll of tape.

"Now what?"

"Now we are going to take all your notes and make our picture. Create your story, on the wall. First, we start with—" he strode to the coffee table, scooped up the notepad, and scribbled on it "—the victim." In capital letters, he'd written the words FRANK WYLER. "Here, give me a piece of tape. We'll put it at the top."

Amused, I asked, "What comes next?"

"The suspects, of course. Then their motives, means, and alibis."

I began to see where Gavin was going with this idea. He picked up the same note from earlier this morning. "C. Higginbottom. Five grand. The hefty fellow?"

"Cedric Higginbottom loaned Frank Wyler five thousand dollars to get this inn off the ground. Frank has yet to pay back the loan." I taped it underneath Frank's name. "Frank also lied to Cedric about investing the money in Donna Morgan's new film to put off paying back the loan."

"Sounds solid. Does he have an alibi?"

I perused the papers and pulled one out. I'd written *wheezes like an accordion.* "He can't climb up and down the stairs with any sort of speed or quiet, much less out a window. I would have heard his retreat."

"I can't imagine him shimmying down the drainpipe. What about the wife?" He bit down into his pastrami sandwich and watched me pace back and forth in front of him.

"Dottie wants Cedric to purchase a lake house. She is desperate for that five grand." I put D. Higginbottom next to Cedric. "She also threatened to confront Frank herself, though her husband did *not* want her interfering in his business."

"And did she?"

"Well, there was a rather nasty message written in lipstick on Frank's bathroom mirror." I unfolded my sandwich finding a pickle spear inside.

"What did it say?"

"'Pay up or else,'" I said in a dramatic tone and my teeth snapped down in the pickle.

Gavin gave a slight wince. "You think Dottie Higginbottom wrote it."

"I can't imagine Connie having written it. Kitty, on the other hand . . ." I held my palm in the air. "Maybe. There's a bit of spine in there, but last night she particularly taunted Cedric and Dottie for having lent Frank the money."

A plop of mustard fell onto Gavin's pant leg. "Damn." He tsked scrubbing the mustard with a paper napkin and smearing it further. "Good thing these pants are dark."

"Wait." I retrieved a wet facecloth from the bathroom. "Here, dab at it with this."

"I think the Higginbottom woman wrote the message too," he said patting the stain.

"Oh? And why is that?" I turned up the soda bottle allowing a gulp of cola to tingle on my tongue before swallowing.

"She and that tall, manly woman—"

"Connie," I supplied.

"Right. They were standing just inside the doorway to the billiard room, and *Connie*," he said her name with exaggeration, "was hissing at Dot. I specifically heard her say, 'I know that shade like the back of my hand.'"

"Mm, my, my. The plot thickens. Did you eavesdrop any longer?"

"No. The plump one saw me, scurried back to her room, and slammed the door." He finished with the washcloth and passed it back. His voice followed me as I returned it to the bathroom. "That Connie woman is as cool as they come."

"Oh? What did she say?"

"She nodded at me and lit a cigarette. Does Dottie have an alibi?"

"Her husband, no doubt." I envisioned Dottie sneaking past my room, and down the stairs.

The thought brought me to another piece of paper. *What was the crash?* It went next to Frank's name.

"I thought the crash was the murder."

"That's the problem. It didn't sound like someone falling to the floor. That's a thumping sound. It was more like a door or window slamming hard." I tacked another note on the other side of Frank.

*Squeaking.*

"Squeaking? Like a mouse?"

"Not an animal squeak. It was more like a rubbing sound, or a squeaky bicycle tire that needs oiling." A small nibble of pastrami hung off the side of my sandwich. I popped it into my mouth enjoying the sweet tang of coriander.

"Did anyone else hear the squeaking?"

"Dunno." I shrugged and taped another name to the wall. "Kitty Conrad. I can't quite figure her out. She has contempt for her husband and Dottie. She claims to be friends with

Frank's mother, but Connie and Dottie seem to think differently. They feel a high school falling out was never mended."

"High school! That's a long time to be mad at someone," Gavin said with skepticism. "They've got to be what . . . in their sixties?"

"Something like that. Dot called them 'mortal enemies.' Apparently, Irene stole Kitty's fiancé."

"I see. And he was Frank's father?"

"No, his name was George Poppleton." I bit off another bite of pickle. "Irene dumped him, and George tried to get back with Kitty, but she was having none of it."

Gavin thoughtfully chewed his sandwich. "A woman scorned, eh?"

"So, it would seem."

He glugged half the bottle of soda to wash down the sandwich and wiped his mouth with the back of his hand. "Where is Frank's mother? Has she been notified of his death?"

"Doubtful. She's at a sanitorium that Frank pays for. I guess she's gone senile." I made a swirl motion with my finger.

"I don't understand." Gavin's face scrunched. "What does Frank have to do with an ancient rivalry between his mother and this Kitty person?"

I picked up the pastrami and eyeballed it, unsure how I'd be able to open my mouth around the jampacked sandwich without making a mess. "I don't know exactly. Taking revenge on the son would mean no one pays for her health care. She'd have to leave her nice sanitorium and go into a state facility." Daintily, I nibbled a corner of the sandwich.

"Isn't there any other family member to take care of her?"

I thought of Johnny and his antipathy toward Frank. I imagined his feelings for Irene fell into the realm of loathing. This would put Johnny at the top of my suspect list, except for the fact that, according to Walter Sullivan, Johnny was absent from the inn last night.

"Not that I know of. Frank was her only child, and I believe her parents are dead." I put the sandwich down and went to stare at the wall. "It's as if Kitty has been sabotaging the success of the inn."

"How do you mean?" He polished off the last bite of sandwich.

"I'm certain she released the mouse that caused a ruckus on the first night I arrived. And I *think* she may have been the one who caused the flood in your room."

"My room had a flood?"

My head bobbed. "Two days before you arrived, the bathroom faucet leaked and flooded."

"That would explain the wet roll of toilet paper I found under the sink in the bathroom." The paper napkin crinkled beneath his fingers as he balled it up. "What makes you think Kitty had something to do with it?"

"She lied to me about looking for Connie," I mused. "Kitty had a coat on last night and was fully dressed beneath it."

"You don't buy the insomnia alibi?"

"Not necessarily. But I don't know if her motive is strong enough to kill Frank. It seems a bit of a stretch. Unless she's got another motive I'm unaware of."

"Back to the Higginbottoms." He flicked the napkin like a basketball player shooting a free throw, and it dropped right into the center of the wastebasket. "I have a problem with their motive."

"What's that?"

"It's tough to get money from a dead man," Gavin stated.

"I considered the same thing. I doubt there was any paperwork drawn up for their deal. No contract. Just a handshake and Frank's word. Which means it will be difficult for Cedric to get his money back now that Frank is dead."

"Would his wife know that?"

I lifted my shoulders "Maybe Wyler caught her in his

230

apartment with the lipstick. They argued. She lashed out?"

"Did you hear an argument?"

"No, but I wasn't home until later." I taped W. Sullivan next to Kitty. "Mild-mannered Walter Sullivan, whom I never would have guessed, cheated on his wife years ago. Someone's got the pictures to prove it and sent him a blackmail note."

Gavin reached into the paper sack and pulled out a bag of Wise rippled potato chips. "Does Sullivan think Wyler is the blackmailer?"

"Walter wasn't sure, but clearly Frank couldn't pay Cedric back immediately."

He peeled the bag open and held it toward me. "How much was he ransoming the photos for?"

"Five thousand." I crunched into a greasy chip.

A low whistle escaped between Gavin's lips. "That's how much Frank owes Cedric."

"I know. Walter's been waiting for another letter to tell him where to leave the money."

"You think Frank asked for the money last night, and Walter killed him instead?"

I chewed my lip, recalling the conversation I had with Walter in Frank's apartment. "Walter said, he and Cedric were the last ones awake. They shared a bottle of port, and then went to bed. Wyler went up maybe an hour before them. At least that's according to Walter. But if he's the murderer, then we can't trust his timeline and accounting of events to be truthful," I mused.

"Was he agitated? Anything in his demeanor leading you to believe he did the deed?"

There was something I found comforting about Walter—maybe his confession about the affair and deep regret sounded genuine to me. Or the way he treated Connie, with love and respect.

I realized; I was being foolish. I didn't know the man from Adam and needed to put aside my feelings to look at the facts as they stood the way a true reporter would do.

I closed my eyes and spun around on my heel picturing Walter last night. "He discouraged me from going upstairs with him. When I told him to phone the police, he called me hysterical and argued. He is fit enough to have come down the stairs quietly, and he wouldn't have had to walk past my room." I chewed my lip in thought. "Was Frank the one to take the dirty photos? Or did he come across them in some other manner?"

"Something isn't sitting right with me." Gavin loomed above the coffee table searching the slips of paper. "A-ha! Here." He picked up a piece and taped the words *Murder Weapon* next to Frank's name. "If Frank didn't fall off the ladder and bash his head against a piece of furniture. Then he was clubbed with something."

"Yes! Something that sat on the fireplace mantel. Something with a round base, diameter of about six inches." I held my fingers in position to demonstrate the size of the dust pattern. "Something the murderer took with him."

"Okay, let's list all the things it could be." He picked up the pad, pencil poised above it.

"A vase, or candlestick," I supplied.

"Any broken glass? Could that have been the crash you heard?"

"Maybe, but Walter and I were on the scene quickly. The murderer didn't have time to clean up a shattered glass vase. On the other hand, it could have been a pewter or heavy ceramic vase that didn't break."

"Hm. What about the base of a lamp?"

"Perhaps, but I don't recall seeing an outlet next to the fireplace. Seems an odd place to have a lamp."

"Silver plate? Sculpture?"

Details of the apartment were already starting to fade out of my mind, and I sighed, "Could be any of those. I'd love to get another look at Frank's apartment."

Gavin paused his scribbling. "What are we waiting for?"

"Uh, I think there are laws about disturbing a crime scene."

"We won't stay long, just take a quick look around."

"It's probably locked."

"What if it isn't?" Gavin's dimples peeked out and his enthusiasm got the better of me.

"Fine," I sighed.

No one was in the hallway when we came out of my room, and we quietly tip-toed up to the third floor. Even so, the floors creaked, and I worried someone would catch us. The police left a rope across the door into Frank's apartment.

Gavin toyed with it.

"See, I told you. It's been roped off," I pivoted to go back down to my room. "We can't go inside."

*Creak.*

Turning, I found Frank's apartment door gaping open. Gavin stood in front of it with wide eyes, and a grin playing around his mouth.

"It wasn't locked," he innocently said.

I groaned. "Don't go inside."

I might as well have been speaking to an obstinate toddler. One of Gavin's long legs stretched over the rope, and the second soon followed.

"*Gavin!*" I hissed grabbing at him.

He was too quick and sidled away from me. "Well, would you look at that."

My resistance collapsed. The room seemed different in the light of day. The body was gone, but the telltale dark stain remained. It had turned brown. The furniture hadn't been moved, but something seemed out of place.

Something was missing . . .

My gaze roved the room. Footstool, coffee table, couch, rug, chair, lamp, photograph.

I gasped.

"What is it?"

"The candlesticks are missing."

"What candlesticks?"

"There were two silver candlesticks sitting on the mantel." I pointed. "They were there last night when Frank was killed. But today they are gone."

"Perhaps the police took them as possible murder weapons?"

I studied the denuded mantel with narrowed eyes. "They were solid silver. Hefty enough to bash a man's skull."

My gaze fell upon the window, where I saw Frank's silhouette. Something in my deductive reasoning wasn't connected. The answers shimmered beyond my vision like a desert mirage. Hairs on the back of my neck rose, and a shiver slid down my spine. Quite suddenly, I did *not* want to be in this room.

"You do what you want. I'm getting out of here."

Distracted, Gavin replied, "I'll be down in a minute."

Quickly, I retreated down the steps, but a sixth sense stopped my feet from returning to the Rose Suite. Instead, I took a left at the bottom of the stairs to investigate something troubling me about my earlier interaction with Johnny.

‡‡‡

Fifteen minutes later, Gavin burst into my room and breathlessly declared, "The message was still on the mirror!"

Polishing off the pastrami on rye, I lifted my brows at his pronouncement.

"What happened to you?" He plopped down on the divan next to me, throwing his arm across the back of it. "You darted out of there like a startled gazelle fleeing from a hungry lion."

Warmth flooded my system. I became very aware of his leg pressing against mine. Jumping up, I snatched the first piece of paper my fingers touched. "Nothing. I just don't want to get caught mucking around the scene of the crime. Unlike you, I was *here* when it happened."

Gavin laughed at that. "Why would you be a suspect? You barely knew the man."

I responded with a noncommittal lift of my shoulder and stuck Melvin Conrad to the wall.

"Melvin Conrad. What's his story?"

The whine of a siren interrupted my reply.

I joined Gavin at the front window. A squad car, and an unmarked black vehicle pulled in front of Ivy Tree Inn.

"I wonder what this means," Gavin muttered.

We watched Detective Kingsley, and two police officers enter the premises.

Someone screamed.

# Chapter Thirty-Four
## Ariadne

"What's going on?" Walter thundered, on his way down the stairs, with Connie following on his heels.

Chasing after the pair, I came up short.

Two policemen led Maria through the foyer. Detective Kingsley watched with a tight face.

"Mom?" Edward trailed the officers. "Where are you taking her? *Mom*!" his voice pitched with panic.

Cedric watched from the library doorway, while Kitty stood in the back hallway, their mouths agape.

"What's happening? *Move*, I can't see." Dottie pushed Kitty aside and gasped. "Well, my, my, my."

"Don't worry, *Niño*. Everything will be fine. Stay here. I'll be home soon," she reassured him with a shaky voice.

"Detective Kingsley, I demand to know what this is about?" Gavin commanded.

Watching Maria being led out by his men, he replied, "We're taking Mrs. Massey down to the station to answer a few questions."

I chased after the police and hollered from the front porch, "You don't have to answer any questions, Maria! I'm calling you a lawyer! Don't say anything!"

Johnny burst out of the front door shaking his fist and shouting, "What the hell do you think you're doing?"

The officer in the rear paused midway along the front walk, putting a hand to his waist where a baton rested.

I grabbed Johnny by the wrist and hissed, "Don't! You'll

only make it worse for her."

"Worse! They're taking her to jail. What can be worse?" he yelled.

"They are taking her to the station for questioning. Unless you care to join her in the back of the car, I suggest you put a damper on it," I said through clenched teeth.

The other officer ushered Maria into the backseat, ducking her head low to keep it from hitting the side of the vehicle. He shut the door, leaving Edward standing outside, his hand pressed against the window, silent tears running down his face.

"Mom?" he whimpered.

"Don't worry. I love you." She matched her hand to his against the glass.

"Son, step back," the police officer warned.

Johnny wrenched free of my grip and called out to the boy, "Edward, come along now. Do as the officers say. Step back from the car."

"You'll keep an eye on the boy?"

He shot me a dirty look. "Of course."

I returned to the foyer, to find Gavin, Walter, and Connie surrounding Detective Kingsley demanding answers.

*"Detective Kingsley!"* I pushed my way past Walter to come face-to-face with the detective. "Are you charging Maria Massey with Frank Wyler's murder?"

The voices faltered and the foyer went quiet.

Unruffled, his taught lips softened, and he let out a breath. "That depends."

"On what?" Connie inquired.

"On Mrs. Massey's answers . . . and what we find in her apartment," Kingsley added.

"Don't you need a warrant or something for that?" Walter asked.

"I have one. Right here." The detective produced a piece of paper.

Walter adjusted his glasses, and his lips moved as he read

the document.

"Well? Is it a warrant?" Dottie breathlessly asked.

"It would seem so." He handed it back to Kingsley.

The detective tucked the paper into his pocket. "Now I have a few more questions for you. Ladies and gentlemen, if you wouldn't mind gathering in the front room, like last night." He gestured with a hand. "It will only take a few minutes."

I didn't care how long it would take; I was going to phone my father first and foremost. I started toward the booth, then realized my change purse was upstairs in my handbag. Instead, I stepped behind the reception desk, to use the inn's telephone, while the crowd shuffled into the parlor. A frightened Edward entered, with Johnny's arm slung around his shoulder.

"I'll need the two of you in there as well," the detective with authority.

Johnny gave him a foul glance but didn't argue.

"Miss Winter, you too," he chided.

Watching the police officers head in the direction of the garage, I picked up the handset. "I'll be right in. After I phone my lawyer."

Kingsley grimaced but didn't argue further, instead he remained within listening distance.

For privacy, I turned my back to him and stared at the room cubbies. While the operator put my call through, I prayed my father would answer the phone rather than my mother or Sylvia the housekeeper.

My prayers were answered, when a deep voice I recognized and loved answered, "Winter residence."

"Daddy?" my voice faltered.

"Ariadne? Is that you? Pumpkin, what's wrong?"

"I need your help." After explaining the situation to my father, he promised to send a lawyer to the precinct for Maria. "In the meantime, I want you to come home. The police can't seriously believe you're a suspect in this Wyler fellow's murder. They've no legal standing to keep you there."

"I know that, Daddy." I lowered my voice and went on, "I'm staying for the story. This could be my big break."

He went quiet for a moment. "I don't like knowing you're there by yourself with a lunatic on the loose. If the murderer figures out you're on a mission to solve the case, you *will* be in danger."

The hairs on the back of my neck rose. My father made a good point. I'd have to be very careful how I went about my investigations.

"Miss Winter," Detective Kingsley growled in warning tones. He'd moved to stand across the reception desk and looked none too happy.

"Don't worry about me, Daddy. I'll be fine. I've got to go." I hung up.

"You must join the other guests now, Miss Winter."

"Yes, I will detective. Before I do that, may I have a word . . . in private?" I tilted my head indicating the library.

"What is it?" he demanded not moving an inch.

In quiet but firm tones, I stated, "First, a lawyer will be coming for Maria. Second, it's my belief you've arrested the wrong person."

"And why is that Miss Reporter? Do you know something I don't?" the detective taunted.

"Well, uh—"

"For instance, did you know Mrs. Massey's son is the main beneficiary of Frank Wyler's estate?" he asked.

"Er . . . as a matter of fact, I am aware he's in Frank's Will," I murmured fidgeting with the hem of my jacket.

He strode to the parlor's entryway and announced, "All of you remain there. Miss Winter, may I see you in the library." It wasn't a question.

"Alone," he grunted when Gavin approached the foyer.

"It's okay, Gavin. We'll only be a moment."

Kingsley followed me into the library and closed the doors.

Gavin was not to be deterred and loitered outside keeping an eye on things through the glass doors. I wasn't afraid of the detective, but I did appreciate Gavin's protectiveness.

# Chapter Thirty-Five
## Ariadne

"I'm curious to know how you came by this information," Kingsley said.

Leaning against the snooker table, I crossed my arms. "Overheard a conversation."

"Then you understand why she would be a suspect."

"I'll admit, it's a possibility, but not the right one."

"No? Mrs. Massey would be able to manage the boy's assets until he comes of age." Flipping open the cigarette box, the detective took one out and put it in his mouth. "Cigarette?"

"No, thank you. By your reasoning, it could have just as easily been Edward."

"It's not the boy. His alibi checks out."

I was relieved to hear it.

"Moreover, both Mrs. Conrad and Mrs. Higginbottom claim they saw lights in the apartment above the garage *before* Mrs. Massey claims to have woken and found her son missing."

I rolled my eyes. "Did Mrs. Higginbottom also confess to writing the message on the mirror?"

The wooden lid flipped shut with a sharp clap. "What are you talking about? Obviously, Mrs. Massey wrote it."

Ignoring his response, I continued, "Can Kitty explain why she's been trying to sabotage the inn?"

"What?"

I pulled one of the red balls out of the corner pocket. "While I agree, Mrs. Massey may be guilty of something, I doubt it's of killing Frank." Abruptly the puzzle pieces shifted and one slotted into place. "No. She was reeling in a different fish," I uttered under my breath.

He cupped his hands around the lighter, and spoke around the cigarette, "What in tarnation are you going on about?"

I tossed the ball up in the air. It made a sharp smack as it landed in my opposite hand. "I'm telling you, plenty of those folks gathered in the parlor have a motive to want Frank Wyler dead."

His brows rose. "And who is your prime suspect?"

"I have a theory."

"A *theory*," he chuckled blowing smoke out through his nose. "Can you prove it?"

"Not yet, but if you'll give me a chance—"

"I think you've read too many Nancy Drew mysteries, Miss Winter." A smirk played on his lips as he inspected his watch. "But it's getting late, and I haven't time for you to dazzle me with your deductive reasoning."

"But Detective—"

"That is quite enough. You have played hero to Mrs. Massey by obtaining a lawyer for her. Now, I need you to please step into the parlor with the others." He whipped open both the French doors at the same time. "Mr. Turnbull, please escort Miss Winter into the front room."

"With pleasure." Gavin offered his elbow and ushered me across the foyer.

I don't know what I'd been expecting, but the studied nonchalance that encompassed the room was not it.

Connie and Walter played a game of cards at the game table, while Kitty and Dottie sat across from each other on the sofas reading rival fashion magazines. Cedric messed around with his pipe, and someone must have rousted Melvin from his room, for he smoked a cigarette in the wing chair opposite Cedric. Ostensibly, with the owner deceased, the protocols for smoking areas were being cast aside.

"Ah, there you are, Miss Winter" Walter half rose from his

seat. "Were you able to find a lawyer for the cook?"

The members of the room weren't as indifferent as they appeared, for everyone paused and their heads turned.

"Yes, a lawyer is on his way. Where have Johnny and Edward gone?" I inquired.

"I told Johnny to find Edward something to eat," Connie responded. She picked up from the discard pile and laid down her hand. "Gin."

"Ladies and gentlemen, thank you for gathering. While my colleagues and I search the apartment, I need you to remain here. Do *not* leave," Kingsley commanded and strode out of the room before anyone could protest.

The front door closed with a slam and Dottie snapped her magazine shut. "I thought he needed to ask us more questions."

Connie lit a cigarette and took a drag. "Sounds like he wanted to round us up like a flock of sheep."

Dottie reopened her magazine with a huff. "Who else had a motive to kill Frank besides his poor Mexican housemaid who knew she'd get something out of it?"

Connie's lips curled down. "Perhaps the person who needed the money her husband loaned to Frank."

"Hey now," Cedric protested.

Dottie sucked in a breath and threw her magazine on the coffee table. "Just what do you mean by that, *Constance Sullivan*?"

"I mean, where is the lipstick you borrowed from me yesterday? My Red Velvet? The one in the gold case?" Connie shot back.

The petite woman jumped to her feet. "How dare you insinuate—"

"No. How dare you, *Dorothy Higginbottom*." Connie rose to full height. "How dare *you*, cast aspersions when you know damn well, you are not the innocent you claim. Did you think I wouldn't notice my own lipstick color? Perhaps, I should tell the detective."

Dottie's face paled. "No," she whispered.

*"Where is it?"*

"I-I," Dottie's chin waggled. "I lost it."

"Lost it or threw it out after you did the dirty deed?" Connie snapped at her.

Cedric rose as the ladies' argument intensified. "Now see here girls, what's all this? Surely a lipstick case is nothing to quarrel over." He pointed at them with the stem of his pipe.

"It is when your wife uses it to write threatening notes. Who else would have written that awful message on Frank's bathroom mirror?"

Cedric's head swiveled to his wife. "Is this true? After I warned you not to speak to Frank about the money. Did you go up to his apartment?"

"Not exactly," she hedged. "Ceddie, the money—"

"Dorothy Krensky Higginbottom!" he thundered making Dottie jump.

While the room at large watched the three players, Kitty, dressed in her fashionable new purple suit, hid a gleeful grin behind her magazine.

"What did you do?" Cedric's teeth bit down hard on his pipestem.

"Nothing. It was nothing," she warbled. "I-I wrote a note. That was all! I swear! I ran out of his apartment. He never saw me. I didn't think—" She put her fingers to her lips and said in a small voice, "All that money."

"I told you we'd be fine,"

"But the lake house," she pleaded.

The devil on my shoulder induced me to throw gasoline onto the fire. I cleared my throat. "A pair of silver candlesticks are missing from Frank's apartment."

In a moment of confusion, the room went silent. No one seemed to know what to do with the information, I'd just dropped in their lap. Since I'd been watching for it, I perceived when Dottie threw a frightened look my way.

Kitty must have seen it too, for a loud "HA!" burst from her, and she darted out of the parlor.

"Kitty?" Melvin tamped out his cigarette.

Gavin asked. "Where is *she* going?"

I raced after Kitty, who'd beelined toward the guest rooms at the back of the house.

She threw open the door on the left and invaded Dottie and Cedric's room. The yellow chamber was smaller than the upstairs suites. The new bathroom, just inside the door, had a golden toilet and sink, and a stall shower with black and yellow tiles. It smelled of pipe smoke, and Old Spice aftershave.

A pair of Cedric's pants hung over the top of the bathroom door. The twin beds had not been made, but one of the lemon-colored quilts was neatly pulled up, while the other slid haphazardly off to one side. Dottie's cosmetics and hairbrushes littered the dressing table. The heavy spicy floral notes from her Shalimar perfume intermingled with Cedric's aftershave.

Kitty plunked a turquoise suitcase on the bed, and stood next to it, triumphantly laughing. We crowded into the small space to find the silver candlesticks resting inside. But that wasn't all. Next to the candlesticks sat four Hummel figurines, and a green porcelain Ormolu clock that I'd seen on a table in the parlor.

"I can explain." Dottie cried.

"You'd better explain quickly," Kitty sneered. "I'm sure the detective would like to hear how these items got into your suitcase."

Cedric's head shook with disappointment. "Of all the things you've ever done, *this* I cannot believe."

"He owed us and now he's dead!" she screeched. "We'll never see that money again. At least I can sell these and get some of it." Angry tears coursed down her cheeks, and she wiped them with the back of her hand smearing her mascara.

"After the estate has been settled," Cedric explained.

"You don't even have a written contract with him," Dottie cried.

In quiet tones, Cedric responded, "Wife, you've been very foolish. I wrote a check, and in the memo, I wrote, 'Building Loan.'"

"The courts will take that into consideration during probate," Walter put in.

Dottie wiped her nose. "I didn't kill him. He didn't see me leave the message. You *must* believe me!" She glanced around the crowded room. "You believe me. Right, Ceddie?" she whined.

While Dottie and Cedric argued, Kitty sidled over to the wastebasket next to the dresser and subtly dug through tissue-laden trash. "Aha!" she exclaimed once again garnering the attention. "Is this your lipstick, Connie?"

Connie took the gold case out of Kitty's hand, opened it up, and glared at the mashed-up bit of lipstick that smeared down the sides of the tube.

Kitty made a tut-tut.

Dottie's face suffused redder than a matador's cape. She let out an unholy screech before charging out of the room knocking people aside. She was stronger than I'd expected and used her excess weight to make way.

I stumbled into Gavin, whose reflexes were quick enough to catch me, before I ended up on the floor. Poor Walter bounced onto the bed in disarray, and Melvin knocked against the corner of the doorway with an "oof" as Dottie shoved out of the room.

We scrambled to right ourselves when a BANG! reverberated through the hallway.

Kitty must have realized before the rest of us what it meant. She let out a shriek and bounded past those of us recovering from demolition derby Dottie.

I recovered myself and asked Gavin to check on Melvin, who gripped his shoulder and winced with pain. Meanwhile,

Connie helped her husband off the bed while Cedric stood helplessly in the middle of the room scratching his rotund belly. With a look of abject disappointment, he chewed the end of his pipe and shook his head at the open suitcase.

"What do you think you're doing!" Kitty yelled, "*GET OUT!*"

I raced across the hall into Kitty and Melvin's room, a chamber filled with the colors of autumn leaves in oranges and deep maroons. It was at least twice the size of the Higginbottom's apartment, and Dottie was in the process of wrecking it.

"What's good for the goose is good for the gander!" Dottie derided. "You have your secrets, don't you?" Dottie ripped open every drawer in the high boy. Bras, socks, and underthings flew into the air landing willy-nilly onto the bed and floor.

"Stop it!" Kitty grabbed at the lingerie.

"Why do I always find you skulking about, listening in keyholes? What are you hiding?" Dottie raced through the room like an insane woman. She threw open the wardrobe and tossed a pile of Kitty's and Melvin's clothing onto the floor. They gave a distinct clank upon hitting the carpet.

Dottie paused her destruction long enough to dig her hand into the pile and came up with a large wrench, and a screwdriver. "What are these for, Kitty?"

"Excuse me." Melvin walked in and snatched the tools out of Dottie's hand. "Those are mine. I keep them in the car when we travel."

"What were they doing in your wife's pockets?" Dottie panted pushing a disheveled hank of hair out of her eyes.

The congenial Melvin was no longer in evidence, and he said in menacing tones, "Madam, I fail to see how that is any of your business."

"Actually, I'm interested to know the answer," I commented.

Melvin swung around; the heavy tools held tight in his hand and his face a mask of anger.

I stepped back bumping into Connie who moved to stand at my side.

"She's right, Melvin. I, too, would like to know what Kitty is doing with those tools." She tapped a finger against her temple. "I seem to recall, when Johnny fixed the bathroom leak, he couldn't figure out how the screw on the faucet had gone completely missing."

Kitty's lips flattened, her arms crossed, refusing to answer.

Dottie stuck her head deep into the back of the wardrobe. "Oh-ho! What is *this?*"

She held aloft a small white cardboard box with the words Hagen Pet Store written in blue letters across the front. There were holes on each side, and a little metal handle arced over the top of the box.

"Looks like a carrying case for animals. I remember getting something similar when we bought Jeffrey a guinea pig," Connie commented.

"I'd say it's the perfect size for a mouse." Dottie's makeup-smeared face broke into a munificent smile. "Not quite so innocent, eh, Kitty cat."

"Why you pig!" Kitty charged Dottie, and the pair of them fell on top of the big queen-sized bed.

One of Dottie's sleeves ripped, and she pulled Kitty's hair. Nails scratched. Feet kicked. A black pump flew up and hit the ceiling. Glass shattered.

"Ladies! Stop it," Connie's cheese grater voice rasped. "Someone, stop them."

I thought the same but didn't dare with all the slapping and nail scratching.

Melvin and Walter waded into the fray. Walter took an elbow to the nose from Kitty and fell back pressing his palm to it. Connie went to his aid, while Gavin took his place.

"What in the Sam Hill is going on here!" Detective

Kingsley's voice boomed, "I told you to wait in the main room!"

The pair of men finally separated the irate women and held them at bay. Gavin had a hold of Dottie, who seemed to have come off the worst for wear. The torn left sleeve of her pink crepe dress hung down to her elbow. Beneath the ruined makeup her face showed a set of fingernail scratches across her temple, and her hair looked as though someone had taken an eggbeater to it. Kitty's new suit was wrinkled, and her cheek had a burgeoning red handprint, but she'd managed to stay clear of the other woman's claws.

The room was a wreck with the Conrad's clothing thrown asunder covering every square inch of the floor. An errant stocking dangled from the dressing table mirror and one of Melvin's sweaters hung off a drunkenly tilted lampshade. The chamber reeked of Tea Rose from Kitty's broken perfume bottle.

Both the women huffed to catch their breath and stared daggers at one another. Connie picked up an overturned chair and placed her husband in it. I retrieved a deep maroon towel from the bathroom, and Walter tilted his head back holding it to his injured nose.

The detective stamped into the room. "I *demand* an explanation!"

"Well, detective, I tried to give you one earlier . . . but you didn't have time," I imparted.

Cedric meandered into the room behind the detective. His eyes bulged, and he let out an enormous, "Achoo!" It didn't stop there. Two, three, four, five, six sneezes. He pulled a handkerchief from his pocket and staggered back into the hallway.

Kitty shook herself free from her husband's grasp and her perfectly manicured finger pointed. "*She* stole candlesticks and those ugly Hummel things from Frank."

Dottie gave a squeal, and her own, red-tipped finger pointed back at Kitty. "*She* broke the faucet and set loose a mouse."

The detective scanned the room scrutinizing the mess, his features drawn and grim. "All of you, return to the front room immediately! Or I'll call up the paddy wagon, and have my officers arrest the lot of you," he said in barely controlled tones.

I pivoted on my heel and led the way.

## Chapter Thirty-Six
### Ariadne

"I'd like an explanation."

Dottie's suitcase, with its ill-gotten booty, lay on the game table. She stood in her stocking feet next to the front windows, turned away from all of us.

When no one responded, the lawman turned to me. "Well Reporter, it seems like you've got all the answers, why don't you explain it to me?"

"Hm . . ." I tapped a finger against my chin.

Outside the window, I watched the police car idling with Maria in the back, and one of the officers at the wheel.

The other officer remained with Kingsley. He had not been introduced to us and stood in the entryway to the foyer, his feet shoulder-width apart, elbows out to the side, and hands behind his back. Despite being indoors, his dark hat remained upon his head. He ignored my stare.

"Miss Winter!" Kingsley thundered.

My shoulders jerked.

"Hey, now, I believe we discussed your tone last night," Gavin scolded.

"I'm not ignoring you, Detective, I'm trying to determine where to begin the story. There are so many aspects to cover," I calmly replied.

My gaze rested on Edward sitting on the same slipper chair I'd occupied last night. Poor Edward. A boy innocent of the shenanigans going on at Ivy Tree Inn, but whose world would surely be changed by the information about to be revealed.

"Perhaps it would be best if Edward could wait elsewhere," I suggested.

His face paled and he replied in resolute tones, "I'm not leaving. As a matter of fact, I-I have a confession." He stared down at his hands. "I killed Mr. Wyler."

I sucked in a breath. This, I did not see coming.

"Edward, no!" Johnny grabbed for the boy's shoulder, but he slipped out of reach.

"Yes! I did it!" He held his wrists out towards Kingsley. "Let my mother go and take me."

Kingsley eyed the boy. "Okay son, why did you do it?"

Momentarily stumped, Edward stuttered before answering, "I-I needed money to go to camp this summer and tried to steal it from Mr. Wyler's apartment." Edward pointed at me. "She knows about the money."

"Edward, dear, no. This isn't the way," I pleaded with him.

But Edward seemed determined to play savior to his mother. "He-he caught me digging through his, um, well . . . you know, the apartment. And-and he yelled at me. I panicked. It was an accident."

"How did you murder him?" Kingsley stroked his chin.

"Why I, uh . . ." Edward glanced wildly around the room as if searching for the right answer. "It was . . ." His gaze stopped at the hearth. "I clobbered him with a fireplace poker. Um . . . yeah, that's what happened. So-so, you can let my mom out of the car now. Right? And take me instead."

Everyone could tell the boy concocted the entire story. I glanced at the detective.

His eyes drooped, but he showed no emotion. "What about the ladder?"

"Th-the ladder?" He wrung his hands. "Oh, yeah, the ladder. Well, you know, first I pushed him off the ladder. Then I hit him with the poker."

"Why was he on the ladder?" The detective pressed.

"Uh-uh, no, I meant to say, I was on the ladder. Looking

above the cabinet . . . for the money. He caught me and told me to get down."

Kingsley nodded. "So let me get this straight you were on the ladder . . . where?"

"In his kitchen."

"In the kitchen, and he told you to get down—"

"Yelled at me." Edward nodded. "And I yelled at him to give me some money."

"So, you're saying it was a robbery gone wrong?" The other policed officer asked.

"Yes?" Edward's voice swung up like a question.

"And the ladder?" Kingsley pressed.

A cloud crossed the boy's features. "What about it? I left it in the kitchen."

"Let me get this straight, you went into Mr. Wyler's apartment to rob him, but he caught you, and instead you murdered him?" The detective was leading the boy, and I'd had it.

"Edward, stop!" I spoke sharply and Edward finally looked toward me.

"What?" the boy plaintively cried.

"The ladder was not in the kitchen," Johnny uttered.

"Son, while I understand your valiant effort to save your mother, you realize making a confession could land you in jail for life," Kingsley said quietly.

Edward's Adam's apple bobbed as he swallowed, but he put his shoulders back and nodded.

Walter piped in, "That's enough, Edward. We all appreciate the effort, but we know you didn't do it. Right, Detective?"

Kingsley must have had enough of the charade. "Your friend Dickie Johnson and his parents confirmed you were at the party the entire time."

Edward deflated, his head and shoulders drooped.

"Now, enough of your fables, son. Go sit down and let the

grown-ups talk." Kingsley pointed to a chair. Defeated, Edward shambled over to it.

# Chapter Thirty-Seven
## Ariadne

"Now, as you were about to say, before we were interrupted, Miss Winter," Kingsley made a swirling motion with his hand.

I bit my lip. "Perhaps Edward should wait elsewhere."

"Why shouldn't the boy remain?" Johnny challenged leaning against the back of the sofa. "He's got just as much at stake as his mother does."

Annoyance speared through me.

Johnny had done very little to stop the boy from making his asinine declaration, and he must have known there would be shocking revelations about Maria. So much for the "Concerned Uncle" act.

With a mocking tone, Kingsley addressed the room, "Miss Winter, our collective breath is bated. Do enlighten us."

"Fine." I sniffed and began to pace across the carpet to the opposite side of the room. "I'll start with the items in the suitcase."

Dottie squeaked.

"Sometime last year, Frank Wyler borrowed money from Mr. Higginbottom." I motioned to Cedric hunched on the sofa, still dabbing his runny nose. "The money went into the inn's renovations. Considering how much time our innkeeper spent looking through his ledger, I'm assuming the inn has yet to turn a profit, and Mr. Wyler couldn't pay back the five thousand just yet. Antsy to see a return, Mr. Higginbottom approached Mr. Wyler. Who then lied to Mr. Higginbottom, implying the money was invested in Donna Morgan's latest movie."

Cedric let out a small moan.

"However, from recent disclosures made in the newspapers, it became clear Mr. Wyler had lied. Mrs. Higginbottom knew about the money and feared their investment would not be returned. I'm assuming those items are in her suitcase, because she decided to take what she could from the house to reimburse the loan."

Kingsley frowned.

"As for Mrs. Conrad—" I rotated to lock onto Kitty "—I'm not sure I've got the entire story, but I have a theory."

Kitty, standing by the fireplace as far from Dottie as possible, harrumphed.

The detective took note but continued to watch me and prompted, "Please, present us with your theory."

"Mrs. Conrad has been sabotaging the success of the inn. To what aim, I'm not exactly clear." I walked back toward Gavin, who maintained a mild sense of amusement while watching the events unfold. "Years ago, Mr. Wyler's mother, Irene, stole her fiancé—"

"They were never engaged," Dottie remarked with a disdainful sniff.

Kitty's gaze narrowed at her enemy. "My father wouldn't allow it, until I graduated. We planned to announce our engagement at my graduation party."

Dottie rotated to face the room.

Kitty continued, "Until that slut, lured George away from me. She was always jealous of me. But since her Daddy was the president of the company, where George's father worked, he felt *compelled* to date her."

Dottie's face wore a mask of disbelief.

"George told me so," Kitty cried. "Irene threatened to tell her father that George took advantage of her at their vacation house, if he didn't take her to the dance."

The other woman's lips rolled in.

"Kitty! That was years ago," Connie chided. "Why are you making trouble for Frank now?"

"*Because Irene ruined my life!*" Her eyes blazed with madness. "She took him from me! And then, after she'd wrung the last drop of happiness out of him, she dumped my beautiful George like he meant nothing. A toy she'd grown tired of."

"But . . . he came back to you," Dottie whispered.

"Do you really think I'd take Irene's hand-me-downs?" Kitty's face pinched into disgust. "Did you think, I had no pride?"

"But Kitty, you married a successful man. Your work at the hospital is important—you said so. *And,* you can have whatever you want, including a new home at the lake," Dottie countered with a whine.

"Ha! A man who laughs like a donkey," Kitty viciously delivered.

I knew she disdained her husband, but her cruelty took my breath away. Melvin's mouth fell open as his face reddened with shame.

"A man who couldn't give me children. And after the last miscarriage, he found me so repulsive, that he moved out of my bedroom and found his pleasure elsewhere," she choked out the last. Her eyes turned shiny with unshed tears of anger and incredibly deep hurt.

"Kitty!" Melvin cried, "I've never—"

"Meanwhile," Kitty cut him off, "Irene got everything. First a successful Broadway choreographer husband. A child. A boy to boot."

"But my dear, he left her . . . for another woman," Connie softly corrected.

"She made her choice to stay behind while he went out west. She stayed with her beloved son, coddling him . . . living in the luxury of her husband's and father's money. When

Robert died, she got everything." She pointed at Johnny. "Going so far as taking it all away from her son's half-brother. Leaving him to a life of squalor. Irene's father bankrupted the company for his own greed, putting hundreds of people out on the street, including my brother! Who I've been supporting ever since."

Clearly Kitty's abhorrence of the family ran deep and wide.

Melvin's mouth dropped. "Ralph?"

Kitty put her hands on her hips. "Where do you think my pin money and the money the hospital pays me goes every month? Ralph has been bouncing from one job to another ever since the company went under."

"Kitty, I could have helped."

She ignored her husband and swiveled back to Dottie. "And yet, Irene still managed to live like a queen! Leaving a wake of despair and destruction behind her."

Connie's head shook back and forth. "Her father committed suicide ten months after the company shut down."

"Ha! I don't believe it! The papers said it was a hunting accident," Kitty challenged.

"Really, woman. He was shot in the head with his own pistol," Walter chided.

"So? So what?" Kitty's quavering voice pitched and rolled.

Pity crossed Connie's features as she observed her old friend. "Irene found him in the study. Everyone knew it was a cover-up, for the papers."

"Well! I didn't . . . she should have . . . I mean—" Kitty's lips twisted with vexation, and she went back on the offensive. "Have you seen that facility Frank put her in?"

Johnny's head moved up and down.

Kitty clamped her teeth together and bit out, "It's a Georgian mansion, for Pete's sakes. Even in her senility, she's living the life of Riley. But, if Frank's business failed—" Kitty's face broke into a tight, close-mouthed, smile. "She might have to finally come back down to earth like the rest of us."

Silence hung heavy in the room, and I began to doubt my own conclusions.

Johnny scratched his chin and asked, "Did you damage the stove?"

Kitty picked at a loose thread. "Sorry, Johnny."

Detective Kingsly stared at the woman, "You're telling me *you* murdered Frank?"

She gasped. "Absolutely not! I didn't go anywhere near the man. I didn't want Frank dead. Just poor enough, his mother would have to be put in one of those institutional nursing homes." Kitty stared down at her nails. "You know the kind, with strained peas and gray meat for dinner."

"In light of this new information, I'll need you to come down to the station, so we can go over your statement." Kingsley told her.

Kitty's fists clenched together. "Forget it!"

"I wasn't asking." The detective strode over to Kitty, who scuttled behind the couch to get away from him.

Unfortunately, for Kitty, the move put her directly in the path of the other officer. He walked over and clamped a hand on her shoulder, effectively putting an end to her evasion.

As damning as Kitty's confessions were, I still believed she didn't do the murder. In the depths of my being, I felt a compulsion to solve this puzzle, and Kitty was only a minor part of it.

"Detective," I spoke up. "You're on the wrong tack. Kitty isn't your killer."

Kingsley turned his attention to me. "Oh? And how can you be so sure?"

I squinted at her and tapped my lips. "While she's shown to be crafty and vindictive, her height makes it rather difficult to wield a weapon high enough to crush the top of Frank's skull."

"She'd be tall enough standing on the step stool," Johnny replied.

My mouth snapped shut, because I hadn't thought of that.

However, Johnny's comment clarified my theory.

"How did she get out of Frank's apartment without any of us noticing?" Connie asked.

"She's obviously been sneaking around this inn undetected for the past week," Johnny drawled.

Kitty's eyes widened, and she spat out, "I didn't do it! I was in my room. Melvin can vouch for me!"

Cedric sniffed. "You went out for a walk. Remember?"

I raised my hand. "Detective, if you would allow me to ask one question. I believe Kitty can be cleared."

He eyed me. "What question would that be?"

I turned to the suspect, "Kitty, who do you think would get Frank's inheritance?"

"I assume it's Irene. She's his next of kin," Kitty spit out. "It seems to be her lot in life, to get every blessed penny the men around her worked and scraped to earn."

"And there goes Kitty's motive." I fluttered my hand toward the ceiling like a bird flying away.

"Irene always got everything she wanted. She was a spoiled brat!" Kitty burst into tears. Her shoulders shook beneath the officer's heavy hand.

"Oh, Kitty, you're mistaken on so many fronts," Connie said pityingly. "Irene was never happy. She was working for her father when the company went bankrupt. She took Robert's inheritance because she was in debt up to her neck. She was desperate."

"Let her go," Kingsley jerked his head at the officer.

Kitty crumpled onto the sofa sobbing.

Melvin passed her a handkerchief and placed a gentle hand on her shoulder. "Kitty, it wasn't like that. I've never been with another woman," he murmured.

She turned her face away from him but didn't shake him off.

"Johnny, it wasn't right, what she did to you," Connie stubbed out her cigarette. "I hadn't seen much of Irene during those years, but when we spoke at the funeral, I told her you were innocent in all of this, and she should settle some of the money on you."

The man's stoic face revealed none of the thoughts in his head.

"Miss Winter, you've told us who *didn't* do the deed. So, who *did* commit the murder," Edward asked.

"What about Higginbottom, over there?" The police officer said.

Everyone turned when the man spoke.

His face reddened with embarrassment. He caught the detective's eye. "I mean . . . Mr. Wyler had the fellow's money. Did he do it?"

Flustered Cedric stuttered, "Why I-I . . . you can't mean—"

"Fortunately," I interjected for the officer's edification, "Mr. Higginbottom can be removed from suspicion due to his, erm, difficulties with the steps. As plenty of us witnessed last night, he barely made it up to the top floor without having a heart attack. There is no way Mr. Higginbottom could have done the deed without the household hearing him go up or down the stairwell."

It was Cedric's moment to wear an embarrassed flush. "Got a bum knee during the war. Stairs are difficult," he mumbled in defensive tones.

"Which leaves us with Mrs. Massey," Kingsley declared.

"If Mrs. Massey could be brought inside, I believe she has something of importance to reveal." I briefly made eye contact with the detective, my expression earnest. Silently begging for him to trust in me.

Edward got to his feet and put his hands together like one does to pray. "Detective, please."

Kingsley scanned the room and scratched his head. His jaw flexed and he said through thin lips, "Very well, bring her in."

# Chapter Thirty-Eight
## Ariadne

Maria sat on the sofa, wrapped in her son's arms, shaking and vehemently denying any part in Frank's murder. "I didn't do it. I didn't kill Frank. He was a good man. He gave me a job and a home for my son. Why would I want him dead?"

"Madame, I've explained the reasons," Kingsley gravely replied. "Your son's inheritance—"

"You're wrong! I told him not to do it!"

"I don't understand, Mom," Edward plaintively cried. "Why did Mr. Wyler put me into his Will? Why would he do that? Johnny or-or his mother should be the ones to inherit everything."

A few of us directed our attention to the handyman. His neck reddened under scrutiny, and he busied himself searching through his pockets for a pack of cigarettes.

"Don't ask me that!" Maria snapped at her son. He recoiled as she returned to defending herself to the police, "I didn't murder him!"

I went down on one knee and took her hands in mine. "Mrs. Massey . . . Maria, calm yourself. I believe you."

"You do?" She gazed at me with a hopeful light.

"I do. But I think it's time to tell Edward his relationship to Frank Wyler."

Edward frowned. "Mom? What is she talking about?"

Maria's eyes darted from Edward, to Johnny, back to me. "I-I don't know what you mean."

"Maria, it's going to come out. Best he hears it from you." I patted her knee and pushed upright.

"You'd better tell us what Miss Winter is referring to. We'll figure it out soon enough," Kingsley said. "Especially if it has to do with the letter we found in your apartment."

She emptied her lungs and drew a deep breath to begin her story, "*Mi Niño*, your father loved you dearly."

"I know Mom. He used to say, 'I was the star in his eye and the apple in his heart,'" Edward solemnly recounted.

"And you were his son, in all the ways that matter."

Edward's lips twisted. "What do you mean—all the ways that matter?"

Her head bowed and she gripped her son's young hands between her work-calloused fingers. "When your father was a boy, he was so ill, he almost died."

"But he didn't die."

Maria shook her head. "When we met, he swept me off my feet and told me I was the most beautiful woman he'd ever seen."

Edward nodded. "I remember, as a child, watching you dance in the living room. He said you were the reason he existed."

The hint of a bittersweet smile crossed her face. "We married a mere five months after we met. For years we tried to have a child. When it didn't happen, your father confessed to me—he had the mumps as a child. A doctor told him he might not be able to have children. He believed we hadn't conceived because of the illness."

Realization lit the teen's face. "That's why he used to call me his little miracle."

She patted his hand. "I remember his joy when he found out we were to have a baby. He swung me into his arms." Maria's face softened as she reminisced.

"As touching as this little story is, I fail to see what bearing it brings on the case," the detective inserted with impatience.

"Maria, you need to tell Edward," I murmured.

Maria's fear studded gaze met mine.

I gave her an encouraging nod.

She visibly swallowed. "Your father and I took a trip to Niagara Falls, but there was a problem at the hotel, and Jack had to leave early. Since we wouldn't be able to get our money back, he told me to stay and enjoy the falls. Frank . . . was there."

Edward's head bobbed. "I remember you told me he was a good friend to you. And you'd known him from school."

"Sort of." She pulled at her dress pocket. "We rekindled our friendship in Niagara. I confided in Frank. Told him how I struggled to have a baby. I-I asked for his help."

Edward nodded interested but confused by the turn his mother's story had taken. The rest of the adults who weren't aware of the relationship leapt to the proper conclusion. As the realization dawned, plenty of eyes darted between Johnny, Edward, and Maria.

Dottie breathed out a quiet, "Oh."

Unfortunately for Maria, her son remained obtuse. "How could Frank help? He's not a doctor."

Dottie cringed with understanding pity and looked away from the pair. Melvin cleared his throat, while Cedric chewed his pipe and stared out the window. The Sullivans became very interested in collecting the cards spread across the game table. I pressed my fingers against my closed eyes, regretting forcing Maria into this confession in front of an audience. I hadn't expected her story to unwind in such a manner.

"I . . . uh . . . we . . ." she stuttered searching for the right words.

Johnny blew smoke toward the ceiling and blessedly put Maria out of her misery. "What your mother's trying to say, she had a tryst with Frank. Nine months later, you were born."

Edward froze. His mouth bobbed like a giant Oscar fish. "Did Dad know?" he whispered.

Maria's head vehemently twisted back and forth. "No. He loved you as his own. For a long time, I couldn't be sure." She stared down at her hands. "It wasn't until you turned ten, that your face began to change. I saw the similarity . . ." she tapered off, unable to utter the end of that sentence.

Emotions flitted across her son's face clearer than a plate glass window—shock, confusion, fear, and finally it landed on anger. His cheeks went from pale to a hot red as the truth settled on him. He jumped up knocking a knick-knack off the coffee table, it crashed to the ground. Lickety-split, the boy darted past our gatekeepers.

A pale Maria stood up, a hand to her mouth. "Edward?"

The front door slammed so hard, the chimes in the clock jingled against each other.

One officer stepped forward as if to go after Edward, who was probably halfway down the block by now. "Should I?"

"I think—" Maria stepped forward, halting when her gaze met Kingsley's frowning demeanor.

Slowly he shook his head.

Johnny pushed upright from the bookcase he'd been leaning against, and said, "I'll go after him."

Before I could object, Kingsley did it for me. "Remain where you are, Mr. Wexler. Officer Briton, please follow the boy to make sure he's safe. Jones can remain here with me." He pointed at one of the uniformed officers. "Do not take him into custody unless you find he's a danger to himself or others."

Briton nodded and swiftly trooped out the front door.

"This is all very interesting." Kingsley strolled into the center of the room; his hands gripped behind his back. "However—" he spun around to face me "— I fail to see what bearing it brings on the murder. Mrs. Massey has confessed to having a personal relationship with our victim. She's also revealed her knowledge of recent changes to his Will."

"Yes. We're getting to that, but I have one tiny question." I pinched my thumb and forefinger together to demonstrate how small. "You mentioned a letter, you found in Maria's apartment. Did it happen to be a blackmail letter?"

"As a matter of fact, it is." He pulled an unsealed, unaddressed envelope out of his pocket and waved it in the air. "More evidence against her."

I felt rather than saw Walter Sullivan's presence as he rose from his chair. Connie's gasp, though quiet, still reached my ears.

"Normally, I would agree with your conclusions, except, the blackmail letter wasn't meant for Frank." I spun to face the distraught woman. "Was it, Maria?"

She'd gone stiff, staring out the door her son had exited.

I raised my voice, "*Maria!*"

She gave me a sideways glance full of malice, but I pushed forward, "The blackmail letter wasn't for Frank. Was it?"

Her eyes slit at me, and she didn't respond.

I let out a breath. "Come now, Maria, I know you're angry, but we must get through this. Unless you prefer to be booked for murder."

We held each other's gaze. Mine steady and unwavering. Hers full of hurt, fear, and misplaced anger. Or maybe it wasn't so misplaced, as I'd done my darndest to air the inn's dirty laundry. It wasn't enough. This group of people twisted in around each other's lives, and we still had a few more secrets to uncover.

"No," she hissed at me. "It was for him." Her eyes didn't leave mine, but her arm straightened, and her finger pointed at Walter Sullivan.

"How on earth did you—" he started.

I cut him off. "It was your husband's hotel. Right?"

Sharp nod.

"Who took the photos?" I fisted my hands so tight, I felt the nails dig into my palms.

Her lips flattened. "One of his assistant managers. He fired the man, and the waitress when he found out what they were doing."

"But he kept the photos, and you found them after his death."

She didn't respond.

Softly, I murmured, "Were there more?"

She broke away from my gaze turning her head, so I could see the profile of her tightly clenched jawline.

"Was this your first attempt?" I asked.

Fear replaced anger. She swallowed and muttered, "You don't understand."

Connie stood, and said with asperity, "I think we understand very well, and I'm here to tell you, it's not going to work, you dirty little blackmailer. Because *I know*."

Maria's eyes darted to Connie, then Walter, and away.

"That's right, missy. I was the one who intercepted your letter the other day."

Another puzzle piece slid into place. On the stairs, Connie's distress over the letter addressed to her husband. And later, the arguing I'd heard, when I came up to my room.

Connie strode across the room to plant herself directly in front of Maria. Bending at her waist she came within millimeters of being nose-to-nose with the woman. "I imagine you were wondering why the money never showed up."

Maria's entire body shook, and she replied hoarsely, "I-I never meant for you to know."

"Don't think for an instant, that *you* were the one to reveal the information." She straightened to full height. "And don't for an instant believe that your husband didn't know about that kid. A spouse knows. We *always* know."

Maria folded over with a wail as if she'd been punched.

At that point, Connie swung around and directed her ire at me. "Well, well, well, Miss Winter. You are *quite* a busybody, aren't you? Digging your nose into everyone's business. Uncovering long past secrets. Ones that should stay buried."

I stepped back. As she stalked closer to me, fear flooded my system. Connie was not a woman to mess around with.

"Dottie is a mess. Kitty has damaged her marriage. Maria has confessed a secret to her son she never planned to reveal, and now he's run off." Her hand flailed toward the foyer. "If I hadn't already known about Walter's infidelity, you would have ruined another marriage in the process. Are you proud of the destruction you've wrought?" she hissed.

"Sometimes secrets have to come out," I muttered. Taking another step backward, I came up against the game table.

"To what end, Miss Winter? *To what end!*" she bellowed.

Connie towered above me, her fury palpable. And I finally understood my father's warning about my safety. I began to wonder if I'd made a grave mistake—there were more people to fear in this household than just the murderer.

Her hand raised to strike me.

I flinched in anticipation.

"*Mrs. Sullivan!*" Kingsley roared.

Gavin jumped in between the two of us and met Connie eye-to-eye. "You need to step back."

Her mouth worked, and she grit out in menacing tones, "Get out of the way."

"Connie," Walter's even voice cut in, "It isn't her fault. You're taking your anger out on the wrong person. I'm the one to blame." He pointed to his chest.

Connie lowered her hand, spun away, snatched up a pack of cigarettes, and helped herself to one of them. She threw the smoldering match in the fireplace, and leaned on the mantel, smoking as if her life depended upon it.

Gavin turned to me and softly asked, "Are you okay?"

My entire body shook, and I bore down, clenching my fists so tight my fingernails dug into my palms.

"Fine," I croaked, cleared my throat, and said with more conviction, "I'm fine."

# Chapter Thirty-Nine
## Ariadne

Kingsley observed Connie, then each person in turn, his gaze landing last on me. "Mrs. Sullivan raises a good point. You've uncovered quite a few secrets, some even illegal. To what end, Miss Winter? You haven't revealed the killer. Do you even know?"

"Yes, about that." I grasped my hands behind my back and paced to the center of the room. "Detective, I must apologize for giving you an inaccurate statement about the night of the murder."

That got the room's attention.

"Inaccurate how," Kingsley prodded.

"You see, I told you that Frank Wyler was awake when I returned home."

"You said, you saw him in the window," Walter supplied.

"Indeed." I nodded. "I was wrong."

Kingsley crossed his arms over his chest and asked with a touch of asperity, "You're stating now that you *didn't* see him in the window?"

"Au contraire. Indeed, *someone* was at the window. I've now realized who I saw, was not Mr. Wyler, but his murderer," I said to the room at large, turning in a slow circle as I uttered the last word.

"Puh-lease," Connie dripped with sarcasm as she blew a plume of smoke into the air.

"As a matter of fact, our innkeeper was dead, before I

returned home," I continued turning to face Walter. "Possibly before you and Mr. Higginbottom went to bed."

Mr. Sullivan frowned. "I don't see how. I told you, no one went upstairs after Frank, until I went up. Unless now you're accusing me." Walter gave a bored stare.

"No, Mr. Sullivan, although I did consider you as one of the suspects." Walter's features turned grim, and I hurried to explain, "You see I realized, I never would have mistaken your lanky figure for Frank's silhouette. Perhaps someone went up *before* you and Mr. Higginbottom had your nightcap," I suggested."

Walter's gaze darted to Connie. "Surely, you're not suggesting—"

"Your wife? No. While she's got the height, and I daresay, strength of a man, Mrs. Sullivan is quite clever, and never would have admitted to knowing the shade of lipstick on the mirror, if she had done it," I explained my reasoning.

Connie let out a snort.

"I didn't do it! He wasn't there when I wrote the message!" Dottie insisted, slamming her fist into her palm with each word.

"Calm down, Dot. She's not foolish enough to believe *you* did it?" Connie said taking another drag off her cigarette.

"What *are* you suggesting?" the detective asked striding up to me.

"Dottie did go up and write the message." I tapped my chin and mused, "Perhaps the killer was already in the apartment . . . waiting for Frank."

Dottie gasped, putting a hand to her throat. Maria glanced warily at me, while Johnny continued to smoke and watch the proceedings with an amused smirk.

"Then again, perhaps not. Maybe the killer came in *after* Mr. Wyler went up."

Walter shook his head in disbelief. "I don't see how."

I allowed my fingers to walk across the back of the armchair "I believe you and Mr. Higginbottom shared a nightcap. Where did you enjoy your drink?"

"In here, of course," Walter asserted.

"No, we didn't Walter," Cedric corrected. "Remember, I needed a corkscrew. I went to the kitchen. You followed me. We took glasses out of the dish drainer and sat at the kitchen table."

Walter placed a hand on his forehead. "Heavens to Betsy, you're right. I'd forgotten."

"You're saying, the stairs were unmonitored during that time," Kingsley directed and accusing tone at Walter.

"Except, you've forgotten the fact that Frank had locked the front door. The killer didn't force the door." Melvin pointed out moving to the game table. He sat in the chair Connie had vacated.

"That wouldn't have mattered if the killer was already inside the house," Gavin said taking the seat next to Melvin. He crossed his legs and began absentmindedly shuffling the deck of cards.

I pointed at Gavin and drew out the word, "Or, if the killer had a key. Let's say, the killer came in the front door, while the Mr. Sullivan and Mr. Higginbottom shared their drink in the kitchen. He went upstairs to confront Mr. Wyler about something."

"Something like what, Miss Winter?" Kingsley snapped.

I rubbed my hands together. "Now, we know the Higginbottoms needed the money. Frank's death doesn't help their cause."

"Can't secure money from a dead man." Gavin overhand shuffled the cards from his right hand into the left.

"And Kitty's pranks were more about putting Frank out of business rather than putting him in the ground," I added.

"By your reasoning, the young boy could have been the one to kill Frank for his inheritance," Officer Jones suggested pointing a thumb over his shoulder in the direction Edward had exited the inn.

271

"Except, he *didn't* know about the inheritance," Maria insisted.

The officer's furrowed brow created a canvas of skepticism, as if challenging the validity of Maria's claim.

"Detective Kingsley stated, Edward has an alibi," I clarified for the doubters in the room. "As I was saying, the murderer went upstairs while Mr. Sullivan and Mr. Higginbottom were having their nightcap. The Conrads were in their beds, as were Mrs. Higginbottom and Mrs. Sullivan. Maria and Edward had gone to their apartment."

I paused as another thought occurred to me. "Maria, when did Edward sneak out?"

Maria hesitated, "I-I'm not sure. I fell asleep on the couch, reading a book. Elevenish?"

"Congratulations, Miss Winter, you've just accounted for everyone's whereabouts," Connie sneered. "There's no one left. Unless you're suggesting a phantom murdered our innkeeper. Or was it you?"

"Hardly." I flashed a sharp smile. "I've got a roomful of partygoers to supply my alibi."

"Yes, you do." Noticing my surprised expression, Kingsley added, "We checked."

"And I *haven't* accounted for everyone," I allowed the comment to dangle, before quietly saying, "There's still, Mr. Wexler."

Gavin's card shuffling came to a halt. In unison, the group shifted their focus away from me to direct their attention to Johnny.

Johnny stopped chewing his thumbnail. "Me?" he guffawed. "I wasn't in the area. I had to go up to Pawtucket for a part."

"And then where did you go?" Walter asked.

"I was at the Lucky Dog. People saw me there," Johnny tapped his chest.

"Who?" the detective asked.

"The bartender for one. And . . . and," he struggled to recall another name. "Adam Clampett! He had a drink with me!"

"Adam Clampett picked up his daughter after the basketball game. He asked me for a pot roast recipe," Maria said quietly.

"So? We had drinks early," Johnny retorted, anger in his tone. "I stayed late."

I tilted my head, squinted at him, and said with deceptive calm, "I don't think you did."

"What the hell do you know about it?" He swept a derisive gaze up and down my body. "You think you know it all! Mrs. Sullivan is right. You go around sticking your nose into everyone else's business. You're nothing but a loudmouthed busybody?"

He switched his attention to Kingsley, who'd begun to scrutinize Johnny with a new gleam in his eye. "You need to put a stop to her wild accusations, Detective. She's way off base," he spoke with a shrill note in his voice.

I pressed my advantage. "I know Edward's exit was blocked by a truck at the end of the alley, and he had to take the long way around. It was the backfiring of *your* truck that awoke Maria as you left the crime scene."

"The popping? Yes? Yes! I heard it!" Maria exclaimed. "You mean it wasn't a dream?"

I continued, ticking off each point on my fingers. "When I saw the silhouette in the window, I assumed it was Frank Wyler. But that was not the first time, I'd mistakenly confused the two of you. Was it Johnny?"

He didn't answer.

"No, as a matter of fact, my first morning, I saw you on the ladder and assumed it was Frank. Didn't I?"

Again, he didn't respond.

"I bummed a cigarette from you. A Chesterfield. I know those were your cigarettes in Frank's apartment. Just as I know the blood on your jacket wasn't from Maria's cut." On a roll, I pressed forward, "You brushed your bloody sleeve against the kitchen door when you ran out the back. You probably heard Dottie heading your way, which is why you didn't have time to close and lock it properly behind you. It blew open, when Dottie went to get the Sherry bottle."

Dot sat up straight and drew out the word, "That's right. I told you, the door was open." She turned to Cedric, and asked, "Was it open when you two had your port?"

"No. It was closed," Cedric answered swiveling his head to his friend for confirmation. "Walter, you checked to make sure it was locked before we turned out the lights to go to bed."

"Correct. It was locked tight," he confirmed.

"I saw something moving by the garage!" Kitty called out.

Johnny waved his hand at Kitty. "You're talking nonsense." Then he pointed at me. "She's being ridiculous. It's utter nonsense."

But Kingsley wasn't convinced. As a matter of fact, the detective scrutinized Johnny as a mountain lion eyeing his prey.

Johnny's features morphed, and he put on that oily grin he'd been wearing earlier and scoffed, "Detective, surely you're not buying this cock and bull story." However, his tense shoulders belied the nonchalance he tried to exude.

In deceptively calm tones, I asked, "How did you know the step ladder wasn't in the kitchen?"

Johnny's casual manner dropped away. "What?"

"You told Edward the step ladder wasn't in the kitchen. If you weren't here last night, how did you know that?

The detective steepled fingers in front of his nose, his hardened gaze locked on Johnny. "How did he get out of the house without anyone noticing?"

"That's the one thing I couldn't figure out." I waggled my finger. "Until just before you arrived."

Hands behind my back, I sauntered closer to Johnny and met his arrogant gaze. "I didn't understand why you were so irritated when you found me in the linen closet. Initially, I chalked it up to Frank's death. However, it all became clear . . . when I went back later."

Johnny's smirk disappeared, and his eyes turned to slits. If I'd been alone with the man, I would have been worried. However, with a crowd that included police, I felt very secure.

I'm not sure which was greater, my arrogance or my own stupidity at those assumptions.

# Chapter Forty
## Ariadne

"Follow me!" I chirped.

Into the dining room, I sailed, leading the crowd like the Pied Piper. It took a few moments for everyone to assemble inside the room, and I whistled beneath my breath as they gathered. The Sullivans, Higginbottoms, Conrads, and Maria shuffled into the dining room in murmuring confusion.

"Come on, Mr. Wexler, you don't want to miss all the fun." The detective drew a reluctant Johnny into the room by his elbow.

Once inside Johnny jerked free and sauntered away, taking up a casual pose against the wall by the swinging door. With a silent head jerk, Kingsley directed the police officer to stand guard by the swinging door, while the detective remained by the pocket door entrance. Gavin joined him there.

"You see, as foreman of the renovations, Johnny is intimately familiar with every inch of this house. Aren't you?" I said over the general murmurs.

He didn't deign to answer, and I continued, "This house is close to eighty years old. Back in those days, people often had live-in help. Thus, the third-floor rooms where Frank Wyler slept. To make things easier for the maids, a dumbwaiter, was installed for sheets, towels, and probably the lady of the house's morning coffee."

If I didn't know what I was looking for, I would have missed it. Two small fingerholds were intricately concealed by the carved chair rail molding above the wainscot. I grunted, gave it a shove, and up it went.

The occupants of the room gasped.

To my horror, a heavy object rolled at me, and I jumped back, bumping into Maria. She cried out as a heavy figurine spun off the platform, and bowled across the floor over my sneakers, leaving a reddish-brown stain in its wake.

"That's an Oscar," Dottie said in reverent tones.

I picked up the golden statuette being careful not to touch the base where the innkeeper's blood soiled the inscription making it unreadable.

"Put that down!" Detective Kingsley barked.

As if it bit me, I dropped the statue on the closest table. My gaze sought Johnny Wexler. To my surprise, I found he'd moved through the crowd and was barely five feet from me. "Robert Wyler's, I presume?"

The handyman gave me a glare that could strip the flowered wallpaper off the dining room walls.

The detective bent at the waist and examined the statue. "That looks like blood to me."

"It's the murder weapon," I declared.

The base was just the right size for the dust ring on the mantel in Wyler's apartment.

"Did I come home before you could make a clean getaway?" I taunted.

Johnny kept his mouth shut.

I shook my head. "No answers?" I tsked. "I would imagine the doctors will find the injury Wyler sustained is of similar shape to the base of the statue."

"But why did you do it?" Melvin asked scratching his bald noggin.

Unfortunately, it was too late for me to realize; I'd made a tactical error allowing Johnny within arm's reach. Before anyone could comprehend what was happening, he grabbed my elbow and pulled me in front of him. The little snub-nosed revolver fit keenly in his hand. It's no wonder we didn't notice him carrying it in a pocket.

The cold metal now pointed at my head.

"Stay back!"

Kingsley stiffened. Gavin's mouth dropped. Adrenaline jolted my system.

"That means you cops as well. Stand over there, away from the door." He pointed with the gun and the crowd shambled away from the pocket doors.

"You too, boyfriend!" he waved the gun at Gavin.

Fear clouded Gavin's demeanor as he stalked into the dining room.

My heart raced in my ears, and my breath came in rapid, shallow gasps. I struggled to calm my breathing, trying to avoid slipping into full-blown panic.

"*Dios mío,* Johnny, no!" Maria cried. "Don't do it!"

"Shut up, Maria," he growled. "Have you any idea why I went up to Frank's apartment that night? No? To request he do the right thing by *your* son. When I saw that damned Oscar sitting on his mantel. *His mantel!* By God, I saw red. Not only wasn't he taking care of his kid, but he dared to take *my mother's and father's award and to display* it!" he shrieked. "Like he had anything to do with it!"

I winced as his fingers bit into my arm.

"Robert loved my mother! Frank bought this stupid inn with *my* father's money. Money he wouldn't have made if it weren't for the talent of *my mother!*" Johnny jerked me against his hard chest.

"The pair of them earned that money together. Every movie they did turned to gold. That Oscar should have been left to me!" His voice reverberated in my ears as he shouted and waved the gun in the direction of the gaping crowd. "Frank and Irene took *all of it* when he died. After my father begged her for a divorce. Time and again Irene refused. Dad foolishly never changed his Will. That woman is a conniving, stealing bitch!"

Spittle landed on my cheek. I feared he'd lose control of the gun as it returned to point at my head.

Johnny snarled, "You were right, Smarty-pants. I took the dumbwaiter down the three flights and was about to make a clean exit when I heard Miss Porky here—" he waved the revolver at Dottie who cringed and shrank behind her husband "—coming toward the kitchen. I didn't have time to close the back door properly."

"Why did you leave the statue behind?" Dottie's voice warbled from behind her husband.

"I hadn't planned on it. I planned to have Frank discovered in the morning. When the door slammed waking the household, I left the Oscar behind and figured I'd get it after the dust settled." His sleeve fell back revealing a watch I'd seen around Frank's wrist.

Before I could think better of it, out popped, "Looks like you took your brother's Rolex too."

"It was my father's," Johnny sneered. "I was with my mother when she bought it for him in Santa Monica."

"Johnny, let the girl go. We can work all of this out," Walter's voice rang with authority.

"Ha!" Johnny scoffed. "You must think me a fool, old man."

The policeman by the swinging door made a jerking movement toward us. Quick as a whistle Johnny turned the muzzle at him and fired off a round.

The officer cried out and his face crumpled with pain. He clapped a hand over his left shoulder and staggered into a dining chair.

Gasps and shouts filled the air. I'm certain one of the screams was mine.

"*Johnny!*" Maria's high-pitched cry rose above all the rest.

Before I could register what happened, and make a move to pull away, Johnny twisted my right arm behind my back and placed the muzzle against my ribcage. I smelled the scent of burnt fabric as it singed the wool.

Dottie dived under the center table knocking a chair to the ground. Her husband followed. He couldn't fit all the way under, and his corduroy-covered rearend stuck into the air.

"Enough!" Kingsley snapped holding his palms out. "Everyone back away. Wexler, you don't need to shoot anyone else."

Walter gripped Connie's shoulders and pulled her further into the corner of the dining room behind the buffet. Melvin seemed stymied, his head darted in all directions, unsure what to do. In the end, it was Kitty who snatched up one of the linen napkins and rushed over to help the injured man.

"I know you're carrying a gun beneath your jacket, Kingsley. Very slowly, take it out and lay it on the table next to the Oscar." Johnny pulled me in front of him, as the detective did as he was told, and gradually removed the weapon. "Very good. Now, step over with the rest of them."

Hands up, Kingsley backed away from us. "You have the gun. Let the girl go."

"No. I think I'll be taking her with me. As insurance."

Sweat popped out along my upper lip and my heart raced faster than a jackrabbit.

"Pick up the statue." He shoved me toward it.

With my free hand, I gripped the cool metal award.

"Good job. This way." Slowly, we shuffled toward the pocket doors.

Gavin's face was a mask of helpless fury, and he kept opening and closing his hands into fists. "If you hurt her—"

"You'll what?" Johnny jerked my arm hard enough to make me cry out in pain.

Gavin made an animalistic noise in the back of his throat.

"I think, I'll take Miss Smarty-pants on a little ride."

The weapon dug deeper into my side, and I clenched my teeth tight to keep from making a sound.

"What no snappy comeback?" His cigarette breath whispered across my neck, and I felt the prickle of sweat drip down my temple. "Don't worry, I'm not interested in having you with me for long."

Someone gasped. It might have been me.

If Johnny had left the gun pointed at my head, I would have considered going limp on him. With it digging into my side, and the painful angle of my arm pushing my chest forward, going limp would more than likely get me a shot in the gut or separate my shoulder. My mind frantically searched for a way to escape. I did not want to get into his truck. I feared Johnny would shoot me and leave me on the side of the road.

"Come on Smarty-pants, let's go." He pulled me with him.

I stumbled and dragged my feet to slow him down.

My gaze darted between Gavin and Kingsley, and I prayed one of them would come up with an answer to my dilemma. However, they remained in place unwilling to take the risk.

Help would not come from that direction.

As we exited the dining room, I determined to take my chance at the front door. One of us would have to open it. Johnny had foolishly put a weapon in my hands, and I would use it to club him upside the head. The irony of using the Oscar as a weapon against him was not lost on me.

Gavin's facial features spasmed as he leaned forward watching our retreat.

A voice brought Johnny up short. "Let go of her and put your hands up, where I can see them, or you'll get a bullet to the brain."

Johnny hesitated.

"Let. Her. Go. Now." The gruff words were followed by the distinct cock of a gun.

My captor withdrew the weapon from my side, released my wrist, and delivered a shove that had me stumbling with my arms flailing.

Quick on his feet, Gavin lunged to catch me, before I planted face first onto the hardwood floors.

"Gotcha," he murmured in my ear.

My right arm hung limp at my side, but I wrapped my left around his neck still holding on to the Oscar.

"That's right. Now, very slowly, put your hands in the air."

I peered over my shoulder to see Aunt Ruby holding a deadly black pistol aimed at Johnny's head. She wore a red swing coat and black stilettos and looked notably confident handling the weapon. She bore a calculating expression, and the pistol did not waver in her grip.

For a moment, Johnny seemed to have a mental debate over which action to take. The room held its collective breath.

"I said, hands up, Johnny," she repeated. "Don't kid yourself, any good will I held toward you, because of Mitzy, was just obliterated when I found you holding my niece at gunpoint. If I must put a bullet through you—" She licked her lips "—I will do it. Without a qualm."

Johnny's arms gradually rose, but upon reaching his ears, he rotated the revolver to his temple and threatened, "Don't come any nearer! I'll pull the trigger!"

"Don't do it, son," Kingsley discouraged.

Ruby gave a sharp head shake and tsked. In a flash, she executed a swift maneuver that twisted Johnny's wrist, forcing the weapon skyward. The gun discharged leaving a hole in the ceiling. Johnny grunted, trying to recover his grip on the revolver, but it was no use, she dug her nails in, and he dropped the gun. At which point Kingsley sprang into action, to subdue Johnny and retrieve his weapon.

"Good afternoon, Detective Kingsley," Ruby greeted. "It's nice to see you again."

"Ruby," he grunted snapping the cuffs around Johnny's wrists.

Releasing a breath, I hadn't realized I'd been holding; I closed my eyes and laid my head beneath Gavin's chin. His jugular pulsed beneath my ear, and he tightened his grip on me.

"Are you alright, Ariadne?"

I opened my eyes to find Aunt Ruby examining me. Concern rippled across her features.

My head bobbed up against Gavin's chin. "Thanks to you." Reluctantly, I pulled away, although Gavin's grip didn't allow me to go too far. "What on earth are you doing here?"

"Your father phoned. Said he was concerned you were getting yourself into trouble. Suggested I stop in to check on you." She glanced over to Johnny, kneeling on the floor with his hands cuffed behind his back. "Guess he had good reason to be concerned."

"Where did that gun come from?"

"I always carry one, Ariadne. I'm a woman living alone. Sometimes, I work late at the shop," she explained, as if it was perfectly natural for woman to carry a pistol in her Prada purse.

Gavin asked, "Where did you learn that-that thing you did to Johnny's wrist?"

"I learned it during the war."

Still confused, I exclaimed, "During the war? Mom said you worked as a secretary."

The whisper of a smile flitted across her mouth. "Let's just say, I worked for the War Department. Same as your father."

My father worked for the Office of Strategic Services, America's intelligence agency during the war. I came by this knowledge, not because my father ever spoke about it, but because, when I was eight years old, I snooped through my father's desk searching for my Christmas present. Buried at the bottom of a pile of papers was a letter signed by President Truman, thanking my father for his service to the department. It wasn't until years later when I learned about the OSS, that I put two-and-two together.

Did that mean Aunt Ruby worked for the OSS too? It would account for her skill with a gun.

"I think it would be best, if we don't mention this to your

mother," she suggested.

I nodded in agreement. "Or my father."

"Very well," she exhaled. "Why don't I take you, and your handsome friend, out for dinner, and the two of you can explain what this is all about?"

# Chapter Forty-One
## Ariadne

### Sunday

Before we left Ivy Tree Inn, Gavin made a few phone calls to locate an old college buddy who worked at the *New York Post-Journal* to pitch the bizarre murder story. He tracked Budgie down at his parents' summer cottage in Montauk. It took a bit for Budgie to understand what Gavin was proposing, because his friend seemed to be nursing a sore head, the result of a recent break-up that led to a martini binge the prior evening.

Once Budgie clued into the meat of the article, he declared, "Sounds like a home run story. I want five hundred words."

Having crammed as much of my body as would fit into the minuscule booth with Gavin, I'd heard Budgie's answer. I shook my head and mouthed one thousand.

"Seems a bit paltry for such a juicy story, what do you say to a thousand words?"

"I haven't the column inches. Seven hundred. Not a word more," Budgie responded. "Have the fellow drop it by the office tomorrow morning."

I opened my mouth to correct his assumption, however, Gavin effectively cut me off by planting his hand over my lips. "Seven hundred, done. Fetch yourself some breakfast, old man. And a Bloody Mary—hair of the dog, you know."

"Good idea. Now let me see if I can scare up some tomato juice," Budgie muttered, and the line went dead.

"Why didn't you tell him, I'm a woman?"

"We will. All in good time," Gavin replied.

As for the inn's cast of criminals, things didn't go as I'd expected. While Kingsley had been interested in arresting Maria for the attempted blackmail, Walter refused to press charges or testify in court. After the detective left, she'd come upstairs to Walter and Connie's room to deliver the offending photos *and* the negatives, along with a heartfelt apology.

Like any good investigative reporter, I watched the exchange through the keyhole of my door.

Meanwhile, Maria, having been let off the hook, must have been feeling magnanimous. She instructed Dottie to return the items, and she wouldn't press charges. Maria also promised to provide proper payment for the loan once the inn started turning a profit. Since the items never actually left the inn, Kingsley had little avenue to pursue the issue.

As for Kitty, she administered first aid to Officer Jones until the ambulance arrived. The doctors claimed her quick thinking saved the man's life. As the heroine of the day, her minor vandalism was overlooked.

Edward returned home. I'm not sure what was said between mother and son, but I knew the pair loved each other, and eventually, he would forgive his mother for her transgressions.

Breakfast that morning was a quiet affair. Each couple took their table. Maria set everything out, including the coffee in a silver urn, so we could serve ourselves. I read my article that Gavin had sold, in the local newspaper, over breakfast.

Conversation was muted or nonexistent, and the snubs made it clear that I was persona non grata. I ate without making eye contact with anyone but Gavin. Upon finishing, we bolted out of there like Sputnik off the launch pad.

While I didn't expect to make friends on this trip, making

enemies during my pursuit of the truth proved to be more uncomfortable than I had imagined. I realized, if I continued to pursue my dream, I'd have to come to terms with the discomfort of being hated.

When I awoke in the middle of the night, drenched in sweat from a nightmare in which Johnny threw me out of his car into a frozen lake, I realized that having my life threatened was a reality I needed to come to terms with,

‡‡‡

The clouds drifted across the sky covering and uncovering the sun like a mother playing peek-a-boo with her infant child. Gavin sped along the Merritt Parkway, while I balanced the typewriter on my lap tapping out my article. I'd titled it "An Oscar Worthy Murder."

"What's your middle name?"

"Ellison. It was my grandmother's maiden name. Why?"

"A.E. Winter. I like it. Use it as your byline," Gavin suggested.

"Why can't I use my name?" I asked petulantly staring at Gavin's profile. He had a nice one. Only a small bump on the bridge of his nose marred it.

"Come now, Ariadne," he chided giving me the side-eye. "How many newsrooms took you seriously when you applied?"

"Well, it was right after college, I didn't have any experience," I defended.

Silently, I remembered a few cringy incidents. One editor laughed in my face while calling me "girlie." He asked me if my husband knew I was looking for a job in a newsroom full of men. Another simply gave me a lascivious stare and told me they didn't have a place for me in the newsroom—but they could always use "a dolly with gams like yours" for fetching coffee and sorting the mail.

"Did they bother to read any of your work?"

I stared down at the typewriter. Sometimes life was very unfair for a woman who wasn't on track to marry and have a pile of children.

He sighed. "I don't want them to be prejudiced against you before they read your work. Trust me." When I still didn't respond, he added, "Besides, it *is* your name."

"An androgynous name."

"That's why you're the writer. You know all the big words" He reached over and patted my knee.

I could still feel the warmth his hand left behind after he placed it back on the wheel.

I sighed, "Fine, we'll do it your way. A.E. Winter."

"I'll drop it off at Budgie's office tomorrow morning. If he accepts the article for publication, I'll arrange a time for you two to meet in person."

"Sounds like you plan to ambush your friend."

"You're catching on." Those dimples peeked at me, and he winked. "Now, where shall we go for dinner tonight?"

"I need to work on this article. I want to make sure it's perfect."

"Of course, but you *must* eat dinner. Now, do you like Italian? Greek? French?" he drummed his fingers along the steering wheel.

I stared at his profile. "Gavin, are you asking me out on a date?"

"If you have to ask, I must be doing something wrong." He grimaced and muttered, "I suppose, it must be the direct approach." Then he took a deep breath and said formally, "Miss Winter, would you do me the honor of joining me for dinner tonight?"

"That depends. Are you going to insist on calling me A.E. or Miss Winter, all night long?"

He glanced at me and caught sight of the smile; I was doing a poor job of hiding. With a head shake, he replied, "If I don't strangle you first, I promise to call you Ariadne."

The giggle finally escaped. "Yes, Gavin, I would adore having dinner with you. And I prefer Greek or Italian."

"I can see dating you is sure to bring a mix of excitement, vexation, and unpredictable moments that are bound to drive me up a wall," he said with a touch of asperity.

"If you prefer someone staider, may I suggest Mr. Hanson's assistant Bunny Davies."

"*Bunny Davies!*" The car swerved, but Gavin quickly returned the roadster to its lane. "Bunny Davies is at least twenty years my senior and afraid of her own shadow."

"So, what you're saying, a girl like me, who will drive you a bit crazy, is preferable to a staid old maid?"

The car went silent for a few minutes as he thought about my question. "I suppose I am."

For the next ten miles, a grin remained glued on my face, as I tippy tapped away at the typewriter. The words flowed out of my fingertips, and I knew the article would launch me into the next step of my journey.

By the time we drove over the Harlem River, the typewriter lay at my feet and the T-bird hummed along the road beneath us. I had a finished copy of Donna Morgan's exclusive interview, along with seven hundred words about Frank Wyler's murder tucked into my satchel. The setting sun striped the scuttering clouds in shades of pink and orange.

My hand tucked into Gavin's, and we headed to an eatery called Rinaldo's Trattoria, for our first official date.

My mother would be thrilled to know I had a date with Gavin. I intended to promptly inform her of my new situation, hoping it would deter her from digging up a potential suitor to sit beside me at next Sunday's dinner. If Gavin stuck around long enough, I might consider bringing him home for a Sunday dinner.

I glanced at him through my lashes and reconsidered.

If I brought him home, Mother would spend the entire

evening gently needling Gavin about his intentions toward me. She'd ask his thoughts on marriage, and how many children he wanted. As the scenario played out in my imagination, I realized I was getting far ahead of myself and gave an uncontrolled grimace.

"What was that face for? Did you forget something at the inn?"

I hadn't meant for Gavin to see that, and stuttered out, "N-no."

He waited patiently for me to explain. When I didn't, he prodded, "Are you still upset over the initials?"

I shook my head. "Not at all. I agree with your plan."

"Then what?"

No good would come out of describing the wayward thoughts about my mother. Instead, I hurriedly devised a different explanation for my wretched expression. "I hope Johnny never gets out of jail."

The moment the words came out of my mouth, I realized they couldn't be truer.

Gavin's nostrils flared. He squeezed my hand hard and said with passion, "Don't worry. If he does get out, I'll make sure he never comes near you."

The tension ebbed out of my body, and I sank deeper into my seat allowing a sigh of contentment to escape between my lips.

# Author's Note

The character of Donna Morgan was inspired by the story of Princess Grace of Monaco. A few months before she was set to marry Prince Ranier, Grace Kelly played her last Hollywood role as Tracy Lord in the musical *High Society*, along with Bing Crosby and Frank Sinatra. They filmed the movie in Newport, Rhode Island at Clarendon Court, and on a Hollywood sound stage. *High Society* was Grace's last film.

About five years ago, I came across a 1956 *Look* magazine with the Prince and Princess of Monaco on the cover. I was not alive when the wedding happened, but I have enjoyed many of her films. The magazine piqued my interest in Grace Kelly's life, and I began researching her time in Hollywood and with Prince Ranier. As a fan of writing historical fiction, I decided to formulate an Agatha Christie-style short story set in Newport and incorporate a starlet on her way to becoming a European princess. The short story ended up being too long and turned into a full-length novel with Ariadne Winter helming the mystery.

For those unfamiliar with Grace's backstory, she came from an affluent family in Philadelphia—her father was a 3-time Olympic gold medalist. By her late teens, she was modeling and acting in stage plays; she made the leap into TV and movies with the help of her uncle, George Kelly, a Pulitzer Prize-winning playwright. Between 1951 to 1956 Grace catapulted to stardom, becoming a favorite of Alfred Hitchcock who put her in three of his thrillers. During those years Grace won a Golden Globe and an Academy Award.

In 1955, Olivia de Havilland arranged an introduction to Prince Ranier during the Cannes Film Festival. That Christmas the prince came to America to spend the holidays with Grace and her family where he proposed. The engagement ring Grace wore in *High Society* was a Cartier 10.48-carat diamond given to her by the prince.

However, it was not all easy sailing. For the Grimaldi family to accept the union, the Kelly family was required to pay a $2 million dowry to the royal family's coffers. Unlike Donna Morgan's story, the prince did not invest in her movie to pay the dowry. Grace combined her acting fortune with her own inheritance to pay the dowry.

On April 18, 1956, in a private civil ceremony at the palace, the pair were married. Grace was 26 and Prince Ranier was 32. The following day, the pair were formally united in a religious ceremony. The "Wedding of the Century," at the St. Nicholas Cathedral, was broadcast to over 30 million viewers by MGM—an agreement Grace made with the studio to be allowed out of her contract.

Sadly, Princess Grace died in a car accident on September 14, 1982, at the age of 52.

The character of Detective Kingsley was inspired by Rhode Island State Police officer, Henry J. Moniz. Moniz was a Vietnam veteran who served in the United States Marine Corps. When his tour ended, Moniz was accepted into the Rhode Island State Police Training Academy, and he became the first African American to break the color barrier. The year was 1969.

Approximately, two years after he graduated from the training academy, Moniz joined the Federal Bureau of Alcohol, Tobacco and Firearms, where he spent the rest of his 35 years in a law enforcement career.

According to ReporterToday.com, Moniz "received four individual Special Achievement Awards from the United States Secretary of the Treasury for high quality criminal case production. Moniz was the recipient of a Special Citation from the city of Boston, Police for apprehension and conviction of two bombing suspects wherin a police officer was killed. He is the recipient of the Distinguished Law Enforcement Service Award from the Massachusetts Italian Police Officers Association for his criminal investigations, and he received a proclamation from R.I. Governor Lincoln Almond for government services. Henry also received the R.I. State police Certificate of Recognition and Appreciation for Honorable Service to the people of Rhode Island."

# An Excerpt from
# Operation Blackbird

## Chapter One
## The Recoleta

*Argentina, October 1952*

It was merely a glimpse, but, in that moment, memories from almost a decade ago flooded back as if it had happened only yesterday. The pungent scent of gasoline, crackling wood, and black clouds billowing in the air. Screams of terror from women and children trapped inside—only women and children, for the men had already been rounded up and marched off to a camp, the old and infirm shot on sight. Black uniforms of the SS surrounding the burning chapel. Finally, the peppering spray of gunshots, which, at that point, was merciful to those inside. I—on a ridge, too far away to do anything—watching in horror. I could smell the acrid smoke, tasting its bitterness on my tongue. The day's hot breeze only sought to enhance the jagged memory.

The wail of a small child crying for his mother distracted me, pulling me back to the present and away from the terrible memory. The mother snatched the toddler, who was dressed in a sailor suit, by the hand and chastised him for running away from her.

When I looked back, the man had disappeared. My heartbeat slowed and the memory faded. Perhaps it wasn't him. My vantage point was about fifteen yards away. His features had been in profile to me, and he'd been speaking to another person who had been out of my line of sight.

Of course, I followed him. Luckily, I was wearing the new pair of espadrilles I'd purchased at the market yesterday. The rope-soled shoes made little sound as I darted past the extravagant sculptures and marbled mausoleums in the Recoleta Cemetery. He'd been wearing an ocher suit, and I heard dress Oxfords tapping along the tile flag way ahead of me. At the next lane, I turned right and hurried forward, catching sight of a man's brown shoe rounding the far corner. Barely dodging a mourner placing flowers in front of a mausoleum, I received a well-deserved frown and excused myself for disturbing her lamentations. Around the bend, I followed my quarry, only to be caught up short as I practically plowed into a bespectacled, elderly gentleman in a tan linen suit innocently reading the scripture on a particularly ornate angel statue.

*"Un millón de perdones!"* I gasped.

He mistook my anxiety. *"Con permiso, estás perdido? Puedo ayudarle?"* he asked kindly in a soft Argentinian accent.

With effort, I lightened my features. No, I assured him, I didn't need help; I was not lost. I glanced down, observed his brown Oxfords, and realized I'd been chasing the wrong footsteps. Pardoning myself again, I retraced my path.

I put an ear out for the telltale sound of men's dress shoes. Unfortunately, it was Sunday and the Recoleta was full of sightseeing tourists, and families who had come to place flowers for their dead. Similar to the famous above-ground cemeteries of New Orleans, the mausoleums at the Recoleta were packed tightly together and it was easy to lose sight of someone amongst the ten- to fifteen-foot-high burial vaults. Moreover, many of the visitors had come from church and wore their best dress shoes, which clicked and tapped along the tile avenues.

After twenty minutes of traversing the labyrinth of alleyways, with not another sign of the man, I gave up and asked an elderly nun dressed in full habit if she could point me in the direction of the closest exit. Taking the map from my hand, she used her gnarled finger and drew an easy path for me to follow.

I found myself on a different road from where I'd entered at the busy main gate. A car zipped down the street, but there was little pedestrian traffic. The sun, at its zenith, beat down upon my head and shoulders, and the concrete sidewalk seemed to throw the heat back up at me. My hair prickled with sweat beneath my straw hat, and the cotton of my checked mint green-and-black dress stuck to my back. Parched and desperate for a drink, I spotted a handful of outdoor tables indicating a restaurant and headed straight for it.

Three French doors across the front of the building were open, to allow the breeze to enter. Inside, along the right, a dark walnut bar seated half a dozen diners, and tables were lined up symmetrically from front to back. The open windows, white tablecloths, walnut-paneled walls, and general hum of conversation from the patrons created an open and inviting atmosphere. I chose a small exterior bistro table, beneath a Jacaranda tree, and took the menu from beneath the salt and pepper shakers. A waitress in her mid-forties wearing a chambray dress and a yellow scarf around her neck arrived to take my order. I chose empanadas and iced tea.

The feathery leaves of the Jacaranda fluttered in the breeze, and a purple blossom dropped at my feet. I removed my hat and gently fanned myself with it. Closing my eyes, I allowed the murmur of Spanish conversations to wash over me. I'd been in Argentina for two days, and my ear was now attuned to the language.

The tea arrived, and, using the tiny tongs, I transferred the four cubes of ice from the metal cup into the warm tea along with a twist of lemon. The combined earthy-lemon flavor quenched my thirst, and I reflected upon what I'd seen.

The man must have simply borne a resemblance to the Waffen SS platoon officer who'd helped to carry out the destruction of the tiny farming town outside of Lyon, France, in

1944. The town had been destroyed in retaliation for a successful French Resistance mission which blew up a rail line and killed a dozen soldiers, including an SS-*Sturmbannführer*. Eighty-six people were murdered. I'd been a courier for the team that destroyed the rail line.

Perhaps he had merely been a ghostly vision conjured by my own imagination. After all, I *had* been roaming one of the most famous cemeteries in Buenos Aires. Why my subconscious would have conjured up such a horrible man, I had no idea.

A different waiter—a young man in his mid-twenties wearing black pants and a white shirt—placed a plate in front of me. "*Su empanada, Señora.*"

I thanked him and ordered another iced tea. The outer shell of the empanada had been cooked to a perfect golden color. I poked a hole in the flaky crust of the crescent-shaped meat pie to allow the steam to escape and to cool down the pie before eating it.

Laughter erupted in the bar area, drawing my attention.

My breath caught.

The fork slipped from my fingers and clattered onto the plate. The noise was overshadowed by the boisterous merriment. Now, instead of fifteen yards, the man stood only fifteen feet away—behind the bar. A shaft of sunlight clearly lit his chuckling features, and recognition instantly flooded my senses. His hair was longer and bushier—steely locks mixed with the dark curls—and ten years of age lined his features. An extra twenty pounds made his frame stockier, but not outright fat; after all, he'd been on the thin side during the war, as were we all. He'd removed the suit jacket, rolled up the sleeves of his dress shirt, and wiped down the bar with a white rag. I supposed he would have been considered rather attractive for a middle-aged man. Knowing the atrocities he'd committed, though, I could see nothing but the monster, even when he smiled in response to a patron's comment.

My tea arrived, brought again by the young waiter.

"Who is that man behind the bar?" I inquired in Spanish.

The waiter barely glanced over his shoulder before answering. "That is Señor Cabrera, the owner."

"He is popular with the customers," I remarked as another round of laughter burst forth. "Has he always owned the café?"

"No." The young man shook his head and put a hand on his hip. "He bought it in 1946. I grew up nearby and remember it was a rubbish street café. Señor Cabrera has made many physical improvements to the place. Now it is a true restaurant. He hired a Swiss chef and expanded the menu to include European dishes, such as the *schnitzel* and *croute au fromage* . . . my favorite," the young man said with pride. "Europeans living in Buenos Aires come often to enjoy a taste of their own food." He placed my empty ice cup on his tray.

The boy seemed quite proud to work at the establishment, and I needed him to continue talking. "It is quite an inviting place. Is Señor Cabrera from Spain?" I peeped at the waiter from beneath my lashes, delivering a tentative smile.

Not immune to my charm, the young man reddened. "No, he grew up on a farm in Mendoza and only came to Buenos Aires in 1945."

"I see. But he speaks other European languages?"

"Oh, yes, French and German, some English. He spent time traveling the continent . . . when he was younger," he said with pride.

*Yes, I remember just how well he spoke French as he ordered the women and children into the village chapel before his men set it ablaze.*

A patron flicked his wrist at my waiter, indicating he wanted the check.

"You have other customers; I mustn't keep you any longer."

He bowed and retreated.

The perspiration on my neck had dried. I replaced my hat,

pulling it down onto my forehead, and shifted my chair further behind the Jacaranda tree trunk, out of the bar's line of sight.

There were a few things I knew—first, Señor Cabrera did *not* grow up on a farm in Mendoza, Argentina. Second, German was his first language, not the adopted Spanish which he spoke fluently. Third, his real name was Helmut von Schweiger, and he was from Reinsberg, Germany—a small farming village west of Dresden. Finally, Helmut von Schweiger looked mighty sprightly for a supposed corpse.

‡‡

Visit Ellenbutler.net or your favorite book retailer to purchase *Operation Blackbird*.

# About the Author

Ellen Butler is the international bestselling author of the Karina Cardinal mystery series. Her experiences working on Capitol Hill and at a medical association in Washington, D.C. inspired the mystery-action series. Book critics call the Karina Cardinal mysteries, "intelligent escapism" and "unputdownable adventures that will take readers on an electrifying yet light-hearted and humorous journey." Butler is also the author of the award-winning historical suspense novel, *The Brass Compass*. *The Brass Compass* has won multiple awards for historical fiction including: a Speak Up Talk Radio Firebird Book Award, Indie Reader Discovery Award, Readers' Favorite Silver Medal. The second book in the duology, *Operation Blackbird: A Cold War Spy Novel*, is inspired by true events, and won a Next Generation Indie Book Award gold medal for historical fiction. Reviewers are calling it "riveting," and "a thrilling adventure."

**You can find Ellen at**:
Website ~ **www.EllenButler.net**
Facebook ~ **www.facebook.com/EllenButlerBooks**
Instagram~@ebutlerbooks
Goodreads ~ **www.goodreads.com/EllenButlerBooks**